I0544042

FIGHTING BACK

CHARLES ALVERSON

WATCHFIRE
PRESS

Copyright © 1973, 2014 Charles Alverson. All rights reserved.

This book is a work of fiction. Similarities to actual events, places, persons or other entities is coincidental.

Watchfire Press

www.watchfirepress.com

www.watchfirepress.com/alverson

Cover design by Kit Foster

www.kitfosterdesign.com

Fighting Back/Charles Alverson. – 1st ed.

Print ISBN: 978-1-940708-29-4

ISBN: 9781940708317

ALSO BY CHARLES ALVERSON

Caleb

The Word

Goodey's Last Stand (A Joe Goodey Mystery)

Not Sleeping, Just Dead (A Joe Goodey Mystery)

Fighting Back

Mad Dog Brewster

Apache Dreaming

Imagine Me

Hooligans

The Triple Shot Box (3 Crime Novels)

The Coming of Age Box (3 YA Novels)

For a current list of titles and further information, please visit
watchfirepress.com/alverson.

GET A FREE SHORT STORY COLLECTION

To instantly download ***Ryan's Way and Other Stories*** completely for free, sign-up for Charles Alverson's author newsletter at watchfirepress.com/alverson.

HARRY CASTER PUSHED A BOTTLE OF CRÈME DE menthe two inches to the left, back an inch to the right, and then stood back with a smile of satisfaction on his round, friendly face. Everything looked right—the gleaming mirrors behind the rows of liquor bottles, the quiet glow of indirect lighting on the curved, rubbed mahogany bar, the casual but careful arrangement of small tables and booths. The intimate sound of soft music came from hidden speakers.

Even the smell was right—a rich, dark, comfortable odor of relaxation and companionship—and, Harry hoped, success. He had sunk nearly every cent he could raise into the Lamplighter, and everything depended on its catching on in the well-to-do little river town of Parker's Landing.

Open just over three months, the Lamplighter began to look like a winner, although early on this Monday evening in October business was slow. At that moment, only one young couple sat at the bar talking quietly with Marco, the regular bartender. The only other customer in the place moved his bottle of beer several feet down the bar toward Harry and said:

"You Harry Caster, the owner?"

"That's me," Harry said, shifting his attention to a man who until that moment had been no more than a stick figure at the bar. From habit, he took a quick reading of the man who now sat close to the spot where Harry leaned on the bar.

The clothes were good—high quality, maybe even sharply elegant—but they didn't go with the man. They were soft, understated; he was sharp, quick, a little tense but cocksure at the same time.

"This is a nice place you've got here," the stranger said.

Harry slightly revised his first, harsh judgment. The man had taste in something besides clothes.

"Thanks," Harry said with genuine pleasure. "We only opened in July, but I think it's going very well."

"Can I buy you a drink?" asked the man. "And could we sit over there in a booth for a moment? I've got something I'd like to discuss with you. I think you'll find it interesting."

He's selling something, Harry told himself, but I'm not buying. Sullivan Street and Little Italy rang clearly in the man's voice, although it was cloaked with something smoother and suburban.

"I've got a drink, thanks," Harry said, picking up his short glass of straight whiskey. "And I've got some paperwork to catch up on." He half-turned to show his disinterest in any deal this sharpie might have to offer.

"Let it go for a while." This was more an order than a suggestion, and it turned Harry around with reluctant interest. "And let's sit over there where we can be more comfortable, okay?" the stranger added in a tone of deliberate appeasement which made it obvious to Harry that the other had been an order.

"Okay," said Harry cautiously, "let's do that." As he ducked to get from behind the bar, he gave himself a mental slap for getting too complacent about good fortune. What could this schlemiel want?

When they were seated in the dark, tall-backed booth, Harry asked flatly: "What do you want?" He'd brought his drink, but now he ignored it, keeping the palms of both hands flat on the table as if in readiness.

"Like I said, this is a very pretty little bar you've got here. And I hear you're getting the kind of customers that just about guarantee success. The quality people of Parker's Landing."

"So?"

"So, I like what I see so much that I want a piece of it. I think you could use a partner. A silent partner, of course. You run things; you're the operator."

Harry relaxed a little. He felt like laughing in this guy's face. "Partner?" he said. "I've got a partner. The Chase Manhattan Bank. They own every stick in this joint. Sorry, fella, I don't need any more partners. What I need is customers."

The stranger didn't seem very discouraged. "I dunno," he said easily, "a guy can always use another partner. How about it?"

"Look," said Harry, getting very tired of this conversation, "I've told you, Mr.—"

"Rice. Charlie Rice."

"—Rice. I don't need another partner. I don't want another partner. I'm doing fine without one. But I'll tell you what I'll do. I'll think over your proposition. Now, me, I guess a half interest in this place is worth"—Harry reached for a ridiculous figure—"ninety thousand bucks—no, make it a hundred grand, cash. I can't see a penny less. What sort of money were you thinking of investing?"

"Nothing," said Rice.

Harry gave a short, very humorless laugh. "You're a real comedian, Mr. Rice," he said, getting halfway up from his seat, "but the joke is over. I've got things to do. So, if you'll excuse me—"

"I won't," Rice said quietly but so definitely that Harry froze. "Sit back down and listen to me, Mr. Caster. I won't keep you long." Without consciously commanding his muscles, Harry sank back into the booth and sat staring at Rice. His glass of whiskey was forgotten in his right hand.

"Listen to me carefully," Rice went on. "I'm not going to repeat myself. I'm going to be your new partner in this bar. I'm not going to put up any money, but I'm going to take half of the profits. That's the deal I'm offering. Take it or leave it. But the only way you can stay in business and stay healthy is to take it."

Harry said nothing.

"You think it over, Mr. Caster," Rice said in a friendly tone, "and I'll be in touch with you in a day or so. But think real hard. If you come up with the wrong answer, it'll be bad for both of us. But I can promise you it'll be much worse for you than for me."

Rice slid easily out of the booth and stood before Harry. Harry didn't look up. He continued to stare at a point somewhere between the man's eyes and the tabletop.

With an expressionless nod to Marco, now alone at the far end of the bar, Rice walked out of the Lamplighter into the street.

For a long moment, Harry remained motionless. Then he drained his glass unthinkingly and rose from the booth.

Feeling only marginally in control of his legs, Harry moved to the bar, slumped to a stool and shoved his empty glass toward Marco.

"Same again," he said, and when he had the glass back between his hands, Harry sat looking at it, not drinking and not talking.

Marco went back to squinting at his paper in the dim light of a beer sign. He was twenty-five years old, tall and good looking, with a lantern jaw that narrowly saved him from being handsome. Harry liked Marco, but he kept telling him he was wasting his life as a bartender and ought to go back and finish college. Marco always listened quietly, smiled and said, "I'm a bum. I like this business. It suits me."

Harry looked up from the untouched glass in front of him. "Marco," he said with careful control, "do you know the guy I was just talking to?"

"I don't know him," Marco said, folding his newspaper, "but I've seen him around a lot. He calls himself Charlie Rice."

"Calls himself?"

"Yeah. But his real name is Carlo Rizzo. He lives in Guinea Gulch a couple of blocks from my aunt."

"What else do you know about him?"

"Not much. He's not big-time, but he's got a hand in lots of action in Hudson County and a reputation as a very hard man."

For a moment Harry was silent. Then: "Would you say he gets what he wants?"

"Usually."

"Thanks, Marco," Harry said, adding, "Look, there's nothing happening here tonight. I think I'll go home. If things are slow around midnight, close up early. Just throw the cash box in the safe. We can sort it out tomorrow."

"Okay," said Marco, watching Harry get his coat from the rack between the cigarette machine and the front door. As Harry was about to go, the bartender said: "Harry—"

Harry turned in the doorway.

"If I can help you in any way," Marco said, "just let me know. I mean it."

"Thanks, Marco," Harry said. "I'll keep it in mind." He turned and left the bar.

But Harry didn't go home. He walked to the side parking lot, got into his three-year-old convertible and sat thinking in the dark. The situation seemed real enough. He'd heard of such things. But Harry couldn't seem to get his mind to bear on it. Too many things kept intruding: Hildy, Lizzie, the baby, the big house on Elgin Street which seemed to gobble money by the shovelful. And the sweat he had gone through to open the Lamplighter.

All these thoughts seemed so much more real than the fact that a stranger—some hoodlum in a $300 suit—was threatening to take it all away from him. Such things didn't happen to unimportant little people like Harry Caster, he thought. There must be some mistake.

Harry backed the car out of the parking lot, headed it into Parker Street, and drove away from the Lamplighter. He didn't know where he was going, but any motion seemed better than doing nothing. Without consciously directing the car, Harry drove the length of the small shopping district past butcher shop, hardware store, boutique, launderette—all the shops he'd been in scores of times. They occupied a line of mid-Victorian houses, once the best homes in Parker's Landing but now gingerbread-dripping relics modernized with plate glass.

"Why not one of you?" Harry asked the blank windows, all dark but the launderette and the liquor store. "Why not you, Matt?" he asked the owner of Riverbank Liquors, now sitting at home at dinner with his family while old Henry Taubman watched the store. "Why me?"

Facing the shops was the Penn-Central train station, the lifeline of most of the commuting residents with jobs in New York City. And behind that the riverfront park with deserted bandstand and tattered, multicolored summer awnings that should have been taken down weeks ago.

Harry turned right on Pier Avenue and headed up the gently rising slope away from the river. It wasn't a big town, and before long Harry was parked on Hudson's Bluff over-looking all of Parker's Landing and a long stretch of black river.

From the bluff, Harry could see his own neighborhood. Parkland, one of the town's oldest areas. Some of his neigh-bors were still uneasy to find a family of Jews living among them, but most had accepted the idea in the last five years. He could also see Guinea Gulch, as the locals called the slightly indented area where an enclave of Italians lived. It had started out fifty years before as a barren piece of land occupied only by the shack of an Italian caretaker of one of the old estates. But now the thinly treed land was dotted with low-profile modern houses which hugged the brown earth. In recent years, more and more of the new houses built in Guinea Gulch had adopted eight-foot-high fences and offered only flat concrete walls to the outside world.

Somewhere behind one of those little dots of light, Harry thought, lives Carlo Rizzo, alias Charlie Rice, my would-be new partner.

2

AT THAT MOMENT, CARLO RIZZO WAS ARRIVING AT HIS low, pale-green house. Moving with a light step, he pushed open a door leading from the basement garage and started climbing well-carpeted steps. But before he'd gone far, he was waylaid by a six-year-old girl in pink pajamas who clung to his leg and made him haul her bodily up the rest of the stairs.

"Maria," said Angela Rizzo after giving her husband a kiss, "what are you doing? You'll break daddy's leg." She was a short, stocky woman in her early thirties with a pretty, broad-nosed face and spreading hips.

"I don't care," said Maria. "I want to. I want to break daddy's leg in a million pieces."

"I'll break you in a million pieces," Rizzo said, detaching his daughter gently, kissing her hair and tucking her under his left arm. As he walked into the kitchen with his squealing, upside-down burden, Angie was putting dinner on the plastic-topped kitchen table. Rizzo put Maria down and sat down at the table eagerly. "Where's Bobby?" he asked, beginning to spoon soup rapidly.

"He's at night football practice," Angela said. "He won't be home until just after nine o'clock. I gave him an early dinner." After Maria had been sent upstairs to get into bed and pick a story to be read to her, Rizzo leaned back at the littered table and lit a cigarette. "A great meal, Angie," he said. "Nobody cooks lamb like you do."

Angela sat down at the table with her own cup of coffee. "You're in a good mood tonight. Carlo," she said. "Is there some word from Abe Montara?"

Rizzo's face darkened. "No. Nothing. Not a word. He's still sore, I guess. But listen, Angie, I'm onto something that I think could take the place of some of the money I'm losing since Montara has been down on me."

"Oh, what is it?" Angie asked like a big-eyed child.

"You know that new bar on Parker Street—the Lamplighter? The one Vince said was pulling in the big-shot commuters. Well, it looks like your Carlo is going to be a partner in that bar. I don't want to talk too soon, but it just could be."

"That's wonderful," said his wife, "but, Carlo, do you know anything about running a bar?"

"I don't have to," said Rizzo. "It's run by a smart Jew named Caster who seems to be doing a very good job. All I've got to do is give him a hand now and then and draw my share of the profits."

"Give him a hand?"

Rizzo laughed. "I'm going to be Caster's adviser, his partner. I know a thing or two about business, you know."

"Well," she said, frowning, "I hope it works out all right."

"It will, baby, it will. Let's go read that story to Maria. There's some boxing I want to watch on TV."

IT WAS GETTING LATE AND COLD, BUT STILL HARRY didn't want to go home. There was something that wouldn't let him. He had to tell somebody about this, somebody who would care and maybe have some ideas. So he decided to go see his oldest friend, Arnold Gerstein, a commercial artist he'd known since high school in the Bronx. Harry rehearsed how he'd tell the story all the way on the half-hour drive up the river.

"Harry! Come in," Gerstein said when he found Harry on the doorstep of his large comfortable house. "Adele," he shouted, "Harry is here." He turned back to Harry. "Is Hildy with you?"

"No, Arnie," Harry said, "I'm alone, and I've got to talk to you about something serious."

Gerstein, a slight, bald man with the face of an animated basset hound, responded immediately to Harry's urgency. "Sure," he said, "we'll go up to my studio where it's quiet." He led the way up to his attic workroom. And there, perched on a stool and surrounded by unfinished illustrations, Harry told him about Rizzo's visit.

"You've got to be kidding."

"I'm not," Harry said. "Arnie, I've never been so serious in my life."

"Then this Rice or Rizzo or whatever he calls himself has got to be a joker. He's been watching too many gangster movies. He can't just move in on you like this."

"He thinks he can," said Harry, "and I'm not so sure myself."

"Well, I'm sure he can't. Have you been to the police?"

"Arnie, it happened less than a couple of hours ago. Besides, what am I going to go to the police with? My word that Rizzo is trying to deal himself half of my bar? They'd think I'm crazy."

"You've got to do something," Gerstein said. "When did this guy say he was going to get back in touch with you?"

"A day or two," he said.

"It's your problem, Harry," Gerstein said, biting on a drawing pencil, "but if it was me I wouldn't wait. This schmuck is convinced that you're his pigeon, that you're so scared that you'll just lie down and let him run right over you. You've got to let him know right away that he can't. Here, I'll tell you what you ought to do. You ought to pick up this telephone and tell him that it's no soap."

"But Arnie, this guy belongs to the Mafia."

"How do you know? Did he say so?"

"No, and it wasn't engraved on his business card, either. But I believe it. Marco, my bartender, all but came out and said it."

"Yeah," said Gerstein, "and it's to this gonif's advantage for you to believe it. If this Rizzo can get even fifty bucks off you with this scare tactic, he's ahead of the game. Here, I'll look up his number. Rice . . . Rice—here it is: 232 Bedford Grove, Parker's Landing. Do you want to dial or shall I?" Gerstein offered Harry the telephone.

"What the hell am I going to say to him, Arnie? Lay off or I'll have my friend Arnold Gerstein rub you out? For Christ's sake!"

"No, stupid, all you've got to do is be very cool and businesslike about it. Just get him on the phone and tell him you've considered his proposition but you're not interested. As simple as that."

"Don't I wish."

"Get yourself ready. I'm dialing."

Rizzo had turned the television off in the fifth round of

a very dull fight and was worrying over some figures in a big black ledger when Angie answered the telephone.

"Carlo," she said from the hallway, "it's somebody asking for you. A man. He asked for Charles Rice."

"Let me have it, sweetheart." As soon as Rizzo recognized Caster's voice, he put his hand over the mouthpiece and said to his wife: "Honey, could you make me a cup of coffee?" When she'd gone, he said: "Sorry, Mr. Caster, I was interrupted. You were saying?"

Rizzo listened to Harry Caster with a perfectly impassive face. When the voice on the other end of the line ended, he didn't say a word for nearly thirty seconds.

"Yes, I heard what you said, Mr. Caster. I heard you very good. But I think you're making a bad mistake. I'm offering you a good deal, and I'm sure you'll be sorry if you turn it down." He held the receiver away from his ear. "There's no reason to shout, Mr. Caster," he said in a reasonable voice. "You'd better do some more thinking. Good night."

"Who was that, Carlo?" Angela asked, coming into the room with a cup of coffee and a piece of chocolate cake.

"Nobody important," Rizzo said, and he looked at his watch. "Hey, it's getting late. I thought you said Bobby was going to be home about nine. It's nearly ten o'clock."

Rizzo drank his coffee and ate the cake silently. Not long after he'd finished, he stood up abruptly. "I feel like having a beer," he said. "I think I'll run down to Aldo's for a while."

"All right, dear, don't be late."

"I won't. And if Bobby isn't home in ten minutes, call up the Swensons. He's probably over there playing Halford's records."

At Aldo's Club, near the Hudson Road, Rizzo nodded a

greeting to the bartender and stepped into a telephone booth. After making a short call, he sat down at a back table with a beer and waited.

———

Harry Caster was still holding the silent receiver to his ear. "Rice...?" he said. "Are you still there?" He put the telephone down.

"He says I better do some more thinking," he told Gerstein. "A lot of good that did. Now that he knows I'm not going to give in without an argument, he could be dangerous."

"Don't be silly. He couldn't have expected you to hand over half of your business just like that. Without an argument."

"Oh, no? I think that's exactly what he expected."

"If you're really worried," Gerstein said, "you'd better go see the police tomorrow. Just for safety's sake."

"Yes," Harry said, "maybe I will."

As Harry unlocked his front door, Hildy Caster looked up from the television set. "Is that you, Harry?"

"No," Harry said, "it's the Boston Strangler."

"We don't want any. We take from Jack the Ripper. What are you doing home? I'll bet Marco threw you out for cramping his style with the stewardesses."

"There was nothing much doing, so I thought I'd come home. The stardust sisters are asleep, I presume."

"Yes, thank the Lord. Whatever you do, don't disturb the sleeping monsters."

At forty-two, Hildy Caster was thin, still pretty, and deeply cynical. The unplanned birth of the baby Sophie the year before had done nothing to temper her habitual misanthropy, lightly disguised by a flippant manner.

"What's on?"

"Robert Taylor and Greta Garbo in *Camille*," Hildy said. "He's just asked her to give up the mad social whirl for a country cottage with painted scenery. Just like you and me."

"Yeah," Harry said, "well, tell her not to do it." He joined Hildy on the couch. His conscious mind took in the love story, but at the same time he was trying to come to grips with his own more unbelievable situation.

Later, in bed, Harry turned from his sleeping side onto his back. "Hildy," he said.

"What?" groaned Hildy, snatched back from the brink of sleep.

"Do you remember a movie where a gangster demands money from a small businessman with the threat of breaking the place up?"

"I remember a hundred movies exactly like that. Why?"

"Well, I was wondering what the businessman usually does in that sort of situation."

"Did you interrupt my elopement with Robert Taylor just to play Cinema Quiz Time? Let me ask you one: In what obscure home movie is the husband brutally murdered for waking his lovely wife with silly questions?"

"No," Harry insisted, "I'm serious. What does he do? Does he pay the money? Does he call the cops? Or what?"

Hildy was silent so long that Harry thought she'd fallen asleep, but then she spoke. "This is just a generalization, mind you, but he usually refuses to pay at first, and then the gangsters break a few windows and arms until he sees reason. Then he pays off for a while until he decides that a man has to make a stand somewhere."

"And then what happens?"

"Usually the mobsters bump him off," said Hildy nonchalantly, "as an object lesson to the rest of the business community. But then the good guys get outraged and rub out the bad guys."

"That's not much help to the businessman, is it?" Harry asked. "I mean the one bumped off."

"No," Hildy admitted, "but they pass the hat and collect enough money for a classy tombstone and to send his kids to a good military school."

"That's nice."

"Any more questions, Mr. Quizmaster?"

"No. Your prize will be delivered within seven days by a famous mystery star himself, right to your own doorstep."

"Goody," Hildy said, and she was asleep.

Sleep did not come so easily for Harry Caster, but it came.

3

THE NEXT MORNING JUST BEFORE NOON, HARRY WAS IN his tiny office at the Lamplighter making up a new liquor list when he heard an odd noise from out on the street. It sounded like the small explosion heard when you wait too long to light a gas oven—sort of a smothered bang.

Then he heard a crashing sound in the main room of the bar and a boy's voice shouting, "Mr. Caster! Mr. Caster! Quick!" Ernie, the errand boy from the liquor store, came lurching into the doorway of the little cell. "Your car!" he gasped.

"What's happened?" Harry asked, getting up.

But Ernie just repeated, "Hurry, hurry, your car!" and ran back the way he had come, sending more chairs flying in his wake.

"What the hell!" Harry hurried after the boy, nearly tripping over a fallen chair. When he got to the street he saw nothing, but Ernie was standing at the corner of the building gesturing frantically.

As he came around the corner, Harry saw that there hadn't really been any need to hurry. There in the Lamplighter's parking lot his car was solid mass of flames. From the tires to the soft top, red and orange flames were in total possession. Paint blisters rose in big patches, and the leather steering-wheel cover curled up as if in final salute. There was no question of saving the car.

Around the parking lot stood a silent fringe of shoppers and merchants watching the fire with solemn appreciation.

"Has anybody called the fire department?" Harry asked nobody in particular.

"I did," said Ernie, "as soon as I saw the smoke."

Harry never heard the sirens, but a red fire van soon appeared, and firemen were pushing onlookers back so that they could get near the car with their fire extinguishers. The extinguishers released a flood of white foam, and the automobile was all but lost in a cloud of smoke and steam. The stench of burning rubber, fabric and chemicals descended on the remaining crowd, and most of them began to cough and splutter and hurry away.

In just a few minutes the fire was out, and Harry's car was a steaming, gap-windowed, stinking hulk resting on four half-melted tires. All that remained of the convertible top was a tangle of metal supports.

"How did this start?" a chubby young fire lieutenant asked Harry.

"I don't know. I heard a funny noise, and Ernie Hollister came running into my office yelling. I came out and saw this."

"We'll finish off here," the fireman said. "You'd better notify your insurance company and arrange to have it towed away late this afternoon. Christ, it sure stinks, doesn't it?"

"It sure does."

Harry became aware that a policeman was standing at

his side listening. "I'll be writing this up, Mr. Caster," the policeman said. "Will you be at your bar for a while?"

"Yes," Harry said, "I'll be there."

Before Harry got to the door of the Lamplighter, he heard the telephone ringing, and he knew who was calling. The telephone shrilled persistently as he walked back to his office.

"Hello, Mr. Rice," Harry said as he picked up the receiver. "I was expecting to hear from you, but not quite so soon."

"Hello, Harry," said Rizzo. "Have you been doing like I said, thinking over the proposal I made to you?"

"It's 'Harry' now, is it?"

"Well, we're going to be partners, aren't we? You call me Charlie."

"Are we?" asked Harry.

"Yes, I think so," said Rizzo. "I really think so. I think we're going to get along just fine."

"Yeah, there's something about a burned-out car that really brings two people together. Don't you think?"

"I wouldn't know about that, Harry, but what about our deal?" Harry was silent.

"Hello?" said Rizzo with the beginning of an edge to his voice.

"You've got to give me more time to think," said Harry. "I need more time. Everything is so sudden."

"Okay," said Rizzo, "okay. But don't take too long about it. I want to get this deal settled before something happens."

"You mean something else, don't you?" Harry asked, but the line was dead.

Roy Beddell, the Chief of Police of Parker's Landing, slumped in his scarred wooden desk reading studiously from an FBI report on interstate automobile theft. His lined face was wrinkled with concentration, and periodically he ran a thick hand through stubble-short, prematurely white hair. A pair of black-framed reading glasses perched unfamiliarly on his bony, vaguely Indian nose.

Chief Beddell's major experience of the West had been a two-week vacation in Arizona several years before, but he had a curiously Western look about him. In his ten years as Chief, the force's uniforms had changed from New York City blue-black to a crisply pressed, sage-colored gabardine and a high-crowned Stetson. And the majority of his men copied Beddell's highly polished tan boots.

The men the Chief played poker with on Friday nights were sometimes allowed to refer to him as "Cowboy," especially if he was winning. But the few persons who had tried to use the expression to ridicule him soon found that this was a dangerous practice in Parker's Landing.

Beddell looked up with annoyance as Vern Hodges, his assistant, entered with a knuckle rap on his office door. "There's a citizen name of Caster here," Hodges said. "Says he wants to talk to you."

"What's he want?"

"He won't say. Says it's very important, and he has to speak to the Chief himself."

Beddell knew Harry. He knew everyone who'd been in town for more than a year or so. The Chief knew Harry as a relatively new resident, one of the few Jews in town and a reputable and potentially successful businessman. But they'd never done more than pass a few polite words.

They'd never had any reason to be acquainted professionally.

"Okay, Vern, send him in. But for Christ's sake, come back in a few minutes so I can get rid of him."

Harry walked into the Chief's office with the diffidence of a man with a natural aversion to the police and police stations.

"Hello, Mr. Caster," Beddell said, gesturing to a curve-backed chair in front of his desk. Before Harry could quite sit down, he asked: "What can I do for you today?" Beddell's manner was cordial but brisk, and Harry knew that the Chief of Police didn't want him to linger.

But Harry didn't know how to start. To him, the problem was simple: to get Rizzo off his back and behind bars if possible. But how could he say this to Beddell? The Chief sat looking at him with quizzical impatience, and Harry had to start somewhere.

"You've probably heard that about an hour ago my car burned up in the parking lot of my bar," he began.

"Yes," said Beddell. "Sergeant Shaw called it in, but I haven't seen his report yet. That's a hell of a thing. I hope you're insured."

"Yes," Harry said. And then he decided that he might as well plunge right in. "But it wasn't an accident. Somebody deliberately destroyed my car."

Beddell didn't say anything, and Harry was disappointed at the lack of response. But then the Chief spoke with deliberation. "You say someone burned your car on purpose?"

"Yes," said Harry. He looked nervously around at the opaque glass walls of the office and asked, "Do you mind if I close the door?"

"Go ahead."

When he returned to the chair, Harry felt a little more at ease. But he tensed immediately when Beddell said in a hard voice, "Now suppose you tell me what this is all about, Mr. Caster. You claim that someone has set fire to your automobile. I think we'd better get an official statement from you." He pushed a button on the edge of his desk.

"Well, look," Harry said in a rush, "do you know a man who calls himself Charlie Rice?"

At the name, a slight but definite change came over Beddell's open face. It was as if a transparent shield had fallen over his features, giving them a frozen wariness. Before he could speak, a middle-aged woman in a white, frilled blouse gave a token rap on the door and came into the office. She carried a stenographer's pad.

"Yes, Chief," she said, looking at Harry with benign disinterest.

"Sorry, Shirley," Beddell said. "False alarm...We won't need you for the moment."

With no change of expression, the secretary swiveled and left the office, closing the door firmly behind her. Beddell watched her broad back until the closing door blotted it out. Then he turned his pale eyes back to Harry Caster.

"You said something about Charlie Rice," he said flatly.

"Yes," Harry said, "do you know him?"

"I know him. He's been living in Parker's Landing for several years, and his boy Bobby plays on the Police Athletic League baseball team. He's the best pitcher we've got." He looked very deliberately into Harry's face. "But what has Charlie Rice got to do with this situation?"

Harry knew he had to come out with it eventually. "Do you know the name Carlo Rizzo?"

"I don't believe I do," said Beddell, and his face didn't

alter from the flat, neutral expression he'd worn since Harry mentioned Charlie Rice. "What about this Carlo Rizzo?" His voice was wearing thin with barely concealed irritation.

At this point, Vern Hodges knocked and stuck his head into the office. He started to say something. "Not now, Vern," Beddell snapped, "later!" The policeman pulled the door shut as if it were electrified.

"What about this Carlo Rizzo?" Beddell repeated.

"That's Charlie Rice's real name," Harry said. He decided that he might as well go all the way. "And it was Rizzo who burned my car this morning, or at least had it done."

Beddell said nothing to this, and Harry sat feeling foolish. So he stopped talking. Finally, Beddell said: "Go on."

"Well," Harry said, "right after it happened, Rizzo called me at the Lamplighter and—"

Beddell cut him short. "Mr. Caster," he said, "you'd better go back to the beginning. I think we're both getting a bit confused." Harry didn't feel at all confused, but he went right back to the night before when Rizzo had approached him at the bar. It wasn't a long story, but he told it step by step, trying to stick to the facts and not get sidetracked or long-winded.

The Police Chief listened to Harry without comment, like a teacher hearing a nervous recitation. When Harry had finished he felt both glad to have it all out and anxious about what would come next. Beddell sat silent, as if letting the story sink in. Then he said: "Well, Mr. Caster, what do you want me to do about all of this?"

This was the last reaction Harry had expected. He'd been fully prepared to be disbelieved or even expected that his sanity would be questioned. But Beddell seemed to accept his story completely. "You do believe me, don't you?"

Harry asked, just to make sure. Beddell didn't answer the question. But after resettling himself in his old leather chair, he fixed Harry with his eyes and began to speak.

"Mr. Caster, when I came on this police force nearly thirty years ago, Parker's Landing was a much different place. It was a small town, much quieter and much more simple. We had crime, all right, but it was a different sort of crime: a few drunks, the occasional fight, cars stolen now and then by high-school kids, a few petty burglaries. We even had a genuine murder in 1940. Fellow stabbed his eldest son at the dinner table. Quite a messy business." Harry started to say something, but Beddell stopped him with a gesture that was also a command.

"But as I say, it was a small town. A cop not only knew everybody in town, he knew most everything about them: families, school records, any little quirks about them that might bear watching. More to the point is that you soon got to know the few new people who came into town. You got to know them real well. You know," Beddell gave the practiced smile of the storyteller who is calling on an old favorite, "one of my own ancestors came here with Jedediah Parker's second boat, but some people hereabouts still think of my family as newcomers."

Harry knew he was expected to react, so he smiled weakly. But he wondered what all this had to do with Rizzo trying to muscle in on his business.

"But things are different now, Mr. Caster," Beddell said. "Parker's Landing is not the same town. The war brought a lot of changes. Some people left and never came back. And after the war, a lot of new people came in. Some very good people, mind you. Did you know that Mayor Frost's people came here only in 1946?"

Without waiting for an answer, Beddell went on. "But it

was a different sort of people coming in—city people, people with a lot of money and fancy jobs, people with foreign names. Poles, Italians, Jews." The Chief cut off his narrative, and Harry could detect a hint of slyness in his manner. "You're Jewish, aren't you, Mr. Caster?"

"Yes," Harry said, "I am."

"You know," said Beddell, "it used to be we hardly had any foreigners in Parker's Landing. Oh, there was always a family or two of bohunks somewhere around—I had a cousin married into them— but after the war we began to get a real mixture of people. Nowadays white, home-born Anglo-Saxons are the real minority in Parker's Landing."

Beddell paused again, and Harry decided to wait him out. He had a feeling that whatever the Chief was working around to was going to show up quite soon.

"Take Charlie Rice, for instance," the policeman continued. "As new residents go, he's a pretty old-timer. He's got a damned nice kid, and so far as I know he's a solid citizen. But I don't really know much about him. All I know is that he's never been on my blotter. You say his name is really Carlo Rizzo. A lot of people change their names."

Harry knew what was coming.

"You, yourself, Mr. Caster," the Chief continued. "Caster's not a Jewish name, is it? Didn't your family originally have some other name?"

Harry cursed his grandfather's ambition and pretensions as he answered, "Yes, Kastransky. My grandfather—"

"There you are, Mr. Caster," Beddell broke back in, "times change, names change. Rice may very well be Rizzo, but that doesn't necessarily make him a bad fella."

Harry came back sharply: "It's not Rizzo's name that bothers me. It's the fact that he's trying to take over my business and seems ready to use violence to do it. And I've come to you for help. This is the police department, isn't it?"

Chief Beddell drew himself up behind his desk, and when he spoke again it was not with easy informality. "Yes, it is, Mr. Caster," he said. "I'll be very happy to take an official complaint from you on your allegations against Mr. Rice. Nothing could be easier. But my advice—both personal and official—is to keep in mind that libel is a very tricky business. You are accusing him of intimidation and conspiracy to commit arson, two very serious charges. If you fail to make them stick, you'll find yourself in some very deep water. But if you like, I'll just ring for my secretary again, and she'll take down your complaint."

The Chief's hand moved toward the buzzer, and Harry watched with nervous fascination to see if he really would push it. But just as Beddell's finger got to the button, Harry lost his nerve.

"Wait," he said, and he cursed himself as he saw the hand jerk to a sudden stop. Perhaps if I'd waited, he thought, he wouldn't have rung for the secretary. But Harry also knew that he was no match for the Chief of Police in a battle of nerves. "Look," he said, "I know what I'm saying is true, but I can't prove it."

"You have no witnesses," the Chief said rather than asked. Harry thought he said it a bit too readily.

"No," Harry admitted, "no witnesses."

"Mr. Caster," Beddell began, and Harry could sense that he was relaxed and confident once more. Harry knew that he was about to be brushed off. "My best advice to you is to go home and think this all out very carefully. The situation you have brought up—as you describe it—is a very serious one and should not be proceeded on lightly. Sergeant Shaw's report will tell us what caused the destruction of your car, and I'll be studying it very carefully. It could have been only a short in the wiring, you know."

Harry said nothing.

"And," continued Beddell in an easy manner, "if it will make you feel any better, we'll have a friendly word with Charlie Rice and—"

"No," Harry said with alarm. "If he finds out I—"

"Never fear," said Beddell soothingly, "what has passed between us in this office will go no farther than these walls. I'll just see that Rice knows we're taking official notice of what happened to your car. If it was other than a freak accident, he'll know that we know all about it. I think he may find this information worth having." Beddell got to his feet, continuing: "Don't worry, Mr. Caster. We may be just a sleepy, small-town police force, but I think you'll find we do a pretty good job for our citizens."

Harry knew he'd been dismissed, and there was nothing for him to do but to get up and leave. "If anything else happens," the Chief said, shepherding Harry out of his office door, "you get on the phone directly to me. I'm sure that between us we can sort this thing out." He forced his big, firm hand on Harry and raised his voice slightly. "Thanks very much for coming in, Mr. Caster. Damn shame about your car. I'll get back to you as soon as I get my sergeant's report. Goodbye."

Harry found himself on the steps of the police station no more comforted than when he had gone in. He was more worried, if anything. Harry felt he could expect no help from Beddell, unless it was after Rizzo had wiped out his business and perhaps his family. In his imagination, he could see the Chief on the telephone at that very moment telling Rizzo all that had happened in his office. The image gave Harry a sick feeling in his bowels.

Chief Beddell was not on the telephone to Rizzo, but before Harry had been in the Chief's office five minutes, Rizzo knew about it. His informant wasn't able to tell Rizzo what had passed between Harry Caster and the Chief, but he could guess. Thanking his friend at the police station, Rizzo put down the telephone with a frown of concentration. He took up a golf club and practiced a few putts on the living-room carpet. But Rizzo's thoughts were miles away from the little white ball.

4

No more than an hour later, Harry was on the Hudson Expressway in a rented car headed for Manhattan. It was like going back nearly thirty years to be running to his brother for help. He felt like a sixteen-year-old high schoolboy again going to see his brother at Columbia University. Not Milton, the Hebrew scholar, but by then Mickey Caster, fraternity man, athlete, seducer—or so he said—of incredibly beautiful gentile girls. Rich gentile girls.

And then when the war came, Harry enlisted in the Army Air Corps to be a pilot and ended up painting signs at Fort Carson, Colorado. Mickey—you didn't dare call him Milton any more—waited until he got drafted into the infantry. And this came only after an unsuccessful appeal to a higher court—Ruth Fineman, a congressman's homely daughter who couldn't quite believe Mickey's sudden love for her.

But once the Army was inevitable, of course Mickey had to become a hero. Harry came back from the Army a paint-stained technical corporal, but Mickey emerged a twenty-five-year-old captain with a Distinguished Service

Cross, two Purple Hearts, and a general's daughter for a wife.

Harry had drifted into a series of small businesses and semi-successful bars which had led him to the Lamplighter. For Mickey, law school hadn't exactly worked out. But some of the best companies in New York opened their doors gladly for Mickey Caster, and Mickey started a climb which had some twists that Harry still didn't fully understand.

Harry didn't see his brother more than three times a year. But there were always birthday presents from Uncle Mickey, and at odd intervals and even odder hours, Harry got used to receiving long telephone calls. Mickey seldom bothered to say hello.

"There are only two possibilities," Harry heard one morning at three o'clock when he answered the telephone: "either I buy Kurtzman out or he buys us out. And I'm a son of a bitch if I'll be bought out by that mealy-mouthed..." Finally, Mickey would wind down. "Good to talk to you, kid," he'd say. Then he'd hang up.

Sometimes he'd ask Harry's advice and listen carefully to it, then hang up without comment. Several times over the years, Harry was surprised to see in the newspapers that his advice had been taken. He realized that he could have made a considerable amount of money by acting on the information he gleaned from these late-night calls, but he never did. And, without making a conscious resolution, Harry had never gone to his successful brother for financial help.

But it wasn't money Harry was seeking now; nor was it something he felt safe talking about on the telephone. On Manhattan's East Side, Harry pulled the rented car into an expensive-looking parking garage and surrendered the car to an attendant who looked like a bank manager. I can't wait to see his reaction to a quarter tip, Harry thought as he left the garage.

Mickey's building was a large, old house with no external signs that it was anything but an expensive private residence. The building had no external numbers, and until Harry saw the 66s sewn on the doorman's Confederate-gray collar, he thought he'd passed it.

As Harry set foot on the thick, plum-colored carpet of the foyer, a woman in her late thirties with gray-rinsed hair challenged him. "May I help you?"

Harry told her who he was and she led him to a narrow door which was nearly invisible in the elaborate molding of the walls. She opened the door and ushered Harry into a tiny elevator lined with silvered glass. Pushing an unnumbered black button, she closed the door again, and the elevator began to rise.

When the elevator door opened again, Harry found his brother facing him.

"Kid," said Mickey Caster, "it's good to see you. Come on in. You've never been to this office before, have you?"

A stranger seeing Harry and Mickey together would probably realize that they were related, but he'd be hard pressed to say how he knew. The similarities were many, but they added up to two distinctly different men.

Both were just below average height, but Mickey was fine-boned whereas Harry was round-headed and slightly pudgy. Mickey, too, had begun to lose some hair, but instead of Harry's growing bald spot, his thinning hair, artfully molded by a cunning barber, only enhanced the translucent fineness of his features. Face to face, the brothers were like prince and peasant, related by some quirk of ancestry.

"No, I haven't," said Harry, taking in the outer room of the office. It had the unworn look of a parlor which through no fault of its own is largely unused. Harry didn't know furniture, but he sensed that the few pieces in the room were worth more than his houseful.

"Come inside," said Mickey. He led his brother into a large, rectangular room with floor-to-ceiling windows on two sides opening onto a narrow terrace. A small Regency desk littered with papers stood at the far end of the room.

A slim, blonde girl rose from a smooth-fabric sofa as they entered the office. She seemed to be in her mid-twenties, mature yet youthfully resilient. She looked, to Harry, as expensive as the room.

"Harry," Mickey said, "this is Alison, my secretary." He put an arm around Harry's shoulders. "Ally, this is my kid brother."

"How do you do, Mr. Caster," she said in an accent as English as the best finishing school in New York could make it.

"Alison," Mickey said, "we've got some important things to discuss, and I won't need you for a while. Will you pour us a couple of drinks—Scotch okay with you, Harry?—and take my calls in your place?"

Alison put two cut-glass tumblers of Scotch and ice on a low tubular steel-and-glass table in front of the sofa and with a soft smile at Harry went through a door in the side wall.

"Alison lives here," Mickey explained, seating himself on the couch and picking up a glass. "It's convenient. Now, sit down, kid, take a swig of this ten-year-old poison and tell me what this is all about."

On the telephone, Harry had said only that he was in trouble and had to talk to Mickey right away. Mickey had immediately said come right in and had canceled the rest of his schedule for the day. Now, Harry told him in full detail what had happened from the moment Rizzo had spoken to him to the time he'd left Beddell's office.

"And," Harry finished, "that bastard Beddell says if anything else happens—if I get my head blown off, I suppose—I'm to let him know right away. And he'll give Rizzo a good talking to."

Harry was disappointed that Mickey showed so little emotion at the story he'd told him. There was no question that Mickey believed him, but he just poured them each another drink from the decanter.

"Harry," he said after a long swallow, "how much do you know about this Rizzo character?"

"Not very much. Only what the cop told me. And Marco. Rizzo's been living in Parker's Landing for some time, he wants the Lamplighter handed to him on a platter and isn't too particular what he has to do to get it. Marco, he says Rizzo's very likely a member of the local Mafia family, but not much of a big shot."

"Look, kid," Mickey said, "don't jump all over me because I ask this, but could you make a go of it if you gave Rizzo half of the action?"

"Give him half?" Harry shouted. "What are you talking about? This is advice from a brother? Thanks very much. I think I came to the wrong place." Harry started to get up.

"Harry, Harry," Mickey said gently, putting a wiry hand on his brother's arm. "I asked you not to jump in my face. That was a theoretical question, not advice. Of course, you're not going to give him half of the joint. But—now think a minute—could you, theoretically, that is, and still make a go of it?"

Harry settled back, but he didn't have to think. "Give him half of what? My debts? I went into hock up to my eyeballs to get that place, and every cent that comes in over bare expenses is going against the debt."

"I thought so," said Mickey, "but I wanted to make sure. In business, Harry, you've got to consider all of the possibilities, no matter how insane they seem. And from a strictly hypothetical point of view, letting him have half is one solution if it's financially possible. That's quite aside from the moral side of the question."

"You may be able to get aside from the moral side of the question," Harry said, "but I can't. Do you suppose I could stand to stay in business knowing that I was handing half of the profits over to a gangster?"

"Plenty of people have, Harry boy," Mickey said softly, "but that's beside the point. On to the next possibility. Could you sell out of the Lamplighter and go into something else?" He quickly held up a small, well-kept hand. "I'm not saying you should. I want to know if you could."

"No. A year from now, maybe. But I haven't yet proved I can make a success of it. I couldn't get enough from the Lamplighter to open up a hot dog stand."

"Harry," Mickey said cautiously, "you know I'd be happy to—"

"No," said Harry sharply. "Dammit no, Milty"—the old nickname popped out—"you know how I feel about that."

"Okay, okay," said his brother with regret, "that's out. Do you think you could buy this Rizzo off with a lump sum —say a grand?"

"A thousand bucks!" exclaimed Harry. "Why—"

"No, I suppose not," said Mickey. "Since when could you scare off a shark by giving him a leg to nibble on?"

Both brothers were silent for a while.

"So, Harry," Mickey broke the silence, "what are you going to do?"

"That's what I came here to find out," said Harry hopelessly.

"Har, there's one possibility we haven't considered. I don't even know if it's a possibility."

"What's that?"

"Fighting back. Not letting this guinea get away with it."

"Fight back?" asked Harry. "How? What am I supposed to do— go over and let the air out of his tires? I wouldn't know how to blow up his car. How could I fight a thug like Rizzo?"

"You wouldn't have to," Mickey said. "If you're really serious, I think I know where you could get some help. There are people who know about such things."

"But how could they help me?"

"By scaring Rizzo off. Convincing him that he'd be better off if he left you and the Lamplighter alone. He could be made to see reason."

"There wouldn't have to be any violence, would there?"

"Kid, I just don't know. Look, apparently you've got two choices. Either give in to Rizzo and go on the breadline or fight him. Which is it going to be?"

Harry thought for a long moment. "I won't," he said, "I can't— give in to him. I've got too much tied up in that place. I guess I'll have to fight. But what about Hildy and the girls? You know how the Mafia is supposed to operate. What about them?"

"I don't know," said Mickey, "but the important decision has been made. You want to fight Rizzo. Now, I've got a lot of telephoning to do and I need some privacy." He got up and knocked loudly on the door at the side of the sofa. "Ally, I've got a new gin rummy pigeon for you. He'll be in in just a moment, so make sure you've got something on." To Harry he said: "Beat it. Go take some of Alison's money. I'll come and get you when I've got some things sorted out. Then we'll go and have a good dinner if you've won enough money."

Harry shrugged and walked through the doorway into the secretary's apartment.

5

ALEC HOERNER SAT ON A STOOL IN A DARK CORNER OF Finlay's Knockout Bar on Eighth Avenue, watching the front door. At not quite nine in the evening, only a thin scattering of tourists and regulars clung to the long, curved bar, drinking and gawking at a hundred years of boxing history stuck on the big back mirror or hanging from the high, dirty ceiling on ancient cords.

At first glance, one might think Hoerner had once been a boxer himself—a lean, thick-shouldered light-heavyweight more noted for cunning than brute force. Or sitting there in an anonymous suit with an equally forgettable hat pushed back to reveal dark hair and a narrow forehead, he might have been a plainclothes cop. The eyes—translucent buttons of pale jade in the neon-reflected light—were impersonal enough.

And so he was—in a way. Alec Hoerner was a private detective. The detective part came from spending six and a half years in Vietnam with the Army Counter-Intelligence Corps, followed by nearly two years with the New York Police Department. Hoerner had spent the last six months as a freelance, calling himself Hoerner Associates, and he'd been on the receiving end of one of Mickey Caster's many telephone calls that afternoon.

At the time, Hoerner had been in Central Park enjoying the mild autumn sunshine and keeping an eye on a very foolish bank vice-president for his suspicious wife. The banker's foolishness came in the form of a childlike blonde stewardess, and Hoerner was carefully noting just how justified the wife's suspicions were when his pocket receiver buzzed.

From the corner telephone booth, Hoerner could still see the romantic couple when a strong voice came on the line: "Mr. Hoerner."

"Mrs. Meltzer," said Hoerner, watching the banker light two cigarettes in his best Charles Boyer style.

"A call for you," said the manageress of Hoerner's answering service. "Just a few moments ago. I would have waited until you called in if it hadn't sounded important." He could hear dollar signs in her voice.

"And if I didn't owe you so much money, eh, Mrs. M?"

"Mr. Hoerner," she said sternly yet lovingly, as if he'd just come into her living room with muddy shoes but carrying a bunch of roses, "you know that I don't care about your outstanding account, but Mr. Blavatsky..."

She made the firm's accountant sound like Attila the Hun out of Simon Legree. But Hoerner knew he was a twenty-seven-year-old business-college graduate with a hollow chest and a bad wheeze from too much early-morning bird-watching in Greenpoint Park.

"Is he picking on you again, Mrs. M?" Hoerner asked with mock solicitude. "You just say the word and me and my pals will..."

Mrs. Meltzer sighed deeply and expressively. She was

about to say something when Hoerner noticed that the banker was helping his ladylove from the park bench.

"Sorry," he said, "it looks like my rabbits are making a run for it. What was that call, Mrs. M?"

"A Mr. Mickey Caster," she said, all business again. "He called himself, and he said he wanted to talk to you most urgently."

Hoerner knew the name immediately. And he knew what it could mean. "Give me the number quickly, Mother M," he said, totally unconcerned that the banker's pin-striped back was disappearing into the taxi into which he'd just lifted Miss TWA. "Thanks," he said, hanging up and beginning to dial the number at the same time.

Hoerner's telephone conversation with Mickey Caster was not a long one. He played it cool and distant until Caster explained what he wanted. Those hot-shot businessmen could smell eagerness like they could smell money. He listened without comment until Caster mentioned the name Rizzo.

"Which Rizzo is that?"

"Carlo Rizzo," Caster said. "He calls himself Charlie Rice. He lives up in Parker's Landing near my kid brother and has some small rackets."

"I know the one," Hoerner said. Once he'd made the connection, data about Carlo Rizzo assembled around the name—the Speranza family, Abe Montara, the Lower Hudson Alliance. And his voice told Mickey Caster that Hoerner had lost interest in the proposition before hearing very much about it.

But before Hoerner could kiss Caster off with a "Thanks very much for calling, but..." Mickey mentioned a figure and a name. The figure wasn't high enough to scare Hoerner off, but it was enough to make him stop and think.

The name was only a name, but to Hoerner it offered vistas of opening doors that had been shut tight before.

"Just talk to my brother, Hoerner," Mickey Caster said. "He'll give you all the dope, and then you can decide. From what I've heard about you, I think you can handle the situation, and I won't forget it."

"I'll have a talk with him," Hoerner said, and a date was made for him to meet Harry that evening. Hoerner stepped out of the booth and twenty minutes later was sitting back in his rickety desk chair staring at a two-year-old Playboy calendar without seeing it. Hoerner's "office" was a cubicle with a half-translucent door at the back of an unsuccessful certified public accountant's suite of offices. Little by little, the CPA had rented off more and more space until he no longer had a room there himself. The only time the subtenants saw him was on the first of the month when he lurked in the outer hall trying to collect rents.

Frowning, Hoerner unlocked the cylindrical metal lock on the telephone dial and spent the afternoon making calls. At first what he heard confirmed what he already knew, and it was all bad. The situation sounded even tougher than it had seemed at first. Hoerner was tempted to call Caster and tell him the meeting with his brother was off. But something —mostly the knowledge that if he didn't come up with some real money soon, he'd be in trouble—made Hoerner keep telephoning contacts.

In turn he called friends, street contacts, a couple of guys he still kept in touch with at police headquarters. Hoerner collected a few unpaid debts in the form of bits of information, put himself in debt here and there for a bit more; working the slow but fruitful circuit that was the lifeline of anybody—on either side of the law—who had to know what was happening.

Finally, as things looked progressively less hopeful, a contact casually let it drop that Rizzo was in the shit with Abe Montara. He had been for weeks, and it didn't look like Abe was going to kiss and make up very soon. With this bit of information in his pocket, Hoerner found the rest easy. Within an hour, just as it was beginning to grow dark, he had most of the story. He knew where Rizzo stood with the family—or at least with Montara, and that was what counted—and now Hoerner had to make up his own mind. He sat working out the possibilities in his mind, not even bothering to turn on the light or respond when the last office tenant, a small-time music publisher, shouted his usual goodbye. Hoerner sat silently until the luminous dial on his watch told him it was time to get something to eat and meet Harry Caster.

Hoerner spotted him the moment Harry walked into Finlay's and stood blinking with stranger's eyes. The detective let him get seated in the appointed booth but not settled before he moved in. "Mr. Caster," he said, "your brother said I'd find you here. I'm Alec Hoerner. Let's order drinks before we start to talk."

The glow of satisfaction lent by a very expensive dinner had already begun to melt away while Harry was driving to the West Side. Now it was almost entirely gone. Neither man spoke while they waited for the drinks. Each was studying the other.

"I'm a private detective, Mr. Caster," Hoerner began when the sore-footed waitress had departed. "Your brother says you've got a problem, and I'm here to see if we can help you." The "we" was deliberate. Hoerner had found that it made clients feel more confident if they thought he had an organization behind him. "It will help if you give me all the information you have. Why don't you start at the beginning and take it step by step to this moment?"

Once again, Harry went over the account, which had begun to sound like fiction, even to him. It was hard to believe that it had all started only the night before. The moment that Rizzo had first spoken to him seemed a long time ago. "...and so," he concluded, "Mickey said someone would meet me here just after nine o'clock this evening."

Alec Hoerner sipped his drink and studied the man in front of him. He wondered if Caster had any idea what he was getting into. He doubted it. "Why don't you tell me a bit about yourself and your family, Mr. Caster? Just anything that comes to mind. It might be useful."

With the unself-consciousness of a man with great problems, Harry began to speak of Hildy and the girls. Unknowingly, he revealed more of his true feelings and worries to Hoerner than he'd confided to anyone for years. Despite his hard appearance, Hoerner turned out to be an easy man to talk to. It wasn't only the professional manner; Hoerner seemed to be really listening.

When Harry stopped talking and took a quick, embarrassed sip from his glass, Hoerner made no comment. He had a delicate situation here and he knew it. Hoerner wanted the Caster job—needed it if he was going to keep going, much less get into the big time—but Harry Caster had to know what he was getting into. Hoerner thought he could take Rizzo, but there was a good chance that things could turn nasty, and he wanted that clear up front.

At last he spoke. "How much do you know about Carlo Rizzo?"

"Not very much, except that he's some kind of crook."

"And does he frighten you?"

"You're damned right he frightens me," Harry said with a nervous laugh. "Wouldn't he scare you?"

Hoerner ignored the question. "Mr. Caster, let me put you exactly in the picture about Rizzo," he said. "Aside from the suddenness and intensity of your brush with Rizzo, he may not seem much different from a lot of other people in your town. But he thinks a lot different. He's spent twenty years in an organization with no more respect for your life, your family and your business than you have for an ant you step on in the street.

"You saw how he reacted to your first resistance, as mild as it was. He had your car destroyed. Just like that. No warning, no preliminaries, no second chance. If he hadn't needed you for his scheme, you might have been in the car when it was blown. It would have been nothing to Rizzo."

Hoerner paused, but then went on when Harry said nothing. "This doesn't mean that Rizzo is inhuman. He's not. He loves his wife and kids just as much as you love your family. But this means nothing when it comes to dealing with you. You're not family. You don't count unless he can use you. You're one of them—the big outside world that exists only to be exploited by the Carlo Rizzos.

"As long as Rizzo thinks you're likely to go along, he won't harm you or your family. But once he gets the idea that you're going to seriously resist him, there's nothing he wouldn't do to convince you that it would be better to go along. He's in a lot of trouble now with his bosses, but Rizzo's not alone. He's still got a few friends willing to give him a hand."

"You make it all sound marvelous," said Harry sourly. "I may as well slit my throat right now and save Rizzo the trouble. Did Mickey hire you to come here tonight and scare me to death? He should have saved his money."

"Your brother hasn't hired me to do anything," Hoerner said seriously. "It's up to you whether you want to hire me. I don't care either way. But I'm not going to kid you that if you do hire me it will be easy. It won't be. If you decide to fight Rizzo, my organization will back you all the way. But I warn you that once we start, we're going to have to be faster and harder and meaner than Rizzo to beat him. We'll be playing by Rizzo's rules, not yours. There's going to be no stopping until we win. And we do mean to win."

"But what will you do?"

"I can't tell you that. If you decide to retain my organization, you'll have to put yourself in our hands completely. We'll tell you what to do, and you'll do it. You will have no choice. And it won't be cheap. Our basic fee is a thousand dollars: half when you retain us, and half when the job is done." Hoerner didn't tell Harry that this was only a fraction of the sum Mickey had mentioned earlier.

"That's a lot of money," Harry said.

"Yes, and it could buy you something you don't want." Hoerner leaned back and took a drink from his glass.

Inwardly, Hoerner smiled sardonically at his own speech. He was deadly serious, but Hoerner had no more "organization" than Harry Caster did. Money could buy technical assistance and manpower, but for the most part Hoerner relied on Hoerner. He was deadly confident that he could take Rizzo. And he was willing to take big risks to satisfy Mickey Caster. There was more than one Mr. Blavatsky looking narrowly at Hoerner's growing debts.

In Harry's mind, a whirl of possibilities and considerations was battling for his attention. He'd come to the city seeking help, but he'd found even more complications.

Hoerner looked at that round, harmless, baffled face and took pity. "Don't give me an answer now," he said. "Go home and take some time to think it over. It's not an easy decision." Hoerner knew he wasn't taking any chances by giving Caster a little bit of line to run with. He didn't want to press too hard and scare him into surrendering to Rizzo. He wrote a telephone number on a blank card. "If you've made up your mind or want to reach me for any reason, call this number. Call any time, but don't give this number to anyone else, and don't write it down with my name."

Harry put the card carefully into his wallet.

6

When he'd said a worried goodbye to Hoerner and left the bar, Harry was surprised to find that it was past eleven o'clock. Checking his car out of a parking lot, he began driving north toward the Hudson Expressway. But as he neared the 125th Street on-ramp, he thought that he'd better call Hildy and let her know he was coming. He should have called before.

"Hello?" said Hildy's unsleepy voice, and Harry knew that she'd been watching television. It was a safe guess.

"Hildy," he said, "it's me."

"Who's me? Your voice sounds vaguely like somebody we used to have around here, but he left ever so long ago. No telling when he'll be back."

"Very funny," said Harry. "How's everything?"

"How is it ever? Utterly fantastic. And the boy business mogul, Mickey? I expect he's still prospering in his crooked little way."

"He's richer than ever," said Harry. "As much as I disapprove, I forced myself to eat the food at the Four Seasons."

"How come you never take me to the Four Seasons, or even to the Three Seasons?"

"You wouldn't like it," Harry said. "The food is great, the service is superb, and they sneer at you if you don't eat things like snails and caviar."

"Let them sneer," she said. "Me they sneer at in the Burgerama on Hudson Boulevard." Her tone of voice changed. "Harry, something strange happened today."

"Not Clark Gable again."

"No, seriously. It was a man I don't know. He said his name was Rice. Charles Rice. And he did act peculiar. You know him, don't you?"

"Slightly. What did he want?" Harry asked carefully.

"I really don't know. He said he'd just dropped by to see you about something concerned with the bar. But even after I told him you were gone for the day, he kept hanging around. I finally had to offer him some coffee. What's he have to do with the Lamplighter?"

"Nothing much. He's been around offering me some kind of a business deal. But I don't think I'm interested. What did this Rice have to say?"

"Oh, things like what a shame it was that your car accidentally burned up this morning. And what a nice house we have. I should have offered to sell him the place. He made a really big deal over the baby and Lizzie's picture. Wanted to know how old they were, all about them. Fairly gave me the creeps, I can tell you. He was nice enough in an oily way, I guess, but even I don't like our kids as much as he claimed to."

"Anything else?" Harry asked.

"No. I finally got rid of him by starting the vacuum cleaner. But as he left, he said to give you his best and that he'd be getting in touch very soon. Who is this charming person, anyway?"

"Just a local guy," Harry said. "He's some sort of a businessman. Don't bother yourself about him." He paused. "Hildy, go to bed. I've got a few more things to do, and I might be home very late."

"All right," Hildy said, "but I want you to tell me just one thing."

"What's that?"

"If you're not coming back, I want fair warning so that I can rent your room. I'll put up a little sign in the front window: 'Lonely grass widow seeks young, handsome boarder. Good eats.'"

"Just hold off on the sign for a couple of hours," Harry said. "I won't be home *that* late. I'll see you in the morning."

"If you're lucky," said Hildy. "Good night, sweetheart." She put down the telephone and walked back to the television set.

Harry fished Hoerner's card from his wallet. A sleepy girl's voice answered the telephone. "Oh-two-oh-four."

"I'd like to speak to Alec Hoerner, please."

"At this hour?" the girl said. "It's nearly midnight, you know."

"I know," said Harry, "but I still have to speak to him. Is he there, please? He gave me this number."

"No, he's not actually here. But hold on and I'll try to reach him." The girl put the telephone on hold and dialed another number. She listened to the harsh rasp of a busy signal. From experience, she knew what this meant: Alec Hoerner had taken the receiver off its cradle for the night. She pursed her thin lips with disapproval. "I'm sorry, but I'm unable to reach Mr. Hoerner at this time," she told Harry. "Could you call back in the morning?"

"No, I really couldn't. It's very important that I reach him tonight. I know it sounds corny, but it could be a matter of life and death. Can you try again?"

"I could," said the girl, "but I'm afraid it wouldn't do any good. This is only his answering service." Her voice became confidential. "You see, he's taken the phone off the hook at his apartment. I can't reach him at all."

"Well, where does he live, then?"

"Oh, I couldn't tell you that. I couldn't. It's the first rule: never give out a client's address. Mrs. Meltzer would murder me."

"Mrs. Meltzer?"

"The boss. The manager," the girl said. "The last time a girl gave out anybody's address, it was to his ex-wife's lawyer, and Mrs. M nearly had a coronary. She practically turned blue. Oh, I couldn't risk it even if I am quitting next week to get married."

"Congratulations."

"What?"

"About getting married," Harry said. "That's very nice."

"Oh, thanks. I won't be sorry to leave here, I can tell you. Working from eleven at night until eight in the morning is no joke."

"Yeah, I can imagine," said Harry as sincerely as he could. "But listen, Miss, I don't sound like anybody's lawyer, do I?"

"Well, no," she admitted reluctantly, "but..."

"Look," Harry insisted, "less than an hour ago I was sitting in a bar with Mr. Hoerner. He's working for me. I'm his client. And he gave me this number and said to get in touch if anything came up and I needed him. Well, something has come up, and I've got to get in touch with him right now."

"It can't wait until morning?"

"No, it really can't. I told you it was a very serious matter. And it is."

"You say you saw Mr. Hoerner tonight?"

"Sure. He's a tall guy, sort of thin but strong-looking with a narrow face and strange, greenish eyes."

"I wouldn't know about that," she said. "I've only talked to him on the phone, but he sounds a bit weird to me. You wouldn't believe some of the messages he gets. I could tell you..."

"I'll bet," said Harry, "but really, I've got to get in touch with Mr. Hoerner right now. Can't you just give me his address? Your boss won't know, and next week you'll be gone anyway."

"Well, all right," said the girl, "but I hope you're telling me the truth."

"I am," said Harry. "I am."

She gave Harry an address in the West Forties, and Harry thanked her profusely.

"Oh, sure," said the girl, swallowing a yawn. "G'bye, now." She disconnected the telephone and picked up a thick historical novel.

Before she'd finished a page, Harry was back in his car and retracing his path toward midtown Manhattan. The 500 block of West 45th Street was a bleak, forgotten line of large warehouses and dirty brownstone tenements untouched by the force-fed glitter of Broadway to the immediate east. Cutting in behind a late-model Buick in the final stages of disintegration, Harry carefully locked the car and climbed a tenement stoop squeezed between squat warehouses. Inside, the narrow stairway was littered with a week's refuse, and a man, ragged with age and hard use, lay sleeping on the first landing, knees and forehead pressed against an apartment door.

On the third floor, Harry stopped in front of a thin door with the tin letter G hanging by a nail from its peeling, green surface. One of those fish-eye peepholes was placed slightly off center about chest high in the door. Harry stood for a moment shifting his weight and then raised his right arm as if it didn't belong to him. He laid his knuckles on the green door gently in a light knock. There was no answer. He rapped again, a bit harder, and the door resounded hollowly.

After a long pause, a girl's voice, thin and peevish, answered: "Who is it? What do you want?"

Harry cleared his throat and said, "Is Mr. Hoerner there? This is Harry Caster. I'm sorry to come so late, but—"

The girl giggled. "He's not here. Go away."

Harry didn't know what to do or say.

"You still there?"

"Yes," said Harry. "Mr. Hoerner—"

"Go away. There's no—"

The girl's voice was cut off sharply, and Alec Hoerner, wide awake, said, "The door's open, Mr. Caster. Come in."

Harry turned the knob and pushed into the darkened room. He felt a light cord brush his face.

"Turn on the light," said Hoerner's voice from a black corner. With a jerk of the cord, a naked bulb overhead threw the small room into cruel illumination. Single-windowed and wallpapered, the room was nearly filled with a gigantic bed in which lay Alec Hoerner and a very young blonde girl. The air in the room was warm and stale, and the girl lay on her back covered only to the top of her prominent hip bones by a sheet which looked to be satin or silk. Her full, elongated breasts hung over discernible ribs. Unblinking eyes in a sharp face never left Harry's face.

"Hello, Mr. Caster," said Hoerner. "I'm surprised to see you so soon." He lay back propped up against two black-covered pillows.

"I tried to call," Harry said, seeing at the same time the telephone receiver off its hook on a small linoleum-covered table. "I had to reach you. Rizzo—"

Hoerner stopped him with an upheld palm. "Maureen, honey," he said, "why don't you take a little walk? I've got to take care of a little business."

"Hoerner," she protested, "you said all night. You promised!"

"Move." Hoerner cocked a leg and pushed the naked girl out of the bed into a passive heap on the floor. For a moment she lay there with sprawling dignity, looking not at Hoerner but at Harry's confused face. Then, as if she were alone, the girl got to her feet, walked to the door and opened it.

"What about your clothes?" asked Hoerner.

The girl closed the door behind her without a word.

"One of the neighbors," Hoerner said. "We're mostly swinging singles in this building. And very friendly."

Harry didn't say anything. The contrast between the Hoerner he'd met just a few hours ago and this one he saw in bed before him was confusing. His eyes, not knowing where to look, darted about the small room, taking in the shapeless furniture, the rutted linoleum on the floor, and came to rest on a large clear-plastic clothes bag on the wall across from the bed. In the bag was apparently Hoerner's entire wardrobe, as if it weren't really in this down-at-the-heels room. At one end hung an Army officer's dress uniform, complete with medals and ribbons.

"Welcome to my humble abode," said Hoerner, watching Caster with some amusement while lighting a cigarette from the scarred bedside table.

"I tried to call," Harry repeated.

"Don't tell me," Hoerner said. "That stupid broad at the answering service gave you my address. I'll have her ass out on the street first thing in the morning."

"It won't do any good. She's leaving next week. Says she's getting married."

"Well, bad luck to some poor bastard." Hoerner changed his tone. "You found me, so what's happened?"

"I called home," Harry said, still standing and feeling nailed to the spot by the naked light of the hanging light bulb. "Rizzo was at my house this afternoon asking my wife questions. About our family—the girls. Admiring the house. I think he meant it as a warning to me."

"No doubt," said Hoerner, leaning back on one elbow and letting a thin wisp of smoke flow to the ceiling.

"What shall I do?"

"I can't tell you, Mr. Caster. Only you can make that decision. But have a seat." He indicated a rickety, straight-back chair in the corner. "Throw my robe onto the bed."

Harry sat down and was silent for a long moment. Then he said quietly: "I'll do it."

"Are you sure?" asked Hoerner, keeping his eyes on Harry's face.

"Yes," said Harry with a firmness he didn't feel. "As sure as I am of anything right now. I've got to do something. What happens next?"

Hoerner was completely changed. Gone was the languid, joking manner. He grabbed up the black silk robe and slipped it over his naked body as he got out of bed.

Knotting the belt, he turned to Harry and he was all business.

"Mr. Caster, do you know any place you could send your wife and children for a short while, perhaps a week or two? Someplace that only you know about?"

Harry couldn't think of a single place. But then it came to him. Hildy's uncle had a cabin in a remote area a couple of hours' drive up the river. It would be empty this late in the year, and he knew where the key was kept. He told Hoerner about it.

"That sounds all right. Now, does your wife go shopping on Wednesday mornings?"

"Sometimes. Why?"

"She's going to go tomorrow at just about mid-morning. Have her and the children leave the house as if they're going on a normal shopping trip. They're to take nothing unusual with them—no suitcases, no extra clothes—to indicate that it's anything but a routine visit to the shops. Have her go to the usual stores and buy enough groceries for two weeks. But not enough to raise suspicion. Then I want her to drive around town for at least half an hour, making various stops. Just about noon, your wife is to drive onto the Expressway and go directly to the cabin."

"Hildy's not going to like that," Harry said.

"That's too bad. It's what she has to do. You see that she does it. One more thing: If she suspects that she's being followed, she's to try to lose the follower. If she fails, she's to return home. But once she gets to the cabin, she stays there until you contact her. Is there a telephone in the cabin?"

"There wasn't the last time I was there."

"Then she'll have to stay there until you come to get her. Make sure she understands that. Have you got all that?"

Harry asked a few questions, but soon they had it all worked out.

"Okay," Hoerner said, "go home now and get some sleep. In the morning go to your bar and wait for me to call. If Rizzo gets in touch, or there are signs of him or his friends getting active, call my answering service. I'll get back to you fast. If Rizzo calls or comes in, stall him."

"How am I going to do that?"

"I don't know. Tell him anything, but stall him. Play dumb. Don't raise his suspicions. If he gets really tough, agree in principle to the deal but put him off as long as you can. Give us some time to get moving, and we'll keep Rizzo so busy he won't have time to bother you."

"How?"

"Leave that to us," Hoerner said. "Now, go home, and I'm going back to bed. Get all the rest you can tonight. You're going to need it."

All the way back to Parker's Landing, Harry mulled over the consequences of what he had just done, but he couldn't see them clearly. Nervous as he was, he felt relieved that at least he had some help. He had taken action of some kind. Harry still didn't know what to think of Alec Hoerner.

7

It was past 2 a.m. when Harry got home. Letting himself in the front door, he stood in the darkened hallway listening to the silence of the house. Despite the late hour, he wasn't sleepy. His mind was too busy trying to sort out the jumbled events of the last two days and wondering what was to come. Instead of climbing the stairs, he walked through the narrow passageway into the kitchen at the back of the house. Without switching on the light, he sat down at the big round table and tried to think.

The kitchen light was switched on.

"What!" Harry cried with fright. Then he saw Hildy in her ragged terrycloth robe.

"What indeed," she said. "What are you doing sitting down here in the dark?"

"Nothing much," said Harry. "I thought I was hungry, but I'm not."

"Well, I am," she said, opening the big refrigerator and peering into it. "And while I'm getting something to eat, do you think you could tell me what is going on?" She began to pull small plates of leftovers and covered plastic bowls out of the refrigerator. "It's obvious," Hildy continued, "that something very strange is happening. And it's very likely connected with that nice Mr. Rice who came visiting today."

She settled herself with her food across the table from Harry. "What sort of a protection policy is he trying to sell you? Don't you think it's about time you told me all of the pertinent details? Like exactly how soon we can expect to get blown up like your car?" Hildy had figured out so much that Harry found it fairly easy to tell her the rest. To his surprise, she didn't seem very frightened. "It's exactly like *Shadow of the Mob*," she said, "except you ought to be a restaurant owner, and I ought to be a young and beautiful redhead. I could dye my hair if that would help any."

"There's nothing funny about this, Hildy," Harry said. "If Rizzo finds out I've hired Hoerner, you and the girls will never get out of town in the morning." He quickly told her Hoerner's plan.

"Do you mean to say that you're going to send me off to that rat-trap while you have all the fun here?"

"That's exactly what I mean to say. You and the girls. Now, let's get to bed."

As soon as the last light went out in the Caster house, the curtain of a darkened window of a neat house across from their backyard was closed, and a little woman verging on old age nervously dialed a telephone number.

"Hello, Mr. Rice?" she said. "It's Mrs. Costello. You asked me to call."

"Yes, Mrs. Costello," Rizzo said, sitting in his small office in pajamas and robe. "Thank you very much."

"I'm sorry to call so late, but they just went to bed a minute ago. I thought they were going to sit in the kitchen talking all night."

"That's okay, Mrs. Costello. I understand. Thank you very much for staying up so late to call me."

"It's nothing, believe me. After all you done for my Stanley, it's the least I can do. I'd have stayed up all night if need be."

"I appreciate that, Mrs. Costello." Rizzo fought a yawn and looked at his watch.

"I almost called an hour ago when Mr. Caster got home. I thought he'd gone right up to bed, and I was just about to call you when the light went on in the kitchen and I saw him and Mrs. Caster talking."

"What time was that?"

"I wrote it down here. It was just 2:05 a.m."

"Could you see anything else?"

"Well, Mrs. Caster was eating something. I can't be sure what it was exactly, but—"

"Never mind, Mrs. Costello, you've been very helpful."

"I try to be, Mr. Rice, especially after all you did—"

"I only wish it could have been more, Mrs. Costello," Rizzo said shortly. "It's late, and I think—"

"Mr. Rice? I don't mean to be nosy, but the Casters..." Her voice trailed off.

"Yes?" said Rizzo a little impatiently.

"You see, they're very nice people and good neighbors, and I hope—I just hope there's nothing wrong. I mean, because of my calling you like this."

"Don't worry, Mrs. Costello," Rizzo said in a warm, sincere voice, "it's just a business matter. You know how business is."

"I suppose so," she said, although she didn't know.

"There you are," said Rizzo. "You just go to bed and forget all about this. And one of these days soon I'll see if there's something else I can do for Stanley. He's a nice boy. Would you like that, Mrs. Costello?"

"Oh, yes."

"Well then, we'll just see. I'll say good night, Mrs. Costello, and thank you again."

After hanging up, Rizzo sat for a while smoking. He picked up the phone again, made a call, and then went to bed.

"Carlo," Angela said as he climbed into bed, "is something wrong? It's not like you to sit up late."

"It's nothing," Rizzo said, sliding his arm under his wife's shoulders and pulling her to him. He kissed her worried mouth, and Angela's doubts disappeared in a warming response.

AT MID-MORNING THE NEXT DAY, THE CASTER FAMILY shopping expedition was about to begin. Hildy had assembled eleven-year-old Lizzie and the baby in the front hallway and was checking to see that everything was ready.

"Lizzie," she said, "you may carry the laundry bag, and I'll bring Sophie in her carrycot."

"The laundry bag is too heavy," said Lizzie, a thick-bodied girl with a lively face and light-brown pigtails. "I can't carry it."

"You will carry it," said Hildy, "or I'll cut your head off."

"I might be able to carry it."

"Do your best," said Hildy. "Get going."

"What's with the laundry bag?" asked Harry, coming

down the stairs. "Hoerner didn't say anything about doing the laundry."

"It's not laundry. It's diapers and clothes and silly things like that which people like you and Hoerner don't think about. If you think we're going to sit in that cabin for a week or two in the clothes we're wearing, you're crazy. Don't worry. It just looks like we're going to the launderette, a perfectly normal thing to do. Millions of decent people do it every day."

"Do what every day?" Lizzie asked, returning from Hildy's battered old car.

"Beat their daughters named Elizabeth until their ears whistle."

"They do not," said Lizzie.

"Wait and see," Hildy said menacingly. "Go wait in the car."

"I want to kiss Daddy goodbye," Lizzie whined.

"Go." Lizzie trudged out the door as if going before a firing squad. "All right," said Hildy, "we're off. I'll call you at the Lamplighter from the service station just before we turn off on the dirt road to the cabin. Then we'll wait at the cabin until you come and get us. Or the gangsters do."

"Don't talk like that," Harry said.

"Don't worry. Uncle Herman has a shotgun in the cabin. If anyone but you comes around, I'll give them both barrels—whatever that means."

"For God's sake, just go out there and wait. Read books, eat until you burst, but don't start getting heroic. I've got enough to worry about."

"Okay," said Hildy, "no heroics. And that goes for you, too. You're not much, but you're all we've got."

From the front room, Harry watched Hildy drive her old car down Elgin Street and then turn right toward the shopping district. The last thing he saw was Lizzie hanging out of the window blowing him kisses. What he didn't see as he walked upstairs to dress was a gray Ford sedan pull away from the curb a hundred yards up the block and follow Hildy's car at a discreet distance.

Unaware that she was being followed, Hildy drove directly to the Sav-O-Mart and parked in the large, half-empty parking lot. Leaving Lizzie to mind the baby, she went into the market to shop for their enforced stay at the cabin.

By then the gray car was also in the parking lot and had come to a stop about fifty yards away. The driver, a slender youth with a wispy blond moustache and mottled blue eyes, got out of his car and leaned carelessly against a front fender for a moment. Then he remembered that he was supposed to telephone Rizzo at Mrs. Caster's first stop. He looked around for a telephone booth and saw one just about twenty feet from Hildy's car where Lizzie was reading a comic book and jiggling Sophie's carrycot with her foot.

Casually, the boy walked past Hildy's car and stepped into the booth. "Hello," he said, "Mr. Rice? It's me, Joey. I'm in the Sav- O-Mart parking lot on Bouton Avenue. Mrs. Caster went in about a minute ago."

"Is there anybody with her?"

"Yeah. A little girl and a baby in her car."

"Did you see Caster this morning?"

"No, just Mrs. Caster, the girl and the baby. About ten minutes ago the girl came out of their house with a big blue bag and—"

"What sort of bag?"

"Could be a laundry bag," said Joey.

"Maybe," said Rizzo. "Joey, you keep an eye on them until they get back home, you understand? Even if it takes all day. Don't let them out of your sight. And call me if anything unusual happens. You got that?"

"I've got it," Joey said.

After feeling to see if his dime had come back, Joey opened the accordion door of the booth and stepped out. Humming a tune that had been bugging him all morning, he walked past the car where Lizzie sat, without a glance in that direction.

"Hey!" Lizzie said, but Joey kept walking.

"Hey, you!" Lizzie yelled again in her husky-shrill voice. "You! Boy in the black jacket."

Joey now knew that she meant him, but he still pretended not to hear. Lizzie leaned far out of the car window and screamed: "Yoo boo, yoohoo! You there in the black jacket and white pants." All eyes were now turned their way, and Joey could hardly keep pretending not to hear.

"I think she's yellin' at you, bud," said a fat old farmer.

"Me?"

"Nobody else."

Joey turned toward the car where Lizzie still leaned awkwardly out of the window. "What do you want?" he demanded, keeping his distance.

"Come here."

"What for?"

"I want to talk to you."

"What about?" Now Joey saw that a small, amused crowd was forming to listen to this long-distance conversation, so he walked over to the car. "What do you want?" he asked in a cross whisper.

"I want to ask you something," said Lizzie as the other people moved away.

"What is it?"

"You live on Elgin Street, don't you?"

"Nah."

"You don't? But I saw you there this morning."

"You didn't."

"I did!" insisted Lizzie. "You were parked in front of the Hokansons' house in a light-gray Ford, license plate CAY 090. I noticed because I just learned what a cay is. Do you know what a cay is?" Joey was embarrassed that he'd been spotted.

"It's a very small island, and very low," said Lizzie, "also known as a key. I looked it up in my dictionary. Do you have a dictionary?"

"No. Look, I got to—"

"If you don't live on our block," Lizzie interrupted, "what were you doing there?"

"I was—oh—visiting a friend of mine. A friend of mine who lives there."

"What's his name?"

"You wouldn't know him. He doesn't talk to little girls. Goodbye, I got—"

"It isn't that awful Wayne Bastable, is it?" exclaimed Lizzie. "Ugh. He's horrible, always covered with dirt and oil from that crazy motorcycle of his and—"

"Yes, that's the one."

"But—" Lizzie began.

At that moment, Joey glanced up and saw Hildy Caster coming out of the supermarket pushing a loaded shopping cart. "Look," he said urgently, "I have to go." He hurried away from the car. "Wait," Lizzie called, but then she saw her mother coming.

"How was Sophie?" Hildy asked.

"Fine," Lizzie said. "She didn't make a peep."

Hildy loaded the groceries into the trunk and pushed the empty cart to a collection point.

"Did you get anything I like?"

Hildy got into the car. "Yes, five pounds of frozen pig's noses and a jar of chocolate-covered ants."

"Ugh," said Lizzie.

Hildy then began the series of local stops suggested by Hoerner. With each move, Joey was carefully behind. At the launderette, Hildy washed some clean underwear and packed it, Lizzie, and the baby into the car.

"Just one more stop," Hildy said aloud to herself as she pulled away from the curb, "and then—"

"Mom," said Lizzie, "did you know we were being followed?"

"Followed?" asked Hildy, fighting an urge to freeze. "Just what do you mean by that, child of my heart?"

"A boy in a gray Ford. He's been following us since we left home. He said he wasn't when I talked to him at the supermarket, but I know he is."

"Why don't you tell Mommy this kind of thing?" Hildy searched the rear-view mirror. She saw no gray Ford.

"I forgot," said Lizzie. "Besides, he wasn't very nice, really. He says he's a friend of Wayne Bastable's, but—"

Hildy saw that a gray Ford had pulled behind them at a distance. "Don't let him see you turn around, Lizzie, but sneak a look and tell me if you see your friend in the gray car."

"Yes," said Lizzie positively.

"That's wonderful," Hildy said. "For that you get a prize." But she was thinking: What do I do now? What did Barbara Fane do in *Masked Vengeance*?

Hildy continued driving automatically, not really knowing where she was headed. And Joey stayed a discreet few cars behind, congratulating himself for being a highly skilled tailer. He didn't imagine that Lizzie was paying any attention to him and lapsed into a daydream about a carhop he'd met in Tarrytown the weekend before.

For no particular reason, Hildy made a left turn. A few blocks later she turned right. Joey followed these turns automatically, but then something prodded him. The image of the carhop receded slightly.

Hildy leaned over to Lizzie and said: "Fasten your seat belt, kid."

"Why?"

"Because if you don't, they'll be scraping Lizzie off the windshield. Mommy is going to be doing some very interesting driving in a few minutes."

"You mean fast?"

"Very likely," said Hildy.

"With lots of twists and turns and skidding and like that?"

"It's entirely possible."

"Goody." Lizzie pulled her safety belt tight.

"Keep a tight hold on Sophie's cot," Hildy said. "Pretend you don't see your friend."

"Can I stick my tongue out at him?"

"Certainly not. You're not supposed to even see him."

Hildy had blundered onto a street running parallel to the Hudson Expressway. At intervals on the right side of the street were on-ramps to the Expressway. Carefully keeping to the left lane, Hildy drove along the crowded street. She saw that Joey had crept up to two cars behind her in order to cut down the chances of losing her.

Helplessly, Hildy passed two on-ramps, but there was no way to get on them, much less lose Joey at the same time. Then, nearly a block ahead, Hildy spotted a possible chance. The traffic light was green, and in the closest oncoming lane a big silver bus sat patiently flashing its left-turn blinkers at the unyielding stream of cars in Hildy's lane.

Just past the intersection on the right side of the street, gaping invitingly, was another entrance to the Expressway. Checking on Joey's position, Hildy was surprised to find him right at her back bumper looking bug-eyed and trying to be invisible.

Gritting her teeth, Hildy started her left-turn blinker and slowed slightly at the edge of the intersection. The bus driver, with a slight salute, started pulling slowly out into her lane. Joey, still stuck to her bumper, also signaled for a left turn.

But as soon as she entered the intersection, Hildy whipped the steering wheel all the way around to the right, pushed on the horn button and jammed the accelerator pedal to the floor. "Hold on, Lizzie," Hildy said as the old car lurched, found its balance and shot directly across the path of the bus. Hildy saw the bus driver's face go white, and she pushed even harder on the horn, hoping that some-how the noise would keep the narrowing gap open.

Somehow it did. The car on Hildy's right shot up and over the curb, giving her a vital couple of feet, and with a hurried twist to the left Hildy snaked her car around the stalled bus and gunned it up the on-ramp.

"Sorry. Whoops. Excuse me. Beg pardon," Hildy muttered to the drivers behind her as she roared onto the Expressway.

At the intersection, Joey had wakened to the danger far too late and had tried to follow Hildy's kamikaze charge. But in a split second the hole she had squeezed through closed, and Joey found himself jammed to a stop against the massive bumper of the bus and rammed on the left rear fender by an elderly station wagon. From each of these vehicles, an angry and frightened driver had emerged and was heading toward Joey as a poor substitute for the madwoman who had escaped.

"Jeez," Joey said to both attackers at once, "I got to make a phone call."

Once she was on the Expressway and sure that Joey hadn't followed, Hildy pulled into the slow lane. Her hands began shaking so violently that she couldn't steer, and she weaved into the first lay-by.

"Are you okay?" she asked Lizzie. Sophie still slept.

"Sure," said Lizzie. "That was fun. Do you know what I did?"

Hildy, still shuddering with fright and watching her hands as if they belonged to someone else, didn't answer.

"Just as we got onto the on-ramp," said Lizzie, "I stuck my tongue out at that boy. But do you know what?"

"No," said Hildy automatically.

"I don't think he saw me."

8

ON HIS DRIVE TO THE LAMPLIGHTER LATE THAT morning, Harry imagined that he was a perfect target caught in the crosshairs of a high-powered rifle. He fully expected every moment to be his last. But nothing happened. It was a warm morning full of sunshiny autumn haze, and the most sinister thing he heard was the cry of a wood pigeon.

Automatically, he set about cleaning the bar and setting up for the night's business. Marco had worked alone the night before, and there was much to do. Harry lost himself in the trivial tasks behind the bar, but all the time his mind was with Hildy and the girls. But then, after Harry had begun washing a sinkful of glasses, three telephone calls came which put his mind in new, more complicated channels.

The first was from Marco. "Hello, Marco boy," Harry said. "You must have had a good night here. Every glass in the joint is dirty."

"Sorry I wasn't able to get them cleaned up, Harry, but something came up right at closing time."

"Yeah," Harry said, "I'll bet. Has she gone home yet?"

Marco ignored the intended joke. "Harry," he said in a serious voice, "I'm not going to be able to come in to work."

"I think you're getting old, kid," Harry said, still joking. "Why—"

"Harry," Marco cut in, and the obvious urgency in his voice stopped Harry cold, "I'm serious. I can't come in."

"That's okay," Harry said easily. "You take care of yourself, Marco. If you're not feeling well, maybe you better stay in bed for a couple of days. If it gets too busy, I'll give Hank Sherman a call to come in and help me out. When do you think you'll be back in?"

"I'm sorry," Marco said, "but I can't work for you anymore. I just can't."

"Can't work? I don't understand. Why? What's wrong, Marco?"

"I can't talk any more right now," Marco said in a strained voice. "I just can't work for you, so find somebody else. Goodbye."

"Marco?" But Marco was gone, and Harry put the receiver down with a baffled look on his face.

But Harry had little time to ponder this strange call. The telephone rang immediately. "Lamplighter."

"And about time, too," said Hildy. "What have you been doing—telephoning matrimonial agencies? You'll be interested to hear that we made it."

"Where are you?"

"I'd rather not say. You-know-who or God-knows-what might be listening in. Besides, you know very well where we are. Where did you tell me to telephone from?"

"Of course," said Harry. "But what happened? Did you have any trouble getting out of town?"

"Certainly not. Except for a pimply young man who insisted on trying to join our party. Lizzie spotted him in the supermarket parking lot, and he followed us all over town. But I lost him on Broderick Boulevard near the Expressway. The last time I saw him he was busy discussing motoring etiquette with a big bus driver."

"Are you all right?"

"Yes, but Lizzie's bored stiff already. She wormed it out of me that the cabin doesn't have a TV set. Sophie's still sleeping, but if she knew what she's been through, what little hair she has would be snow white. And the old banger is wheezing something terrible. I think I killed it."

"Hildy," Harry said, "go right to the cabin and stay there until I come to get you. Funny things are going on. Marco just called and said he can't work here anymore. God knows what will happen next."

"Okay."

"And take care of yourself."

"You, too, Harry," she said and hung up.

Harry tried to call Hoerner, and his answering service said they'd have him call back as soon as possible. Then he went back to his work. A half hour passed, and he was scooping a mound of squeezed-out oranges and lemons from a utility sink when the telephone rang again. He knew the voice immediately.

"Caster," demanded Carlo Rizzo, "what the hell are you playing at?"

"What do you mean, Mr. Rice?"

"You know what I mean. Your wife, this morning. She almost got one of my boys killed and then she disappeared on the Hudson Expressway."

"Does that mean you were having her followed?" There

was no answer. "I wouldn't say that was a very friendly thing to do."

"Caster," Rizzo said in a too-calm voice, "this is not a joke. If you think this is a game, you're going to find out that I can play very rough."

"I'm sure you can."

"Well then," Rizzo said, "what's your answer to my business proposition?" When Harry didn't respond, Rizzo insisted: "I want an answer."

"I need more time," Harry said. "This is a complicated proposition."

"There is no more time, Caster. I want an answer right now. What is it?"

"What choice have I, really?"

"None."

"All right, I'll go for your deal."

"Now you're being smart. I'll be right over."

"No," Harry said, "make it tonight. Come around—come around just before closing time. Say a quarter to two."

"Why not now?" Rizzo pressed. "I'm coming over."

"You do and I won't be here," said Harry firmly. "This is still my business, and I've told you when I want you to come here. At one forty-five tonight. I'll talk to you then."

"Okay, okay, Caster," Rizzo said good-naturedly, thinking that Harry was trying to save a little face in defeat by sticking at a small detail, "you're the boss. I'll see you tonight, okay?"

"Okay," said Harry, sweating in the cool darkness of the bar as he put the telephone down.

The twenty minutes which passed before Hoerner returned his call seemed like hours, but then Hoerner was on the line.

"Hello, Mr. Caster. What's happening?"

"Everything," Harry said. "Rizzo called a little while ago. He's getting edgy and he pushed me for a decision. He wanted to come over right then, but I was able to put him off."

"How long?"

"Only until tonight," Harry said glumly. "A quarter of an hour before closing. He said he'll be here, and I don't like the way he said it."

"Christ," said Hoerner, "that's not much time. Couldn't you do any better than that?"

"No. It was tough enough getting that much time. I still can't help expecting him at any moment."

"Just hold on," said Hoerner. "I've got a hell of a lot to do today, but you'll be seeing me about midnight tonight. Don't sweat the rest."

"But what's going to happen tonight?"

"I'll tell you later," Hoerner said. He had only a vague idea himself. "I assume Mrs. Caster got out of town safely this morning."

"Yes, she did," Harry said, "but just barely. Rizzo had some kid following her, and she had to lose him before she got on the Expressway. Rizzo was mad as hell."

"Too bad. That means Rizzo may be getting the idea that something is up, that you're not just lying down so that he can walk over you. And it changes things a bit."

"How?"

"I'll tell you tonight. In the meantime, you go to the bank and draw out five hundred bucks in fifties. I'll want it when I see you."

"Okay. Anything else?"

"No," said Hoerner. "Just take it easy today and be ready for anything tonight. We're going to need your help."

"My help? What doing?"

"You'll find out. See you tonight."

The receiver in Harry's hand went dead and he looked at it questioningly before returning it to the holder. With a sigh, he went back to work behind the bar.

9

IT WAS THE PRIME OF THE EVENING, AND THE Lamplighter was well stocked with customers. Hank Sherman, the relief bartender, was doing most of the work while Harry chatted with the drinkers.

But Harry's mind was far from the Lamplighter that evening. He had no idea what Hoerner was up to. He only hoped that whatever it was would help rather than make the situation worse. And what the hell was going on with Marco?

Harry kept up his usual light banter with the drinkers, gossiping, throwing dice for drinks, settling disputes from his set of reference books near the cash register. And the clock wound around to midnight. At that hour, the bar was packed, and Harry was caught up in a furious game of liar's dice with Doc Schenley when he glanced up and saw Hoerner looking over his opponent's shoulder.

Accidentally letting a die escape from the box, Harry recaptured it and said to Hoerner: "I'll be with you in a minute."

"No hurry," said Hoerner easily. "I'll be over in the corner booth."

After losing the game, Harry excused himself and went over to Hoerner.

"Good evening, Mr. Caster," Hoerner said. "Have you heard from Rizzo this evening?"

"No," said Harry, "but I forgot to tell you something this afternoon when you called." He quickly filled Hoerner in about Marco's curious telephone call.

"That doesn't sound promising," said Hoerner, "but we'll handle it." He looked at his watch. "Rizzo is due in about an hour and a half. There's a back door to this place, isn't there?"

"Yes. It leads to the alley out back. We take deliveries there."

"Show me where it is and the rest of the layout."

Harry led the way through a narrow corridor piled high with liquor and soft-drink cases to the back door. Hoerner inspected the high-walled alley and came back inside.

"Okay. Have you got an empty room back here?"

"Just the liquor storeroom," Harry said. "What do you want it for?"

"Let me take a look at it," said Hoerner, ignoring the question. Harry switched on the light in a small, white-painted room half-full of cases of liquor. The room was about ten-foot square and windowless.

"Can some of these cases be moved somewhere else?" Hoerner asked.

"Yes, I'll put them in back near the door."

"Never mind," Hoerner said. "We'll take care of that. You get back to your customers. When Rizzo shows up we'll know. Stall him until closing time, lock up, turn off the front lights and lead him back here. Then I'll take over."

"But—"

"Mr. Caster, you hired me to do a job. I've already started. You'll just have to trust me."

"Okay," said Harry, and he returned to the front of the bar.

"What's up, Harry?" asked a regular customer. "Got a buyer for the joint?"

"I should be so lucky, Burt."

After one in the morning, the crowd began to thin out. People who had to work the next day slowly began to leave. Only the hardcore of light sleepers and non-workers were left huddled around the bar. A little later, Harry told Hank he could go home and then was left with a small knot of mid-week drinkers who didn't want to go home until they absolutely had to.

Unencouraged by Harry to stick around, even these began to slide off their stools and make their way to the front door. Finally, only Jimmy Allgood, a retired Army sergeant, was left hugging the curved bar with a glass of rye whiskey in his hand. And then Rizzo was in the doorway. He was alone, but his big, cream-colored car was parked out in front with someone sitting in the darkened front seat.

"Hello, Harry," said Rizzo, easing onto a stool. "Hi, Jimmy."

"Hello," Harry said reluctantly, his eyes returning quickly to the glass he was washing. Allgood didn't return the greeting.

"Bourbon and water," said Rizzo. Harry gave him the drink and then retreated to the sink again. "Business good tonight?"

"Fair," said Harry.

"It'll get better. You ready to have that little talk now?"

"As soon as I close up," Harry said. "Jimmy—"

"In Hudson County, the State of New York," said the old sergeant, "establishments which are licensed to serve alcoholic beverages are allowed to serve such beverages until two a.m. It is now one-fifty a.m. I'll have another rye, Harry. A double."

With a look at Rizzo, Harry poured the drink.

"Thanks," said Allgood. "Now you're going by the book. It's a good policy. In thirty-eight years of soldiering, all I had to do was take a little look in the book and any problem was solved."

"Yes, Jimmy," said Harry, not really listening.

"Any problem. In '43 I had a problem with a wop kid in our outfit in England. He was a real cute little fellow who could use his fists like razor blades; flyweight champion of the division, he was. He could have been a champion. He was some cute little guinea."

"Jimmy—" Harry said warningly.

"No," said Rizzo, "I want to hear. What happened to the little wop, Jimmy?"

"Got too cute for his own good. We had a West Point captain, a miserable bastard but a good soldier, and Peruchio, that was the wop, Pfc. Peruchio, took a fancy to this captain's wife. She was a tall blonde from Cleveland. She encouraged the boy to a certain degree."

"Encouraged him?" asked Rizzo.

"Took off her panties and climbed into the back of the captain's staff car with him," said Allgood. "The captain found them all twisted up like a pair of wet overalls."

"What happened?" asked Harry in spite of himself.

"Court-martial. Got out my little book of U.S. Army regulations. Absent without leave, conduct prejudicial to discipline, undue familiarity and failure to obey a direct order. Got three years at hard labor. The captain got his head blown off by a booby trap in France. Don't know what happened to the blonde. Probably went back to Cleveland. Just goes to show you: Always go by the book and things will turn out all right."

"Right," said Harry, "it's now two o'clock and the book says it's time for you to go home."

"Correct," said Allgood. He downed the dregs of his drink with a gulp and started to push himself away from the bar. "Uh-oh, Harry," he said, "I think you've poisoned me. Legs won't work. Look, they've gone as limp as a bishop's pecker."

"Tell you what, Jimmy," said Harry, coming around the bar, "I might be court-martialed for doing it, but I'll give you a hand to the door." Putting the old soldier's arm over his shoulder, Harry tried to hoist him from the barstool. But Jimmy's two hundred pounds sagged limply, and his legs flailed.

"Here," said Rizzo, "we can do it together." Taking Allgood's other arm, he helped pull the old man from the stool.

"It's a miracle," said Allgood. "I can walk again." With ramrod back and rubbery legs, he allowed Harry and Rizzo to pilot him to the door. "I can make it home," he said.

"Good luck, Sarge," said Harry, shaking his hand.

"You're a white man, Harry," said Allgood. "It's an honor to serve with you." He looked at Rizzo. "You, too, Mr. Rice. I'm sorry about that story. I mean about the wops and all."

"That's all right," said Rizzo. "Everybody's somebody's wop." With military formality, the old man saluted them both and walked stiffly into the chilly night.

"So much for that," said Harry, bolting the front door and drawing the drapes at the front windows.

"Now we can have that talk, eh?" said Rizzo.

Harry hadn't forgotten, but it was still a shock to find the moment upon him. "Look," he said in almost a pleading voice, "can't you just—"

"No," said Rizzo sharply. "No more fooling around, Caster. I mean business."

"Okay, Rizzo," Harry was surprised to hear himself say calmly, "as soon as I douse the lights out here, we can talk in my office."

Rizzo leaned against the bar, watching Harry go around the room switching off the old converted oil lamps. One by one they died until the big room was lit only by a neon globe behind the bar.

When the last light was extinguished, Rizzo said impatiently: "That's it, right?"

"That's it," said Harry. "This way." He started toward his cubbyhole office. Rizzo fell in behind him.

Harry looked neither to left nor right as he walked slowly in the near darkness. He imagined his heart was louder than his footsteps. Behind him, Rizzo was humming a tune he didn't recognize.

Abruptly the humming stopped.

"Hey!" Rizzo cried as a dark figure closed in from each side. The larger one gripped him around both arms while the other pulled an eyeless black hood over Rizzo's head. "What is this?"

"Shut up." Hoerner shoved the barrel of a pistol against the bump in the hood which was Rizzo's nose. Lifting Rizzo off his feet, the big man Harry had never seen before wrestled him swiftly into the storeroom and set him down in a straight chair. The light went on revealing a small projector set on an up-ended whiskey case.

Not knowing what else to do, Harry followed along and

stood aimlessly in the doorway as the big man swiftly tied Rizzo to the chair with his hands roped behind him. The stranger was dark haired and blocky with a dime-sized purple-black birthmark at the corner of his nose. His face was expressionless.

Hoerner, with a short-barreled black revolver in his hand, motioned Harry into the room and into a corner behind Rizzo's left shoulder. Finished with the tying job, the big man straightened up and remained looming over Rizzo, who sat faceless and silent. Rizzo had remained mute since his first cry of surprise, partly because of Hoerner's threat and partly because his mind was a whirl of half thoughts he kept plucking up and casting down like playing cards. He cursed himself for being stupid enough to come into the bar alone; he cursed that useless bastard, Pete, sitting in his car on the street listening to the radio. He'd just been too confident, too sure that Caster was an easy mark.

"Is your name Carlo Rizzo?" Hoerner asked softly.

Rizzo said nothing, only gave his hooded head a stubborn shake.

"Hit him," said Hoerner, and the big man cocked his fist.

Rizzo jerked his head back as if he had been hit. "My name is Charles Rice," he said, "and my business is with Harry Caster. It's nothing to do with you."

At a nod from Hoerner, the big man landed a stinging backhand blow to Rizzo's right jaw which snapped his head back violently. Slowly Rizzo lowered his head. Harry put a hand to his own jaw, and the big man silently sucked his knuckles. Harry started to say something, but Hoerner cut him off with a sharp gesture.

"That's where you're wrong, Rizzo," Hoerner said. "It's everything to do with us. Someone very interested in Mr.

Caster's welfare has hired us to see that you leave him alone. We know everything that has happened since Monday night as well as you do, and some things better than you do."

He paused, but Rizzo remained silent.

"It's in your interest," Hoerner continued, "to end this matter right here, tonight. But it's even more in your interest, Rizzo, to drop this business right now and leave it dropped. We know you're in bad with Montara. If you get in trouble, Rizzo, the family is not going to raise a hand to help you as long as you're on Abe's shit list." Hoerner paused again. "And you are in trouble. Carlo, real trouble." He gestured to Harry. "Lights."

The room went dark, and Rizzo felt the hood being untied and lifted from his head. But he could see nothing. Then from behind he heard the same voice say: "Okay, roll it," and a square of light burst out on the white wall in front of him. Rizzo tried to turn his head, but a big, hard hand gripped the back of his neck firmly.

"Eyes forward," Hoerner ordered.

Then a string of garbled letters and numbers flashed on the improvised screen, followed by a blur which slowly focused into a black-and-white image of a low, modern house with a sloping lawn and a basement garage. It was some seconds before Rizzo realized that it was his own house. At first it seemed to be a still picture, but then a starling flew into the frame and perched on a telephone wire.

"What the hell—"

"Shut up, Rizzo. I'll do the talking. I think you'll recognize this scene." The camera zoomed in on the front door. It opened, and Angela Rizzo, wearing a flowered apron, came out and stood, hands on ample hips, on the sheltered porch.

"This is Mrs. Angela Rizzo, known locally as Angela

Rice." Hoerner fell into the narrator's deadened tones. "She's waiting for someone." The camera's eye switched to a distant corner, closed in on that corner and hung there until Rizzo wanted to scream. Finally, the figure of a small girl turned the corner, and the camera slowly backed up into a long shot showing Angela Rizzo waiting on the porch and the girl slowly—so slowly—walking beside a tall wooden fence.

"This is Maria Rizzo, aged six," Hoerner continued tonelessly, "who also goes by the name of Rice."

"You son of a bitch," said Rizzo, but he felt the hard hand tighten on his neck.

"Every afternoon at shortly after three o'clock, Maria Rizzo leaves All Saints Elementary School," Hoerner said, and the scene turned to the exterior of the grammar school and the camera singled out Maria walking away from a group of friends. Rizzo watched with fascination as his daughter, looking even smaller and more vulnerable than she was, moved along, step by step, with childish preoccupation. He wanted to shout: "Faster, Maria, faster!"

"Most afternoons, Maria walks home from school alone. It takes her approximately eleven minutes to cover the two and a half blocks if she doesn't stop along the way."

The film cut to the girl stopped in the middle of a block petting a large calico cat sitting on a cement-block fence. The camera lingered on the girl and the cat until Rizzo knew he had to jump up and stop it. He strained against the rope but stopped when he felt the muzzle of a pistol pushed into the soft indentation where his head joined his neck. Rizzo sank back but did not relax.

With relief, he saw that Maria had begun to walk again. But then something dark and bulky caught his eye at the extreme of the patch of light. Harry Caster saw it, too, and sucked in his breath audibly. That dark something was a big car, purposely out of focus, that had turned the corner behind the traipsing child and was closing in with the inexorable pace of a cruising shark. Rizzo and Harry watched in horror as the big car pulled alongside the girl and seemed to match its pace to hers. Rizzo was glassy-eyed with anticipation; Harry could hardly keep his eyes open.

To their great relief, the film cut once more to the front of Rizzo's house. Maria had just come through the gate and had turned to fix the latch. Angela Rizzo had taken a step toward her daughter. Maria turned toward her mother and started running up the path, her arms out-flung and her hair flying. She hurled herself at her mother's arms, and there the picture froze with Maria's sweet, joyous face nearly filling the small screen.

The projector cut off, plunging the room once more into total darkness. "Have you seen enough, Rizzo?"

Rizzo opened his mouth, but at first he couldn't speak. When his voice came, he didn't recognize it. "What are you guys playing at?"

"We're not playing at anything," said Hoerner firmly. "We're just telling you that if you don't lay off Caster—from this moment on—you and yours will suffer. Someone is going to get hurt, Rizzo, and it's going to be you. And those very close to you."

"You're crazy."

"You think so? Show the man a little more film."

In rapid progression Rizzo saw, flashing on the screen, images of his family: his son Bobby in a line waiting for a bus; his father in his tobacco shop on Prince Street; his mother, stubby and gray-haired, examining a cauliflower at a street stall; his brother Steve, hands in the pockets of his leather jacket, coming down the steps of the building where the Rizzos lived in lower Manhattan. The frame stopped with Steve's foot in mid-air.

"Turn it off," Rizzo said involuntarily, shutting his eyes.

"Okay," agreed Hoerner, "anything to oblige." The projector went dark. "Put the hood back on, and let's have some light."

The naked bulb revealed Rizzo, hooded once more, in the straight-backed chair. He looked unreal, as lifeless as a manikin. The three men stood silently watching him for several minutes. When Hoerner spoke his voice was soft, but Rizzo jerked as if he'd been touched.

"Rizzo," he said, "if we wanted to, we could kill you right now and solve our problem. I don't think many people would miss you. The river is deep enough to hide a thousand small-time punks like you."

At first Rizzo was silent, and when he did speak it was not to his anonymous persecutor. "Caster," he said hoarsely, "are you there?" Hoerner shook his head peremptorily, and Harry shut his mouth again. He realized that he was wringing his hands, and they were wet with sweat.

"It's got nothing to do with Caster now, Rizzo," Hoerner said. "You're dealing with us, not him. You'd better make up your mind. We'll give you a minute's silence to think things out, but then I want an answer. The right answer."

A thin, sour silence fell on the room, and inside the hood Rizzo struggled to swallow. Without waiting for the minute to end, he croaked dryly, "Look—"

"Take the full time. Carlo. Make sure it's what you really want to say. Get our friend a drink from the bar," he said to Harry. "Bourbon and water, isn't it, Rizzo?"

Harry silently left the room. But instead of going behind the bar, he crept over to the Lamplighter's front window and peeked out at Rizzo's car parked half in the arc of a street lamp. A dark figure was still hunched behind the steering wheel, and Harry thought he could hear the thin strains of pop music coming from the car. He dropped the corner of the dark drape and ducked behind the littered bar. Carefully, he poured out a tall glass of bourbon and water and took a little slug from the bottle himself. The ice cubes gently clicked as he walked back down the dark hallway.

Alec Hoerner pulled the hood up over Rizzo's mouth so that he could drink. Rizzo took the drink greedily, not stopping until the ice clinked against his teeth and the bourbon and water was gone. A sigh escaped him.

"That was good, eh?" Hoerner took the glass away and let the hood fall again. "I'm getting thirsty myself, so let's get this over with. What's your answer, Rizzo?"

Rizzo slumped in the chair, falling against his bonds as if he had no backbone.

"Yes," he said, "yes. I'll lay off Caster."

At a nod from Hoerner, the big man plucked Rizzo from the chair, his hands still bound behind him, as if he were a baby. Hoerner opened the door to the hallway, and Rizzo was hustled out of the room toward the alleyway. Harry stood where he was for a moment and then hurried to follow.

"Wait!" cried Rizzo. "No, I told you—you win. I'll lay off. I really will. Help!"

Hoerner smoothly brought the butt of his pistol down on the back of Rizzo's hooded head, and his small body slumped in the big man's arms. Rizzo's expensive shoes dragged along the rough concrete floor. In the alley, Rizzo was thrust into the far corner of the back seat of Hoerner's black BMW sedan. The big man turned to Hoerner as if expecting further orders, but Hoerner reached into the breast pocket of his suit coat and handed him a folded banknote.

"Okay," Hoerner said, "that's it. You did well. Disappear."

The big man took a quick peek at the note and slipped it into his pocket. "Thanks," he said, turning and walking with urgency toward the darkness at the end of the alley. In a few steps he was gone.

Hoerner turned back through the rear entrance of the Lamplighter. Harry met him in the hall.

"Christ!" Harry said. "What a show. Those movies— where's Rizzo? Is he all right?"

"He's fine, Mr. Caster." Hoerner smiled. "Rizzo's taking a little nap in my car back there. But we'll be taking him for a little ride in just a minute or two."

"You will?" Harry asked. "Hey, you're not going to— to—"

"No," said Hoerner, "not right now, anyway. But I'm not going to take Mr. Rizzo for a ride. We are. You and me. And right now."

"Me?" said Harry. "What about him—the big guy?"

"Oh, my friend had a very pressing date someplace, so I paid him off. And speaking of money, weren't you going to have five hundred dollars for me tonight?"

"Oh, yeah." Harry pulled a thick envelope of banknotes from the side pocket of his coat. "It's all there."

"I'm sure it is," said Hoerner. "And now I've got something for you." He reached into a side pocket and came up with a chromium- plated revolver much like his own. He thrust it at Harry butt first. "Do you know how to handle one of these?"

"I—I suppose so," said Harry, reluctantly taking the

revolver in both hands. "But I haven't fired one since the Army. What do I need it for? I'm not—"

"You probably won't need it, but it won't hurt you to carry it. You may be glad to have a gun before this is over. Let's get going. Rizzo's not going to nap out there forever." He turned and started down the hallway.

Harry followed him involuntarily. "But, where…?"

"I'll explain later," said Hoerner, "when we've got more time."

They had reached the car. "I'll drive. You sit in back with Rizzo and keep an eye on him. But don't speak. The less Rizzo knows of your personal involvement in this little adventure, the more off-balance he's going to be. If he stirs, let him know you've got that gun."

"How?"

"Use your imagination," said Hoerner, walking around the car and slipping behind the steering wheel.

Harry locked the back door of the Lamplighter and got in back with Rizzo's slumped form. There was no sign that he was conscious yet. Harry hefted the revolver uneasily in his right hand as the car began moving slowly down the dark alley.

10

RIZZO REGAINED CONSCIOUSNESS SHORTLY AFTER THE car left the alley, but he remained huddled in the corner without moving, pretending to be still knocked out. His hooded face was pressed into the corner of the door and car seat, and his hands had begun to lose feeling. Rizzo's brain, beyond the sharp ache, was a confusion of questions: Who are these guys? What's their game? If they're going to kill me, why the song and dance with the films? Who are they?

He racked his memory. Rizzo hadn't caught even a glance at their faces, and he'd heard only one voice: that of the boss, the heavy. He'd never heard that voice before, but he'd know it if he ever heard it again. But he drew a blank now. Except for the deep sound of the engine and the whir of the tires on the road, all was quiet. Rizzo could sense that someone was in the back seat with him. That made two in the car. Was there a third?

His eyes now adjusted to the darkness, Harry sat in the opposite corner watching Rizzo's inert form and wondering if he were really unconscious. He hefted the compact weight of the revolver. It was strange but comforting to have it in his hand. The safety was on, and out of curiosity he swung open the cylinder to see how many shells were in it. All six chambers were full. With a flick of his wrist, Harry swung the cylinder shut again.

To Rizzo, the soft, oiled click was as loud as a door slamming. He jerked involuntarily, and Harry caught the movement. He started to say something, but then remembered he was supposed to stay silent. He looked down at the gun in his hand and then instinctively reached out and shoved it against the side of Rizzo's head. A little too hard.

"Ow!" Rizzo said without meaning to. He could have bitten off his tongue.

"So Carlo's awake, is he?" said Hoerner. "Take it easy, Rizzo. It won't be a long ride."

Harry pulled the revolver away from Rizzo's head as he felt the captive's body go limp.

"Not talking, eh?" said Hoerner. "That's okay. I can't stand a lot of begging and pleading anyway."

"You're a funny man," said Rizzo in spite of himself. "I don't know what you guys think you're doing." His voice was muffled from the hood and from the way his face was shoved into the corner.

"We're just doing a little job, that's all, Rizzo," said Hoerner. "For somebody who doesn't like your business methods much." Abe Montara. The name flashed through Rizzo's mind. But Abe wouldn't do this. The freeze-out was bad enough. Speranza wouldn't let him go this far. Hiring outsiders.

Just then, Rizzo felt the car leave the smooth highway for the roughness of a secondary road. The tires didn't whisper now; they muttered and grumbled at the resistance of the roadway. He sensed that they were approaching their destination.

"Hey," he said, trying to sound casual, "where are we going? Look, let's talk about this. I mean, Caster's place doesn't mean anything to me. What do I want with a small-time joint like that?"

"You keep thinking like that, Rizzo," said Hoerner, "and you'll live a lot longer."

They rode a few minutes more in silence while Rizzo searched for something to say, some argument that would carry weight. Harry felt mingling apprehension and a sense of power over the man who had been his tormentor. The car slowed to a stop, and Rizzo imagined that his heart stopped, too. But after a few seconds the car started again, turning onto what felt like a dirt road. On one bump Rizzo bounced so hard that his head hit the window ledge with a sharp rap.

"Don't hurt yourself," said Hoerner coldly.

The car jolted to another stop, and Hoerner killed the engine. Rizzo went rigid as stone.

"Get him out," he heard the driver tell the gunman in the back. The other door opened and slammed, and Rizzo waited like a man on a hanging scaffold. The door opened and Rizzo fell like a sack of flour into a soft bank of fallen leaves. He didn't move.

"Up you go," said Hoerner, jerking Rizzo up by the coat and making him stand on tiptoe. Rizzo tottered unsteadily on muscles stiffened during the ride.

"Walk him." Rizzo, at the reluctant prod of Harry's pistol, began to shamble forward at a blind man's hesitant, hurtling pace, fearful at every moment of running into something.

"Hey, take it easy," he complained.

"You'll have a long time to take it easy, greaser," Hoerner said. He brought Rizzo to a rough halt by the rope around his hands. "Untie his hands."

Harry fumbled at the tight knots for a moment and then undid them and unwound the rope from Rizzo's hands. Rizzo's arms moved out from his sides involuntarily, and he felt the fizzy pain of the circulation returning.

"Whoever you are," he said, "be reasonable. I—"

Hoerner cut him off. "Okay," he said, "waste him." At the same time he brought his revolver up next to Rizzo's head and squeezed the trigger once.

Rizzo was engulfed by the roar, felt the sting of pain in his face and sensed that he was hurtling through space. He gathered breath to scream, but then the black inside the hood was filled with blinding light, and he lost consciousness.

Hoerner started back to his car and then noticed that Harry had stayed behind looking down into the blackness that had swallowed Rizzo.

"Come on," Hoerner said.

"You're just going to leave him there?"

"That's right. Come on; we're leaving."

Harry followed Hoerner silently to the car. But as they got moving on the bumpy back road, he burst out: "Christ, I never saw anything like that before."

"You didn't do so badly yourself, Mr. Caster," said Hoerner with a hard smile. "The way you were handling that gun in the back seat, I thought you were going to cool Rizzo and put me out of a job."

"I didn't know what to do."

"You did the right thing."

"I don't know. Rizzo's not badly hurt back there, is he?"

"He'll be all right," said Hoerner.

"How'll he get back to Parker's Landing?"

"That's his problem. Our problem is what he's going to do once he gets home. If he jumps the wrong way, we may be in a bit of trouble."

"What do you think he'll do?"

"If he's sensible, he'll nurse his hurt feelings for a while and then go off to find somebody else to lean on. If tonight didn't convince him that we mean business, he'll have to learn his lesson an even harder way. What you mean, Mr. Caster, is what are we going to do. Don't think that you're going to be able to just sit back and cheer from the sidelines while Rizzo and I cut each other up. I didn't give you that gun tonight just for show. If worst comes to worst, you'll have to use it."

"Me?" said Harry, all innocence. "I hired you to—to..."

"To what, Mr. Caster? To fight Rizzo? To put a bullet through his guinea head so that you can go back to your peaceful little bar? Is that what you thought you hired? A murderer?"

"No, of course not."

"No," agreed Hoerner, wheeling the car back on the highway, "you hired me to help you fight back against Carlo Rizzo. To help you protect yourself, your family and your property."

"But your organization..."

Hoerner laughed shortly. "My organization consists of exactly two people—you and me."

"But those movies, and that big guy at the Lamplighter tonight. What about them?"

"Yeah. What about them? The movies were a favor by a documentary filmmaker I know who's not working now.

And the geek with no forehead was casual labor who needed a fast twenty. I never saw him before tonight, and with luck I'll never see him again. So you see, like it or not, it boils down to you and me. Mostly me, but you've got to understand I may need backing up."

"Christ," said Harry. He couldn't think of anything else to say.

"Of course, if you're not satisfied, just say the word and I'll drop the case right here and let you hire somebody else." Hoerner took one hand from the wheel and reached for his inside breast pocket. "I'll just give you your money back and…"

"No, no," said Harry. "I don't want that."

"It's a good thing, Mr. Caster," Hoerner said, "because I've already spent a big piece of it, and if I didn't have the rest tomorrow, the finance company would be driving this car and I'd be walking."

"You mean," Harry asked, "that you're a phony? That you've been running a big bluff?"

"I'm no phony," said Hoerner angrily, unconsciously stomping down on the accelerator pedal. "Don't get that idea. I may be running a bluff, but I mean every word I say. I can take Rizzo. I know it. You've got to believe that, Mr. Caster, or we're through before we start. You don't know how many agencies your brother went through before he got to me. I'm your only chance, Mr. Caster, and you've got to know it."

"I believe it," said Harry without too much certainty. "I don't see that I've got much choice. All right, let's say that you—that we can take them. Now what? To begin with you can knock off the Mr. Caster stuff. Call me Harry. What do I call you?"

"Suit yourself. Call me Alec or Hoerner. It doesn't matter."

"All right, Hoerner, what next?"

"We wait," said Hoerner. "And we hope that Rizzo learned something tonight. We hope he stays off your back."

"And if he doesn't?"

"Well," said Hoerner, "he can't do much alone. Like you, he needs some help to fight this kind of war. Unless my information is terribly wrong, he's not going to get much joy from the Speranza family." He told Harry how Rizzo stood with Abe Montara, the real power in the family, and why.

"But what if Montara does forgive Rizzo?" Harry asked.

"Then we're in the shit, Harry. Up to our pretty little necks. But it won't happen. Believe me. I wouldn't have jumped into this situation just for the sake of getting smashed by Abe Montara. I'm not that crazy." They were entering the scattered outskirts of Parker's Landing. "I'll drop you at the Lamplighter, right?"

"Yes," said Harry, "my car is there. But what about Rizzo's friend? The one he left sitting in front of the place in his car."

"It's after four in the morning. If that monkey is still sitting there, Rizzo's going to be an easier touch than I thought."

The street in front of the Lamplighter was empty.

"Thank God for that," said Harry. "I wonder where he is."

"He's wondering the same thing about Rizzo. I wouldn't want to be him when Rizzo gets home. You go home and get some sleep now, Harry. If I've figured Rizzo right, he's going to be closed up tight and licking his wounds for a bit. I don't think you'll be hearing from him immediately. Don't forget, he thinks he's up against some pretty tough operators. He'll be seeing a gunman around every corner for a while."

"So will I," said Harry. "Call me tomorrow morning just to check. If I don't answer the telephone. I'm dead. Rizzo got me." He got out of Hoerner's car and watched the detective drive smoothly away. He was very conscious of the weight of the gun in his pocket.

11

It was the cold, damp and insinuating, that woke Rizzo. He fluttered his eyes and then opened them to the shock of total darkness. Then he remembered, and his first thought was, *why am I not dead?*

With impatient, cold-stiffened fingers, Rizzo ripped off the hood, and the light of a full moon attacked his eyes like sunlight after a long tunnel. When he could see again, Rizzo found that he was at the bottom of a sharp fifteen-foot slope jammed against the thick trunk of a squat tree.

Except for a terrible ringing in his ears and the pain in his head, Rizzo seemed to be in one piece and unharmed. Gingerly, he felt his body for broken bones and then put his hand to his smarting face. It came away black with blood.

Rizzo looked at his hand and felt sick. Then the smell of gunpowder and burnt cloth came to him, and he knew what had happened. The gunman had fired very close to his head but missed him —either on purpose or by mistake—and the blast of the gun had scorched the hood and peppered his cheek with tiny bits of powder. He picked up the hood and found it charred and bloody. Rizzo carefully patted the singed side of his head and felt burned hair fall away.

Patting his face with a handkerchief, Rizzo leaned back against the tree that had stopped his fall. He could see nothing at the top of the slope. Through the shattered crystal his still-running watch told him it was a quarter after four. Listening carefully, he could hear only the rustling of branches and the sound of an occasional night bird. He felt better. His head still ached, but his cheek seemed to have stopped bleeding.

Home seemed the answer, so slowly and stiffly Rizzo edged up the steep slope. He feared, almost expected, at any moment to hear voices or feel the impact of a bullet. Nothing happened. Rizzo got to the dirt road and found nothing but darkness and silence. He trudged warily up the dirt road wondering where the hell he was.

Soon he found the rough macadam road and turned onto it without thinking. But then there was a flash of lights and a screeching of brakes.

"You trying to get yourself killed, mister?" asked a loud voice from a pick-up truck which had slammed to a stop just a few feet behind him.

Rizzo was blinded by the headlights until he got past them to the driver's window. "Sorry," he said, "I didn't see you." He tried to keep the right side of his face away from the driver. "I've had some trouble with my car. Are you going toward Parker's Landing?"

"Part way." The driver was dressed in the rough clothes of a farmer and wore thick, round glasses. "Get in. I'll take you as far as I go."

Rizzo gratefully eased himself onto the plastic-covered seat and closed the door. They had driven in silence for about five minutes when the driver spoke. "You're bleeding."

Putting his handkerchief to his face, Rizzo said, "I had a bit of an accident back there." He wondered if the farmer believed him. "Look," said Rizzo, "I feel lousy. Could you drive me clear into Parker's Landing? I'll pay you."

The driver said nothing.

"I could pay you five dollars."

"Make it ten," said the farmer.

"Okay," said Rizzo, sinking gratefully back into his worrying thoughts.

Rizzo had the farmer let him out a block from his house and paid him. As he turned the corner, the first thing he saw was his car parked in front of his house with Pete sleeping behind the wheel.

Rizzo raised enough strength to rip open the car door, causing Pete to nearly spill out into the street.

"Wha—" Pete grabbed for the steering wheel to save himself and reached for the gun inside his jacket at the same time. Then he recognized Rizzo. "Mr. Rice. Where did you go? I waited in front of that bar for hours."

Rizzo raised his hand but then let it drop futilely. "Go home and get some sleep, Pete," he said. "I want you here at eight-thirty to take my kids to school. Bring Ernie with you, and come prepared to stay for a while."

"What's up, Mr. Rice?"

"I'll tell you in the morning. Go now."

Rizzo limped up the walk and opened the front door quietly. Behind him the first gray of predawn was showing. As the door swung open, the flash of a large white envelope on the hall carpet caught his eye. Stooping stiffly, Rizzo picked it up and carried it into his small den. Switching on a shaded light over the expensive, carved desk, he ripped open the envelope and a large photograph slid out and fell face down on the desk.

Rizzo turned the photograph over and found that it was an enlarged frame of the film he'd been shown that night at Caster's bar. It was a full-face photo of Maria, eyes downcast with childish preoccupation. Slightly soft and out of focus, the picture emphasized the girl's delicate features and vulnerability. Superimposed on her face was the spiderweb sighting of a telescopic sight. The effect brought flaring back to Rizzo's mind all of the shocks he'd been through in the last few hours. He started to rip the photograph up, but couldn't do it. He shoved it quickly under the desk blotter. The envelope was blank except for "Rizzo" scrawled on the front.

Crumpling the envelope and throwing it at the waste basket, Carlo Rizzo embarked upon a series of miscalculations and errors of judgment. First, he remembered only the humiliation and pain he'd suffered that night, discounting the cool efficiency and deadly seriousness of his captors. He was no longer grateful to be alive. Rizzo knew only that he'd been had, and for that someone was going to suffer terribly. He had only contempt for those who'd had his life in their hands and let it slip.

Second, Rizzo refused to accept that they could seriously hurt him and his family. The lesson of the night was already fading away. It was others who were hit, who were punished, who felt the pain.

They were the victims, the suckers, the fish—not Carlo Rizzo. He dealt out the fear; they bent under it. Helped by his family, his friends, his bosses, his subordinates, Rizzo could take on these lucky amateurs—they had to be amateurs—that Caster had foolishly called upon for help. They'd see who would win.

At once more relaxed, Rizzo walked through the darkened house to the bathroom at the rear. In the mirror he looked like a man who had been shot at and very nearly hit and then pushed off a cliff. Stripping off his ruined clothes, he showered and did what he could to doctor the side of his face. Then, taking blankets from a cupboard, he bedded down on the couch in his den to try to sleep the dawning hour.

Only a couple of hours later, Angie Rizzo woke in their big bed and reached out to touch her husband. Finding herself alone, her plump face clouded with worry and she got up and slipped on a robe. The children were still asleep. There was a cold, gray light outside, but the house had the stillness of night.

Angie padded down the stairs to Rizzo's den. Carefully she opened the door and saw his blanket-shrouded figure on the sofa. She walked into the room until she stood over her sleeping husband, drawing back slightly as she saw the raw and blackened cheek above the satin-edged blanket. She placed her hand next to but not touching Rizzo's injured face as if to draw the hurt from it into her own body.

Later, after Pete had taken Bobby and Maria to school, Angie heard the bathroom door shut and the sound of running water. Shortly, Rizzo emerged as dapper as ever except for the white bandage on his cheek and a smudge of soft black which escaped the bandage.

"Good morning, Carlo."

"Morning." Rizzo sat down at the kitchen table and took up the morning paper.

"Would you like some bacon and eggs?"

"No, just coffee. I'm going right out." Rizzo put the paper up as a barrier to unspoken questions and worried looks. As he sipped his nearly boiling black coffee, Rizzo felt an urge to tell Angie everything. But he couldn't. The pull of custom was too strong. A wife could share only so much.

After his coffee, Rizzo kissed Angie goodbye. "Stay in today," he told her, "and when the kids come home, keep them in. Tell Bobbie I said so. Pete and Ernie will be with you all day, and Pete will pick up the kids after school."

Angie nodded silently and stood in the doorway watching Rizzo speak briefly on the sidewalk with Pete and Ernie. After watching her husband's car disappear around the corner, she turned back to her kitchen, her pleasant face taut with worry.

12

Baptiste Speranza was in his garden treating aphids on a tall, late-flowering rosebush when Kathy told him that Rizzo had arrived. "Ask him to wait a few moments," he told his auburn-haired granddaughter.

Kneeling heavily before the ailing plant, Speranza was a man at peace with the world. His long, once-powerful limbs were weighted down with flesh which seemed to pull him toward the earth he had come to love so much in the last few years. Once a rich and flashy dresser, he now wore a pair of baggy overalls, a blue denim work-shirt and a maroon cardigan with one unraveling cuff. Pushed back from his thick, gray hairline was a very old straw hat nine-year-old Kathy had found someplace and had insisted that he wear. Speranza found that it suited him. Once, coming unexpectedly upon a mirror, for a second he had thought he was seeing his father as he had been in the last few years of his life.

In those days, Baptiste, then in the full strength of maturity, had felt fond contempt for the old man and considered him a failure for plugging away at his flower shop while others who had come to America at the same time had carved fortunes out of the raw years of the twenties. But now he understood, and Speranza could see the same look in the eyes of his sons.

They and the others were respectful toward him—at least to his face—but Speranza knew he no longer wielded any real power, and it didn't bother him. Somehow, living here in Parker's Landing with Carmen, his widowed daughter, to look after him, it didn't matter. It was power enough for him to doctor this beautiful plant, to see it bloom again, a strong deep yellow, next summer. Wishing that Rizzo wasn't in the house waiting for him, the old man gave the rose plant a few more bursts from the spray can with the absorbed expression of a physician lost to all else but the needs of his patient.

In the living room of the big, modern house, Rizzo waited with impatience tinged with foreboding. He sat on a blocky leather sofa and unconsciously ran the toe of his shoe against the nap of the thick, wheat-colored carpet, watching its color change to dark gold.

Kathy came back into the living room. "My grandfather asks if you'll wait a little while," she said. Rizzo saw that she was staring at the bandage on his cheek. Embarrassed, Kathy pulled her eyes away. "Would you like some coffee?"

"Yeah," said Rizzo, "please. Black with no sugar."

The girl went to a high mahogany sideboard and poured Rizzo a large cup of coffee from an electric pot.

"Is it hot enough?"

It wasn't; it was lukewarm, but Rizzo drank it. "Just fine."

"I'm out of school sick today," Kathy told him. "I had an earache when I woke up and Mother thought—"

"Hello, Charlie." Rizzo looked up and saw Gino Speranza, the old man's younger son, in the doorway of the front hall. He was a squat, curly-haired man in his mid-twenties wearing glasses with a very light green tint. "What are you doing here?"

"Uncle Gino!" said Kathy, turning around.

"Hiya, Kath," said Gino. "Why aren't you in school?"

"Earache," explained Kathy, putting a dirty hand to her left ear. "Shall I tell Grandpa you're here?"

"Sure, I guess so," said Gino, flopping heavily on the other end of the leather sofa and putting a moccasined foot on the dark, oval coffee table in front of it. When Kathy had gone, he repeated: "What are you doing here, Charlie?"

"A little business, Gino. A little business."

"I think you've come to the wrong address, Charlie boy," said Gino. "These days business is generally conducted over on Ramona Way." Abe Montara lived just over two miles away.

Rizzo shrugged.

"What's wrong with your face?" Gino asked. "It looks like you've been standing too close to a blast furnace. Don't tell me Abe is getting that tough over a few bookkeeping errors."

"I had a little accident. Nothing serious."

"If you say so."

To change the subject, Rizzo said: "I thought you were supposed to be up at that business college in Syracuse. You on vacation?"

"Yeah," said Gino. "Permanent vacation. I graduated myself a little early and told them to stick it." He warmed to the subject. "Charlie, you wouldn't believe—"

"Gino."

Baptiste Speranza was standing in the doorway with his gardening gloves in his hand. Anger showed on his face.

"Hello, Papa," said Gino, taking his foot off the coffee table in spite of himself, "I—"

"In a minute," said the old man. "I've got business." He turned a welcoming but wary smile on Rizzo. "Hello, Carlo, you wanted to see me?"

"Uh, yes," Rizzo said stiffly, "I did. But if you're busy—"

"This is a good time," said Speranza. "Come. We'll find a place to talk." He looked at his son. "Gino," he said, "we'll talk in a little while, eh?"

"Sure, Papa."

Rizzo followed the old man down the hallway. Speranza stopped at a green metal door and put his hand on the doorknob. "We can have some privacy in here," he said.

Rizzo followed, and a blast of warm, moist air hit his face.

"Make sure you close the door tightly," cautioned Speranza. They were in a small greenhouse crowded with plants. Only a walkway of latticed boards was free of foliage. A small heater in the corner exuded a steady blast of warm air.

"Look at this, Carlo," said Speranza, cupping a delicate green-veined, peach-colored orchid, "*Orchis morio*. It's probably the only specimen in New York State. And look, more buds. They don't live long, the flowers, but they've got a beautiful aroma. Smell."

Impatiently, Rizzo bent to sniff the delicate flower. It smelled distinctly of vanilla.

"Very nice," he said.

"Yes," agreed Speranza, "very, very nice."

There was silence for a few moments. "Carlo," said Speranza, "what have you come to see me about? Are you in more trouble?"

"No," said Rizzo. "Yes—I mean—Don Baptiste, I need

help." The whole story of the night before came out in a rush. Even through the embarrassment at telling such a story, Rizzo could see that despite himself Speranza was becoming more and more interested. At first he listened silently, but then he began to interrupt with questions and comments.

"Motion pictures," Speranza said. "They sound very professional. You didn't see them at all?"

When Rizzo had finished, Speranza was in deep thought. Then he spoke. "This Caster, how much do you know about him? Was he—" Then the animation which had risen in the old man's face seemed to die. Once more he was an old man in gardening clothes. An old man who knew he was retired and had resigned himself to it. "Carlo," he said, "you'd better see Abe Montara about him. He's the one who can help you."

"I can't, Don Baptiste. Abe won't even talk to me, not since—" He didn't have to finish the sentence.

"Yes," said Speranza, rubbing his smoothly shaven chin, "it's a very bad situation. But I can't help you, you know. You'll have to see Abe. Tell him I told you to come see him. He'll listen. You'll see." Rizzo found that Speranza was leading him out of the little greenhouse and along the hallway. When they re-entered the living room, Gino was nowhere to be seen. Rizzo noticed the old man looking around for his son, and then they were on the doorstep and Speranza had taken his hand.

"Thank you for coming to see me, Carlo. You go see Abe; he can help. And give my love to Angie and the little ones."

"Sure, Don Baptiste," said Rizzo hopelessly. "I'll do that."

The big oaken door was closed. There was nothing

Rizzo could do but walk down the flagstone path to his car. He started the car and began driving without any real idea where he was going. But not to Abe Montara.

After less than three blocks, Rizzo heard the blast of a loud horn immediately behind his car and saw in the mirror, dangerously close to his back bumper, a black Thunderbird. His first reaction was panic, and Rizzo started to step on the accelerator. But then he recognized Gino Speranza's grinning face behind the wheel of the big car.

Rizzo pulled over to the curb, and in seconds Gino was in the front seat beside him.

"Scared you just a little bit, didn't I?" Gino said.

"What do you want?"

"I want to help you." When Rizzo looked puzzled, Gino cocked a leg over the other knee and exhaled a cloud of blue smoke. "What my old man doesn't know," he said, "is that from my old room on the second floor you can hear everything that goes on in that precious greenhouse of his."

"You heard—"

"Everything. Every word. You're in trouble, Charlie. And it sounds like bad trouble. But I'm going to help you out of it."

"You help?" Rizzo asked incredulously. "How are you going to help me if your old man won't?"

"Can't, you mean," Gino said. "My old man is past it, Charlie. He's only good for tending his garden while Abe runs the Speranza family action."

Rizzo didn't agree or disagree.

"But I don't see it that way," Gino continued. "I don't see why Abe Montara should take over anything."

"And you're going to stop him, eh, Gino?"

"I just might."

"All by yourself?"

"I'm not alone," said Gino. "I've got my friends. What's the matter? Don't you want any help? Are you going to back off just because they got the jump on you? I don't see how you can afford to do that. The way I hear it, your finances aren't all that good these days."

"No," Rizzo admitted, "they're not."

"Well, then. Montara's got you in a hole and is in no hurry to let you out. If you let these imported heavies put you down like this, you might as well pack it in. You're through. Nobody can help you. Not my father. Nobody."

Rizzo couldn't deny that he was boxed into a corner.

On the other hand," said Gino, "if you buck these guys with my help and take over that bar, it's all yours. You don't owe Montara a thing for it. And Abe will come around sooner or later. He'll make a lot of noise, but Abe's a realist. Right now he thinks you're just a punk he can make or break."

"What's in this for you?" asked Rizzo.

"Me? Well, you might want to do something for me now and then—just to show your gratitude. But mostly I've got a little reputation. I show I've got a bit of muscle, that I can do a job. And then maybe my old man and my brother will stop trying to make a college graduate out of me and let me in on some of the action Montara is keeping to himself. God knows, Dom Speranza, the original paper tiger, isn't going to buck Abe, so I guess it'll have to be me."

"That's a big job," said Rizzo, half-amused and half-impressed by Gino's cool confidence.

"I know. But I can do it. What do you say—is it a deal?"

Rizzo didn't have to ponder long; he could see no other way out. "It's a deal," he said.

13

After a night of little sleep, Harry Caster felt like a man on a frayed rope. He was tempted to lock up the house and the Lamplighter and head for the cabin and Hildy.

But fear and stubbornness kept him in Parker's Landing. Rizzo would know he had left, and then what would happen to the Lamplighter? And how could he come back? There was no point in starting all this just to run away and have everything destroyed. So, after fixing himself breakfast, Harry went down to the Lamplighter and spent the day aimlessly cleaning, taking stock and trying to pass the dragging hours. The call from Hoerner never came, but with every move he made, Harry felt the compact presence of the gun Hoerner had given him.

Harry didn't hear from Marco, so he asked Hank Sherman to come in again. The weekend was coming on, and business would be good. Hoerner finally called late in the afternoon to try to bolster Harry's confidence, but he failed to ease Harry's mind.

Just after six o'clock that evening, Harry was in his small

office when Hank called him. "Harry," he said excitedly, "the telephone."

"What is it?"

"I don't know," Hank said, "but hurry. Something's wrong."

Harry threw down his pencil and moved swiftly to the telephone behind the bar. "Hello," he shouted into the speaker, "this is Harry Caster."

The line was silent. The call hadn't disconnected, but he could hear nothing.

"What did it sound like?" he asked Hank.

"It was like somebody gasping for breath. It was a man, I think, calling your name, and it sounded like he was in pain. I don't—"

Harry cut him off with a gesture as a sound came on the line. It was a gasping, choking noise he'd never heard before. Then something that almost sounded like his name: "Har—Har—" The line went silent again, and Harry heard the dial tone buzzing loudly in his ear. He put the receiver down.

"Who do you think it was?" Hank asked.

"I don't know. I didn't hear enough to—Marco!" Harry was certain. "It was Marco. I know it was. Take care of things here, Hank. I'll be back."

Ripping off his apron, Harry grabbed his coat and ran out to the parking lot. Marco didn't live far away.

Marco's cottage, small and dirty white with a sagging red-tile roof, was nearly lost in the drooping branches of willow trees. Harry skidded the car to a stop in front of the cottage. He could see that some lights were on inside it. At the screened front door, Harry knocked and shouted: "Marco! Marco! It's me, Harry. Are you okay?"

There was no answer, but the doorknob turned easily, and Harry pushed into the white-walled living room of the cottage. The room was empty, and Harry pulled back slightly, feeling like an intruder. "Marco?" he said in a quieter voice. Still there was no answer. Harry had his hand on the knob ready to leave, when he turned to have a better look around. The lights had been on.

Harry pushed against the kitchen door, but after a couple of inches it stopped and would go no farther. It stopped with a soft, slightly giving feeling, as if it was held by something heavy but pliant.

"Damn," Harry said, giving the door a heave with all his strength. It haltingly opened enough for him to stick his head into the dark kitchen. At first, all he could see was that something white was on the floor blocking the door.

Then recognition came. It was Marco, dressed only in underwear and wedged between the door and a tall cabinet against the wall. "Marco," Harry said, but he got no answer. He stopped trying to force the door and quickly retraced his path out the front door. Pushing open a half-sprung gate, he ran through the side yard to the kitchen door. Flicking on the overhead light, Harry saw that Marco was lying on his stomach wedged headfirst into the corner behind the door. The receiver of the telephone dangled at the side of his head. His shorts and T-shirt were startlingly white against the worn linoleum. Marco's naked, hairy legs were a bluer shade of white in contrast.

Harry was surprised at how big and soft Marco looked. Grabbing him by the shoulders, Harry tried to turn Marco over and get him out of the corner. But Marco's weight and the close quarters defeated him. He was forced to fall back and pull Marco out by his stocking feet.

When he managed to get the youth turned over, Harry saw his face and gave a grimace of shared pain and sympathy. To Harry, Marco's face looked like a burst fig. The predominant color was a painful purple with swelling black pouches where the eyes should have been. The mouth was split and hung as slack as a slashed innertube. A broken tooth hung on his lower lip by a strip of skin, and another, shattered to a peak, stood out sharply in his black and bloody mouth. One eyebrow, red and furry, hung down over a closed eye.

Afraid to touch Marco, Harry grabbed for the dangling telephone receiver and frantically tapped on the cut-off switch until he got a dial tone.

"Parker Hospital," said a woman's middle-aged voice that soon assured Harry that an ambulance was on its way. Then he dialed Alec Hoerner's home number.

Hoerner was trying to read a newspaper and keep an eye on two frying pork chops on a hot plate when the telephone rang.

"What's happened?" he asked.

"It's Marco," Harry said, "my bartender. He's been very badly beaten up."

"Where are you?"

"At Marco's cottage in Parker's Landing. He called me at the bar, and I came over here and found him."

"Is anybody else there?"

"No," Harry said, "but I called an ambulance."

"Stay there until it arrives. Then go back to your bar and stay there until I contact you. If Rizzo gets in touch, stall him as much as you can. I'll see you or call you later tonight."

"What are you going to do?" Harry asked.

"I think Rizzo needs a little more convincing," Hoerner said, and he was gone.

Harry sat down at the kitchen table across from Marco. He could hear Marco's breathing—deep but ragged, as if something inside were torn and flapping. He became conscious of every breath. With nothing else to do, Harry sat in the darkness—he'd cut off the bright light—and the seconds dragged. There was no denying the certain knowledge that what had happened to Marco was all his fault. Or the premonition that this was just the beginning of a very bad time.

This thought was broken by the dying howl of a siren at the front of the cottage. Out front Harry found a beige ambulance parked across the street, and a man in a white hospital jacket standing looking in the wrong direction.

"Over here," Harry called, but hardly any sound came from his throat. He tried again, and the ambulance driver turned to face him. He was a young black with hair like dirty yellow wool. From the waist up he was dressed in hospital-issue with a fine stipple of rust-brown spots across one shoulder. But below the waist, he was strictly war surplus. Marine Corps green trousers fell over high-zippered jump boots.

"You called for an ambulance?"

"Yes."

Another attendant emerged carefully from the ambulance. With streaked gray hair and a face nearly the same color, he looked like an unsuccessful abortionist just out of jail. By the time he got around to the back of the ambulance, the driver had pulled out a long stretcher and was headed toward Harry. The older man grabbed the back of the stretcher as it was going away.

"Where's the victim?" asked the driver.

"In the kitchen at the back," said Harry, trying to lead the ambulance men and stay out of the way at the same time. "I'll hold the gate for you."

"Never mind," said the driver, plunging on and continuing an old monologue to his partner. "Yeah—so I told the first sergeant..."

His voice trailed off into the side yard of the cottage. This left Harry out front not knowing what to do next. He supposed he ought to see Marco off to the hospital.

But then a big four-door Dodge with an outsized aerial like a deep-sea fishing rod pulled up at the curb and Chief Beddell got out. He leaned against his car, looking at Harry Caster.

Before Harry could speak, the two ambulance men came back through the gate with Marco strapped to their stretcher. The older man was now the motivating force with the stretcher poles slotted into hands like piston guides and his head down. The driver, who floated easily at the head of the stretcher, was still talking; "...picks up this bar stool and flings it through a winder. Well, naturally...."

Beddell stopped them with a gesture. He looked down at Marco's ruined face with seeming indifference. "How is he?"

"Hurtin', man, hurtin'," said the driver. "Somebody tried to grind his head off. But my man here gave him a jolt of sodium pentothal, and he's feeling no pain."

Marco was no longer writhing and gasping, but lay death-still with only a slight raggedness of breath.

Beddell turned his eyes to the other attendant. There was an almost audible click as he put this new fact and face in his memory. "That right?"

"Yes." The attendant still looked down at his hands.

"All right," said Beddell, "get him out of here."

Harry and the Chief of Police watched silently as they shoved the stretcher bearing Marco into the ambulance, and the older man slowly got in with him. The ambulance rolled off down the street with siren moaning.

The few neighbors who had come out to watch receded, leaving Harry and Beddell alone on the sidewalk. "Let's take a drive," the Chief said, motioning to his car. He saw Harry look over at his own car and added: "I'll see that you get back."

They rode silently for a while, and Harry realized that Beddell wasn't heading for the police station. He didn't know what to say, so he said nothing. Finally Beddell spoke.

"That was a nasty thing that happened to young Carradino. His mother's going to take it hard."

"Yes, Marco's a good kid."

"We don't get many crimes of violence in Parker's Landing. You got any idea who might have done it?"

Harry had no stomach for further fencing, so he answered: "You know I do. It had to be Rizzo or some of his hoods. Rizzo thinks that by beating Marco up he can scare me into going along with him."

"Is he right?"

"No. He's not right. He's not right at all. I..."

"Go on," prompted Beddell. "You were saying?"

"Nothing," Harry said. "Just that I'm not going to turn half of my business over to Carlo Rizzo." Harry knew now that Beddell knew he was telling the truth. "You tell me something, Chief. You know that Rizzo really is trying to cut himself in on my bar, don't you?" Harry felt very bold.

"Mr. Caster," Beddell began slowly, "there are some very plausible elements to your story. My sergeant tells me that your car was set on fire with a homemade phosphorus grenade. That makes it arson, and I'm drawing up a report of the incident. But that doesn't mean that Charlie Rice had anything to do with it. Rice was at home at the time—with guests. That's a pretty good alibi, and it could be tough to prove that he hired somebody else to torch your car."

"And I suppose he'll have an alibi for tonight, too?" Harry asked.

"He probably will, but you can be sure that we'll check it out."

"I'm sure you will," said Harry, emboldened, "but how is that going to help Marco? And how is it going to help me when Rizzo decides it's time to get really rough?" Harry felt his gorge rise as an image of Marco's face flashed into his mind.

The Chief of Police aimlessly but carefully threaded the darkened minor streets like an airline pilot in a holding pattern.

"Your family, Mr. Caster," he said, ignoring Harry's questions, "where are they right now?"

"Somewhere safe," Harry said, surprising himself.

"Safe from Rizzo?" Beddell asked, dropping the name Rice for the first time.

"Yes," said Harry, "and from anybody else if Rizzo's too busy establishing an alibi to do the job himself." He suddenly became aware of the revolver in his coat pocket, and for the first time he felt comforted by its presence. He knew Beddell would have him if he knew about it. But he didn't. And he didn't know Harry Caster quite as well as he thought he did.

Beddell knew that in his timid, chickenshit way Harry Caster was challenging him. But he didn't feel angry; he only felt tired and longed for retirement and a pension as, after a hard day, he longed for his soft bed.

The policeman also knew that he could jerk this little Jew down to the station and in a very short time have the whole story out of him: where his family was, what the hell he was up to. It would all come out. Beddell knew that Caster was up to something. He was still scared, but there was a hardening core beneath his soft exterior. Something was propping Caster up or he wouldn't be talking as he was tonight. He'd be running.

But Beddell didn't want to—couldn't afford to—know what Harry was doing. In twenty-nine years on the police force, he'd been a man who had built up a complicated web of ties and interdependencies. Debts and credits. A favor done; a benefit received. The complexity of Beddell's particular situation didn't allow him to interfere actively in the affairs of the Speranza family. And he'd never had reason to.

He didn't like the situation, but he'd grown to accept it. Beddell honored the restrictions as much out of a sense of obligation as out of fear. He made good his debts. So Beddell ignored Harry's comment and sealed his mind to the more unpleasant possibilities of the situation.

"Well, Mr. Caster," he said with conscious finality, "you know what you're doing. I think we'd better go to the station and get a statement from you about Marco Carradino. It won't take long, and I'll have a squad car take you back to your automobile."

Now Beddell was driving differently. No longer aimless, his style was direct, crisp and economic. In a short time the car was in his parking bay at the police station. Harry followed Beddell into the depths of the station to make a statement, true as far as it went but false at the same time. Harry knew the Chief wouldn't ask him whom he suspected. And if he did, Harry would lie. The lie was as necessary as the truth seemed to be a couple of days ago. Harry knew his part and he would play it.

14

"I KNOW, MAMA, I KNOW," RIZZO SAID INTO THE telephone. His sallow face was pale. "I said I'll be there, and I will. But I've got some things to do here first. Mama, don't cry. I told you—I'll be there in just a little while. I won't be long. But let me talk to Papa now, please. Yes, please go get him. That's right. I'll see you soon, Mama."

Rizzo sat under the pale yellow light of a standing lamp in his living room waiting for his father to come on the line. A gentle knock sounded on the hall door.

"Yeah?" Rizzo said.

Angela Rizzo pushed open the door uncertainly. "Carlo," she said, "Gino Speranza is here to see you. He's got two men with him. Gino said you called him."

"Yes," said Rizzo, holding his hand over the speaker of the telephone, "tell them to wait, Angie. I'll be right with them."

Angela pulled the door shut, and Rizzo spoke again into the telephone. "Papa? Yes. Look, Mama is going crazy. You've got to calm her down. Where the hell are Sylvia and Carmela? Well, if they're there, what are they doing—

feeding their fat faces? You tell them if they don't take care of Mama, they'll be sorry. All right then. I'll see you in maybe an hour. What? You tell that goddamned priest he can just wait. Okay? Okay. Goodbye, Papa."

When Rizzo went into the kitchen, Gino Speranza and two young guys were sitting at the table drinking coffee. Neither of Gino's men could have been much over twenty-one years old. One was darker than Gino with a big, high-bridged nose and shiny black hair combed straight back from a bulging forehead. The other was big, blond and soft-looking, with southern handsomeness. His head was large for even his big body, and his hair bulged out under a narrow-brimmed black hat like curly straw.

"Come on in," Rizzo said to Gino and turned and walked back into the living room. Gino and his men gulped their coffee and followed, chewing the last of the raisin cake. When they were all in the living room and the door was closed, Rizzo turned on Gino. "It took you long enough to get here."

"Easy, Charlie, easy," Gino said calmly. "I know you're upset about your kid brother getting cut down like that, and I'm sorry. But don't take it out on us. We're on your side."

"Are you?" asked Rizzo sharply. He glanced at the other two men. "Yeah," Gino said. "This is Injun"—he indicated the dark one— "and Ruby." The big man raised a pale hand, but Rizzo ignored him.

"They look like kids to me," he said.

"Maybe," said Gino, "but they do the job. Okay, we're here. What's on your mind?"

"You know damned well what's on my mind. You and your red-hot pistoleros got my kid brother nearly killed tonight." Gino said nothing. His refusal to deny the accusation made Rizzo even more angry. "Your guys were supposed to rough Carradino up," he said, "not tear his head off."

"He got difficult," said Ruby.

"Shut up," ordered Gino without anger. "Look, Charlie, this just won't wash. You told me to give Caster something serious to think about, put a shot near enough to scare him. And you agreed that Carradino was right for the situation. So we did the job. It was heavy, I admit, but my boys are young and eager. They want to make good, and maybe they lack a little finesse. But are you claiming that because Carradino got hurt bad, the muscle behind Caster hit your kid brother on the street in Manhattan on the same night? Within two hours?"

"Who else?" Rizzo asked. "Who else do you think would have run my brother down like a dog?"

"Abe?"

"No, I don't believe it. Abe's mad at me, sure, but to hit my brother like this, right out of nowhere—he wouldn't do it."

"Maybe he heard you were over to see my old man this morning," Gino said. "And he didn't like it. Have you asked him?"

"I don't have to." But Rizzo didn't tell him that he'd tried to call Montara as soon as he'd heard about Steve. Montara had refused to take the call, just as he'd refused to talk to Rizzo since the trouble had begun last spring. "There's no point. It's got to be those guys who jumped me last night." Unthinking, Rizzo put his hand to his bandaged jaw. "It can't be anybody else."

"If you're right," said Gino, "we're up against some very tough boys. You sure you want to go on with this thing, Charlie?" Gino didn't think there was much chance of

Rizzo quitting, but he wanted a definite commitment for the whole ride.

"Go on? Of course I'm going on. Do you think I'm going to fold up now with my brother in the hospital and maybe could die? I'm going to make those bastards regret they ever threw in against me."

"The way these guys are working," Gino said, "we'd better get cracking. The next hit could be right at your family here. These guys mean business."

"So do I," said Rizzo. "Now listen. I'm going into the city to get my folks straightened around. I'll be back very late tonight. After I leave here, this house is buttoned up tight. Nobody gets in or out. My boys will see to that. Your job is to stay with Caster. Where he goes, you go. But don't touch him. Not yet. Even if he runs for it, stay with him. He could lead us to his wife and kids. Check in with me here early tomorrow. And no more screw-ups, okay?"

"Sure," said Gino, getting up. "You're the boss." He started for the door with Ruby and Injun following him. He paused at the door. "Only one thing."

"What's that?"

"You go ahead and square things with your people in the city, but when you get back, I say we'd better get into some action. Doing nothing could be dangerous."

"Don't worry, you'll get action. I just hope you can handle it."

"We can handle it," said Gino, and he and the others left.

Rizzo went into the kitchen where Angie was ironing clothes. "Angie," he said.

Angie looked up from her work with the frowning expression she always wore when she was worried. Rizzo crossed the linoleum floor and put his hands on her shoulders at the base of her neck.

"Angie," he said again, "stop it. Just stop worrying. There's no need. Just do as I said earlier, and everything will be all right. All we've got to do is sit tight for a few days, stay close to home. Is that so hard? Just keep Bobby and Maria home from school starting tomorrow. A few days off won't hurt them. I've got to go see Mama and Papa now, but I won't be long. We'll all be here tomorrow and—I'll tell you what, we'll send over to Guichi's for a big pizza for lunch. The kids will like that. It's going to be like a picnic."

"All right," said Angie, trying to stop frowning. "Only, Carlo—"

"What is it?"

Angie hesitated.

"What is it?" His voice was a bit more edgy.

"Bobby's football game. It's tomorrow night, and it's the big game against Grosmont Tech. Will he be able to play?"

Rizzo had completely forgotten the football game despite his efforts to keep up on the kids' activities. He was proud that Bobby was doing so well as an athlete. This wasn't going to win him any points with Bobby.

"No," he said very definitely. "I'm sorry. It's just not possible." Rizzo was stuck. He couldn't emphasize the danger to their son in going out to the game without frightening her even more. He tried to put all of the words he couldn't say into his refusal. "Tell him I'm sorry, but he'll have to miss this one. He's not the whole team."

"Can Bobby talk to you about it?" Angela asked, biting her lower lip. "I told him I'd ask you."

Rizzo felt himself being driven into yet another corner. "Oh, shit—I'm sorry," he said quickly. "It won't do any good. We'll just both lose our tempers. I have to go right now.

Mama is climbing the walls. Do as I say. Be a good girl." He pulled his wife to him and kissed her forehead. "I'll be home as soon as I can. I'll make it up to Bobby, you'll see."

Angela Rizzo sighed, returned her husband's kiss and then walked with him to the door. As he drove away, she let the curtain fall and then went upstairs to console her waiting son with the feeble prospect of pizza for lunch tomorrow.

15

AFTER AN EGG-SHAPED, SILENT POLICEMAN DROPPED him at his car in front of Marco's cottage, Harry decided to go by Parker Hospital on the way back to the bar.

Harry hated being a patient in a hospital, but he found entering the brightly lit, timeless atmosphere of these corridors very exciting. In his fantasies, he imagined Harry Caster, M.D., stalking the waxed floors, stethoscope dangling carelessly, short, a bit pudgy perhaps, but all the same poised to use his steel nerves and sure hands to save lives.

But now, Harry entered Parker Hospital with a feeling of dread and fear that they'd tell him that Marco was dead, that his defiance of Rizzo had cost an innocent life. At the reception desk, a nurse who looked no older than Lizzie told him that nobody could see Marco until preliminary examinations and tests were finished. She couldn't think of any reason why Harry couldn't wait a while.

The waiting room was empty except for a gaunt, gray-haired woman of about fifty who sat leafing through a women's magazine without seeing the pages. After a glance at her, Harry sat down across the room on a cold, red plastic couch to wait.

Then it hit him. The woman's face. It was Marco's face, finer, more strained and infinitely more marked by time, but the same handsome-beautiful face. Harry was reminded again of the responsibility for Marco's being beaten and for her presence in this plastic-and-chromium-steel room. He considered avoiding her, burying himself in a magazine, but he couldn't.

Harry walked carefully over to where the woman sat and stood silently waiting for her to notice him. After half a minute or so, the woman raised her eyes to his face hopefully, somberly, in confusion. Her eyes were a soft, mixed color like violet-speckled china. They showed no sign of redness or crying.

Prompted by her questioning look, Harry said, "You're Mrs. Carradino—Marco's mother?"

"Yes," she said, and she stood up. She kept rising until Harry's eyes were level with her nose.

"I'm Harry Caster," he said. "Marco worked"—he couldn't help the past tense sneaking out—"for me at my bar, the Lamplighter."

"I know," she said. Her voice was neither cold nor warm. It fell in a nether region of non-commitment.

"I'm very sorry," Harry began.

"Thank you," said Mrs. Carradino, cutting Harry off with those two unforgiving words and dismissing him to the world of those who are sorry but no more than that.

Harry felt like going away, but didn't know how. He couldn't even figure out how to get back to the neutrality of the cold red couch.

"Has there been any word?" he asked, breaking off the silence that was building up.

Before she could answer, Harry heard clicking footsteps behind him and saw Mrs. Carradino's eyes come nearly alive with recognition. He shifted his weight to look toward the door of the waiting room.

It was a girl. Twenty-two or twenty-three, with long, slightly wavy black hair falling over her shoulders. She wore faded jeans and a thin, blue work-shirt but still managed to look womanly and somehow properly dressed for a hospital. Wooden-soled sandals were making the clicking noise.

The girl's eyes slid over Harry without pausing and met Mrs. Carradino's. Then she was standing at his side, her thin shoulder reaching exactly to his.

"Is there any word?" Mrs. Carradino asked.

"Not yet, but the ward nurse says the doctor should be able to tell us something any time now. She thinks he'll be out soon."

Mrs. Carradino hauled her attention back to Harry. "This is my daughter Sandra," she said. "Sandra, this is Mr. Caster, Marco's employer. It was he who found Marco and called the ambulance after"—Mrs. Carradino paused deliberately—"what happened."

"Hello," said Sandra. She didn't have to raise her eyes to look into his, and Harry saw in her face curiosity mixed with youthful disinterest. To him, her look said: "You exist because of your connection with my brother, but other than that you're a zero."

"Hello," answered Harry blankly. Despite his concern for Marco, Harry couldn't say that he cared very much for his family.

The three of them stood in a little triangle saying nothing but held together by unanswered questions. Harry was about to break away and return to his side of the room when the door opened and an elderly nurse with a tiptoe walk came in.

"Mrs. Carradino," she said. Marco's mother answered with an eager look. "Dr. Burns says you may see your son for a few minutes. If you'll just come with me."

Marco's sister would have followed, but the old nurse stopped her. "I'm sorry, but Dr. Burns thinks it best that only your mother sees the patient at this time. He's very weak, and we don't want to tire him further."

Sandra opened her mouth to protest but glanced sideways at her mother and shut it again. "All right," she said. "I'll wait here for you, Mother."

Mrs. Carradino obediently followed the nurse. Sandra threw herself into the nearest chair and snatched up a fashion magazine. She tossed it back on the table with a snort of impatience.

Harry began to return to his couch, but her voice stopped him: "Do you really think a jealous husband did this to Marco?"

He turned and faced the girl, who was looking at him with bored curiosity. "I don't know," Harry said. He remained standing with most of his weight on his pivot foot.

"Don't stand there in the middle of the room," Sandra ordered. "Sit over here. I hate hospitals. All these white uniforms and hushed voices give me the creeps. They're inhuman. Don't you think?"

"I don't know," Harry repeated, sitting down a chair away from Sandra and not really listening.

"Maybe not," she said, looking directly into his face, "but I think you do know more than you're saying." Harry was certain that the fear he felt showed plainly on his face. "Don't worry," Sandra said. "You won't be giving away any secrets. I know what a lover boy Marco is. Everybody knows, except Mother, and she won't let herself know anything 'distasteful.' Almost every time I've called Marco's cottage, a different woman's voice has answered: drowsy, slutty voices fresh from the hot little bed of Marco Carradino."

Harry didn't answer, didn't say anything. He just looked at the girl's scornful face and felt his fear being replaced by relief and mild curiosity about this family of Marco's. His relations with Marco had been confined to the tight little precincts of the Lamplighter. "Look, miss," Harry said with force, "don't think—"

"Don't call me miss. My name's Sandra. It's a crappy name, but it's all mine. And yours is Harry. I know that from Marco. He thinks you're a good old boy even if you do bug him too much about wasting his life. I know—"

What she knew was interrupted by Mrs. Carradino's return to the waiting room. "I've seen Marco," she said, "and he looks awful. But the doctor says he's getting stronger."

"May I see him?" Sandra asked.

"Not tonight, dear," her mother said. "Dr. Burns says you may visit tomorrow if he continues to make progress. And, dear, the doctor says that he can find a bed here for me tonight if I want to stay. I'd like to in case Marco needs me. Would you mind going home alone?"

Harry considered offering the girl a ride but decided against it. Before the girl had a chance to answer, he cut in: "In that case, Mrs. Carradino, I'll be going. I'll call in tomorrow to check on Marco. It was nice meeting you," he finished lamely, and looked at Sandra as if to include her, too.

"Yes, of course," Mrs. Carradino said absently. "Thank you very much for coming." She extended her ringless hand, and Harry clasped it gingerly and let go. As he walked away, Harry heard Sandra asking if her mother would need anything from home for her night's stay in the hospital.

As he drove slowly along the hospital's tunnel-like exit road, he noticed a figure standing under a bright street light at the end of the drive.

It was Sandra Carradino.

Harry reluctantly pulled up beside her and rolled down his window.

"Can you give me a ride?" Sandra asked. "The goddamned taxi office said it would be at least forty-five minutes before he could get a cab here."

"Okay," Harry said, "get in." He reached over and cracked the other door open for her.

Sandra slid into the front seat, settling not very close to Harry, yet not hugging the door.

"Which way?" Harry asked.

"Just go up Cutler Boulevard, left on Schumann and I'll tell you from there," she directed. "This isn't too much trouble for you, is it? I don't want to make you late for anything."

"You won't," Harry said, and he pulled the car out into the deserted street in front of the hospital.

Harry drove in silence, determined not to make polite conversation with this girl. But in truth it was no inconvenience. He'd never felt so lonely in his life as in these last few days. He was glad of any company, even this cool, almost hostile girl.

Sandra broke the silence. "Do you know what I think? I think Marco wasn't beaten up by a jealous husband at all."

"I wouldn't know," Harry lied, keeping his eyes on the gently sloping dark street.

"But don't you have any idea at all?" she asked. "I mean,

you see Marco a lot more than we do. You must have some idea what he's been doing. Who he hangs around with. There are some pretty shady characters who hang around bars. It could be some of them."

If you only knew, little sister, Harry thought. We've got shady characters, all right. I'll introduce you to a few sometime. "What do you mean by shady characters?" he asked, to avoid telling any more lies.

"You know," Sandra insisted, "crooks, gangsters, that sort of person."

"Oh," said Harry in a nasty voice, "you mean like me?"

To Harry's surprise, Sandra didn't react defensively. Instead, she was silent for a moment and then said thoughtfully: "No, not like you. I don't think you're a crook or a gangster, Mr. Caster."

Harry didn't know what to say.

"But," Sandra continued, "neither can I really believe that Marco was beaten so viciously by some jealous husband or boyfriend. Marco's a big boy. He's not as bright as I wish he were, but he can take care of himself. This is something else, and I'm going to go to the police tomorrow and ask some questions."

"You're going to see Chief Beddell?"

"Yes. Or whoever is handling the case. That's what the police call it, isn't it—a case?"

"Yes, I think so."

"Have they asked you any questions yet about how you came to find Marco this evening?" she asked.

"Some," said Harry. "I was at the police station talking with Beddell just before I came to the hospital. He asked me what I knew, and I told him."

"And what was that?" Sandra persisted.

"Very little," Harry said, annoyed to be questioned and

even more to have to lie again. "I told him about Marco's telephone call to the bar early this evening and that I went to the cottage and found him there. That's all."

"But—"

"This is Schumann Boulevard," Harry said. "Now what?"

"Take the second left after this signal. Then left, right at the third block, and our house is the one with the big lantern out front."

"Okay," Harry said, pretending to concentrate on his driving, but he couldn't shake the girl off.

"But," she continued, "if the Chief of Police is so interested, doesn't that mean there must be something important? He doesn't get involved every time some bartender gets beaten up, does he?"

"I haven't any idea," Harry said. "I stay away from the police. I've only talked with Beddell twice in my life." The second Harry said that he knew it was a mistake.

"What was the other time?"

Harry was saved for the moment by the fact that they were approaching the Carradino's house. "Is this it?" Harry asked, pulling to the curb in front of a large house with a lighted lantern out front. He didn't turn off the ignition.

But before Sandra could either say something else or get out of the car, the door on her side was snatched open and a long-haired blond youth in a sheepskin jacket was leaning into the car.

16

"WHERE THE FUCK HAVE YOU BEEN?" THE YOUTH shouted into Sandra's face. Harry recognized the rotten fumes of half-digested alcohol. He'd spent half his life across the bar from that stink.

"Lenny," Sandra started to say, but the boy grabbed her by the arm and pulled her so violently out of the car that she left a wooden-soled clog behind. Once he'd gotten the girl out of the automobile, Lenny found her too hard to manage and dropped Sandra heavily onto the grass strip between the curb and the sidewalk.

"Come on, bitch," he said, beginning to pull the struggling girl across the grass.

"Stop it, Lenny," Sandra said, fighting to get free. "Listen to me, stop it!"

But Lenny continued to pull at her arm and shoulder, too drunk to move her effectively but strong enough so that she couldn't break loose and regain her feet. In the struggle, her denim shirt rode halfway up her naked back.

Christ, thought Harry, what's this? But at the same time he switched off the ignition and slid out of his door of the car. Harry reached behind the car seat and came up with a lug wrench. Nearly twenty years of handling drunks had taught him that you couldn't do it barehanded.

Moving quickly around the back of the car, Harry found that the youth had succeeded in dragging Sandra to the sidewalk and was laboriously tugging her along on her knees.

"C'mon, you fucking bitch," he muttered. "I want to talk to you." Despite the cool night, the boy was sweating heavily, and a thin white shirt was plastered to his slim body.

Without saying a word, Harry reached out and gave the boy a firm crack on the left forearm with the lug wrench. It was very painful, but not hard enough to break the bone.

"Ow!" Lenny cried, letting go of Sandra's wrist and falling back onto the sidewalk in front of her. "My arm. You broke it, you bastard. My fucking arm is broken!" Clasping the injured arm to his chest, the boy began to rock and croon in pain and outrage, not trying to get up from the sidewalk. Nearly at his feet, Sandra still knelt soundlessly with her hands over her face. Harry saw tears dripping from the heels of her hands onto her shirt.

"Come on," Harry said softly, pulling Sandra up by her shoulders. She was light for a tall girl, and under her hands her arms and shoulders felt fragile, almost brittle. Under the strong lamplight, Harry could see that the right knee of her jeans was ripped open and the knee had been scraped raw. He began to lead her toward the white-latticed front of her house.

"My purse," Sandra said, "it's in the car...my keys."

"I'll get it," Harry said, continuing to shepherd her toward a long porch and finally depositing her on an old-fashioned porch swing.

"He's really a very nice boy," Sandra said, trying to wipe the tears from her face with the sleeve of her shirt.

"I'm sure he is," said Harry. He gave Sandra his hand-kerchief. "I'll be back in a minute."

When Harry got back to the sidewalk, Lenny had gotten to his feet and was rhythmically kicking the rear fender of Harry's rented car with a sneaker-shod foot. He still clutched his wounded arm at the elbow, but it didn't seem to impair his kicking skill. The hollow booms rolled out like slow drumbeats.

"All right," said Harry, touching the boy's right shoulder.

Then Harry's world turned black, shot with purple and yellow sparks. With the pure science of drunkenness, Lenny had whirled and caught him across the bridge of the nose with a perfect, if unintentional, karate chop. A wave of intense pain hit Harry between the eyes, and his hands went instinctively to his face. He felt his dinner coming up and amidst waves of dizziness fought to keep it in his stomach.

Lenny stood watching Harry struggle with pain and nausea. Then the boy made a murky connection between some action of his and Harry's current state, and his young face parted in a boozy smile of self-congratulation.

"That will teach you," he told the back of Harry's hands, "to go around hitting innocent people with steel bars. How do you like it?"

Harry heard this as if from a long distance through a faulty connection. Then he heard, a little bit clearer: "You're getting blood all over yourself."

The cloud that had been hanging around Harry's head cleared enough for him to see that Lenny was right. The front of his suit coat and shirt were polka-dotted with wet, shiny blood, and he had its unmistakable taste in his mouth. Harry reached for his handkerchief but couldn't find it.

"Here," said Lenny, and Harry felt a crumpled handkerchief shoved into his hand. But Harry, even at that moment wondering how clean it was, didn't know quite what to do with it. He didn't want to put it to his face, and it wasn't much good to brush at the blood on his clothes. He compromised by trying to get some of the blood off his hands.

The pain had largely gone now except for a deep throb at the front of his brain, and Harry stood wondering what to do with Lenny.

"Is that a wash-and-wear suit?" Lenny asked.

"No," Harry said, standing bent forward to avoid dripping any more blood on himself, "it's not." Reluctantly, he tried to stop some of the blood with the handkerchief and felt it quickly becoming saturated.

"It's probably going to stain, then," said Lenny with serious concern. "Unless you soak it pretty soon in cold water. That's what my mother says."

"Lenny," Harry said, bored, tired and impatient, "thanks very much, but why don't you go home? It's getting late." It was hardly ten o'clock, but to Harry it felt very, very late.

Lenny then remembered what he was doing there. A mean, petulant look came on his face. "I want to see Sandra," he said sullenly.

"No," Harry said, stepping in his way.

"I've got a right," insisted Lenny. "Sandra's my girl. I want to see her." His face turned soft as if he were going to cry.

Harry felt so weary that he didn't want to waste a single word on this drunken boy. "Lenny," he said with as much menace as he could summon, "if you don't go home, I'm going to get that lug wrench and I'm going to bend it over your head."

"You wouldn't."

"I would."

"Sandra wants to see me," Lenny said, changing the subject.

"No, she doesn't," Harry said, feeling like the oldest sixteen-year-old boy in the world. He tried to take the boy's arm to lead him to his car, a much-dented Mercedes painted a silvery gray. But Lenny shook off Harry's hand and once more gripped his injured arm.

"My arm still hurts," he said as he walked to the car.

"I'm sorry." Harry shadowed the boy until he half-fell behind the steering wheel.

"You should be." Lenny fumbled in his pockets. "I've lost my keys," he said, trying to climb back out of the low sports car.

"They're in the ignition." Harry pushed him back into the bucket seat.

Lenny batted the rabbit's foot dangling from the keys and looked up sincerely at Harry. "Will you take a message to Sandra?"

"Sure."

"Tell her she's a lousy lay," Lenny said, switching the Mercedes to a loud roar. Blinking his eyes to get them to focus, he said, "I'm not going home."

Then he popped the clutch, floored the gas pedal and peeled away from the curb, narrowly missing Harry's car. Halfway down the block, the car backfired thunderously, and at the corner, Lenny, still running dark, took the turn on two wheels and was gone.

17

HARRY THREW THE LUG WRENCH INTO THE BACK OF the car, picked up Sandra's purse with his two least-bloody fingers and walked slowly up the walk to the house. His nose had stopped bleeding.

Sandra met him at the foot of the steps.

"He'll kill himself."

"Good," said Harry, stepping out of the dark shadow of a squat oak that dominated the front yard.

"My God," said Sandra, "blood everywhere." She stepped toward him. She'd felt indifferent, even hostile, toward this man since she'd met him at the hospital. But now, despite his ludicrous appearance, Sandra felt herself drawn to him. Maybe it was because he looked ridiculous and yet somehow wasn't ridiculous at all, just human. She reached out a hand to touch his arm. "Are you all right?"

"I think so," Harry said, feeling as if bleeding were in bad taste.

"You ought to put your clothes in to soak," Sandra said, "or the blood will stain them."

"That's what Lenny said. If you two ever get back

together, you'd make a fortune in the dry-cleaning business."

"Come inside," Sandra said, taking a key from her purse and leading Harry up to the big front door and into an impressive foyer. The house had been built in the mid-twenties when Wall Street money was hitting New York suburbs in great waves. When it receded it left a number of similar monuments to easy money and hard reality.

"Wow!" Harry said, staring up at the acres of rich wood-work. A delicately carved staircase began directly across the foyer and spiraled gently into the upper reaches of the house.

"Yes," Sandra said, "the glory that was Rome. I'll tell you all about it, but now you better do something about getting that blood off you. I haven't a delicate stomach, but you look like an atrocity victim. The bathroom is the third door on the right at the top of the stairs. Put everything especially bloody into the bathtub to soak, and I'll get you a robe to wear. In the meantime. I'll make some coffee. Or would you prefer a drink?"

"Coffee," said Harry as he started to walk up the faded blue-carpeted stairway. A few minutes later he was standing in his underwear watching his bloodstained clothes swim-ming soggily in the giant marble bathtub and slowly turning the water pink. Harry shoved the revolver Hoerner had given him into one of his shoes and stuffed his handkerchief in after it. There was a rap on the door, and a hand reached in holding a dark-blue robe.

"Coffee in the small drawing room in two minutes," said Sandra through the door. "Just follow what's left of your nose."

Harry's fingers discovered that the robe was soft, thick velvet with worn satin edging. He looked at himself in the gold-veined mirror and saw that the fit wasn't bad. Over the breast pocket was an elaborate monogram Harry made out to be ALW.

Something subtle bothered his nose, and Harry sniffed deeply, bringing back a wave of dull pain which made him blink his eyes and vow not to do that again. It was perfume: rich, yet dry and clean-smelling. Harry took one more look at the bruised bridge of his nose—it seemed as though he wouldn't have black eyes after all—and left the big bathroom.

Halfway down the stairs he saw Sandra waiting for him at the bottom. "Very fetching," she said, and Harry felt himself going red. "I was afraid that with the damage the mighty Lenny did to your nose you might not be able to smell the coffee, so I came to lead you."

Sandra couldn't help smiling at the picture Harry presented, but mixed in with the amusement she felt a growing warmth. Watch it, Sandra, she told herself, you're about to demonstrate yet again your absolutely rotten taste in men. This thought only made her smile more broadly. And, she rationalized, he did win me in fair combat.

Harry followed her through darkened rooms to a set of double doors which Sandra opened with mock ceremony. They stepped into a smallish room with a beamed ceiling and a curbed rosewood marble fireplace in one wall. The furniture was like the robe Harry wore: worn but well preserved.

"This is the only downstairs room I can stand," Sandra said. "I think it used to be reserved for intimate gatherings of the very best people." She gestured Harry to a plush-covered sofa facing the fireplace and gave him a big cup of coffee.

"This robe," Harry asked, "it's not Marco's, is it?"

"God, no," said Sandra, "it's a remnant of the wardrobe of the late Alvin L. Wishart, the man who built this monument to capitalism. That's his picture beaming down in the foyer. You'd be lost in Marco's robe. Old Alvin was a squat little devil."

"Thanks very much," Harry said, taking a sip of the coffee. "How did you know I like my coffee black?"

"All civilized people drink black coffee."

"He may have been no giant, but Wishart used a very nice perfume," Harry said. He cautiously sniffed a lapel.

"Oh, that's mine. I confiscated the robe years ago when I found a trunk full of his clothes in the attic. Mother wanted to make me put it back, but Daddy let me keep it."

"This guy's clothes are still up in the attic?" Harry asked. "Who was this Alvin L. Wishart, anyway? He's not still up there, too, is he?"

"Not exactly. Wishart was something very money-making on Wall Street; probably a crook. Grandpa was his gardener. Somehow, during a week of extreme frenzy, Grandpa ended up the legal owner of this monstrosity, and Wishart got all Grandpa's cash. The old boy didn't play the market, so he had some."

"Clever him."

"Yes, clever. They nearly starved on Spode china."

"What did Wishart do with the money?"

"The last thing Grandpa heard was a cryptic postcard from Buenos Aires."

"Clever him, too."

"My dad was about fifteen years old at the time, and he used to love to tell us kids all about Alvin L. Wishart. Mother thought it was sacrilege."

"Your father," Harry said, "he's—uh—"

"That's right. He's dead," Sandra said. "Someone had

the bad taste three years ago to drop several tons of scrap metal on him at the yard. I think that's why Marco won't work there."

Sandra threw her black hair and gave an equine laugh. "This is a cheerful conversation. Bankruptcy, death. Can't we find something more cheerful to talk about?"

"How about Lenny?" Harry asked. "He says he's your boyfriend. Is he?"

"No," said Sandra, "that's not more cheerful. And no, Lenny's not my boyfriend. Not any more. Lenny's just a rich, very crazy boy I once made the mistake of falling in love with."

"But not anymore?" Harry asked out of real curiosity.

"Uh-uh," Sandra shook her head. "I'm a masochist, but I'm not that much of a masochist."

"Tough on Lenny."

"Not so tough," she said. "I can't do anything for him that a bottle can't. And he knows it. That little show tonight wasn't unrequited love. Lenny just didn't have anything to do for a while and thought he'd come over and pick at a few old wounds."

"He could be dangerous."

"I don't think so," Sandra said, ruefully examining her skinned knee and torn jeans. "He always ends up crying and goes away quietly in the end after making as much fuss as possible."

"He didn't go away quietly tonight."

"Ah, but that's because he had a new audience. You were here to add spice to the script. Besides, drawing blood on you gave him a shot of adrenalin. You can't begrudge the boy his moment of triumph. Speaking of triumph, how's your nose?"

"Okay," Harry said. He waggled the tip gently between

thumb and forefinger. "You really despise him, don't you?" Harry felt the protective empathy of kind for kind.

"Not really," she said. "That's bitterness speaking. Frustrated hopes, thwarted expectations, shattered dreams. All that stuff. But I'm tired of talking about Lenny. Tell me about you—no, better yet, tell me about your wife."

"Hildy?" Harry was shocked to find that he hadn't thought about Hildy for hours.

"Yes, if that's her name. Is she sitting faithfully at home waiting for your lordly step at the front door? What's she going to think when you come home wet, rumpled, smelling of my perfume and with a slightly damaged nose? I suppose she's used to that. Will she hit you with a rolling pin?"

"No," said Harry, "Hildy's out of town with the girls—my daughters."

"How many? Daughters, I mean."

"Two. Lizzie is eleven and Sophie, the baby, is eleven months."

"A baby at your age," Sandra said with a smile. "You should be ashamed of yourself, you devil."

"It was nothing, really," Harry said, feeling his ears go red. "It was a cold winter."

"What's Hildy like?"

What was Hildy like? It may seem a standard husband-wife joke, but Harry couldn't answer that question. Would it do to say that she was short, dark, loved old movies and would rather live in fantasy than in the real world? That was part of what she was like, but it didn't sum up Hildy.

"I'd rather tell you about me," said Harry. "I'm forty-five years old; I'm a high-school graduate; I never got to be a fighter pilot, and I scratch out a living selling liquor to people with too much money and too little sense. Very likely, somebody much like me is pouring a drink for Lenny right now."

"No, you don't," Sandra said. "You're not clever enough, Harry, to turn this non-conversation back onto Lenny—and thus back onto me."

Harry noticed that this was the first time she'd called him by his first name. "Maybe not, Sandra," he said, "but I thought I'd try." Sandra finished the rest of her coffee and shuddered at the bitter, cold taste of the dregs. She looked at him.

"Are you going to spend the night?" she asked.

"Yes," said Harry, forgetting Hoerner, forgetting the Lamplighter, forgetting everything, and at the same time he felt the slightly cool softness of her hand on his. Harry put out his other hand and encountered the animal thinness of her rib cage. With an easy pull, Harry's mouth was on her young lips. It was not a passionate kiss but one of searching tenderness.

"But more later," said Sandra, breaking the kiss but remaining in Harry's arms. As tall as she was, it was hard to say who was in whose arms. "First, I think we'd better sort out somebody's gory clothes. Unless of course you want to go home in a pair of Alvin L. Wishart's golf knickers or his tuxedo."

"No," said Harry, letting his hands drop easily to her soft-hard hips, "I don't think I could live up to them."

Sandra rose from the sofa but let her hand linger on the pudgy curve of Harry's jaw. "Right, then, follow me."

Harry followed her back up to the baronial bathroom where his clothes lay in what looked like a pool of weak strawberry soda. "I'm a pretty good bleeder," he said.

"Yes," Sandra said, sitting on the thick edge of the bathtub and pushing the sodden clothes around with her hand. "Help me wring these out and we'll put them in the dryer. I'll see what I can do with a steam iron in the morning."

The suit, shirt and vest were slowly tumbling in the big-eyed clothes dryer when Sandra closed the laundry-room door behind them.

"And now?" Harry asked.

"And now," she said, "I live up there." She pointed at the ceiling. Once again, Harry followed her, this time to a narrow, sharply rising staircase in the corner nearly hidden in shadows. As they climbed, Harry watched the creasing and straining of the jeans over her small, rounded bottom and thought about taking them off her.

18

"I'm sorry," Harry said, lying beside her in the dark.

"Don't be," Sandra said. She lay under his outstretched left arm. She picked up his other hand and placed it on her breast. At the touch, Harry felt again the intense excitement which had so recently failed to translate itself into action. "There's nothing to be sorry about."

"I suppose you're used to failures."

"Failure and success," she said. "There's not much difference."

"Maybe it's because I'm new at this sort of thing," Harry said, hating himself for saying it. At first, in the fresh humiliation of his failure, Harry had tried to move away from the girl. But in the Spartan narrowness of her bed there was nowhere to go, and she clung to him with surprising strength. "Like when a girl loses her virginity," he added.

"I don't know about that," she said. "When I lost mine I couldn't stop giggling. No trauma at all. Poor Lenny."

"I'll kill him," Harry said, but he felt better.

"No," Sandra went on soberly, "I don't think you're

suffering from first-infidelity nerves. I think you've got something much more serious on your mind, and that's what went wrong with our little love scene."

"You're right," Harry said. Then he told her everything. About Rizzo and Hoerner and why Marco was lying in the hospital. Sandra didn't say anything, just listened. As he talked with a fluency he didn't know he possessed, Harry could feel her soft breathing and see the shadows of her face. All she said was: "Poor Harry, poor Marco." Her thin arms snaked around his waist and pulled Harry to her fiercely.

When he had finished telling, they made love with a ferocity Harry didn't recognize in himself. Just before she fell asleep, Sandra told him drowsily: "You've nothing to be sorry about, Harry boy." Shortly after, Harry felt his mind dissolve into nothingness.

Their sleep was short. In the blackness a telephone was ringing with short, persistent bursts of annoyance, and Sandra fumblingly put on a nightlight and picked up the receiver. It was just after midnight.

"Yes?" she said sleepily.

Harry reached over to cup Sandra's breast from behind, but she shook off his hand with an unconscious convulsion. "Mother," she said. "Yes, I'm awake. What's happened?" She listened for a few moments and then said: "I understand. Mother. How are you? Good. I'll be right there." Sandra replaced the receiver and turned to face Harry.

"Marco's dead," she told him. "He died a few minutes ago. A blood clot in his brain."

Harry couldn't say anything. He was grateful when Sandra slipped back into his arms and clung wordlessly for a long moment. He felt her tears on his chest. Then she broke free and kissed him. Her kiss was a wordless release from blame.

"I've got to get to the hospital," Sandra said, sliding out of bed and beginning to dress swiftly. From behind, her waist looked as thin as a child's, and her shoulder blades stuck out like little wings.

"I'll drive you." Harry reached for the old velvet robe.

"Okay. But hurry. Your clothes must be nearly dry now."

They were—nearly. Harry pulled them on quickly, shuddering at the feel of the damp, wrinkled cloth. Putting the revolver back in his coat pocket, he walked back to the vast bathroom to wash his face. He looked like a corpse that had been washed up on a beach. A not very high-class corpse badly in need of a shave.

Sandra was waiting for him in the hallway looking as if she'd never been to bed. She had put on a plain blue wool dress, and her hair was caught up in a loose braid at the side of her head. When she saw Harry, Sandra couldn't quite stifle a smile.

"I know," Harry said, "I know. Let's get going."

They drove in silence, each aware of Marco lying cold and dead in the hospital ahead. Harry hadn't yet said anything to Sandra about her brother. He sensed—he hoped —that she knew what he wanted to say: how guilty and responsible he felt. Harry wished he'd accepted Rizzo's offer in the first place. Marco would be alive. It could have been worked out somehow, Harry thought.

He parked in a dark, shadowy spot within sight of the brightly-lit hospital entrance. An ambulance stood in front of the entrance with its blue top-light rotating slowly. A white-uniformed attendant leaned against its pale side carefully smoking a cigarette. Harry wondered whether its passenger was coming or going—alive or dead.

"I'll let you out here," Harry said. "If anybody saw me like this, they'd throw me down and give me artificial respiration."

"Okay." But she didn't move.

"Sandra," he said.

"I know," she said. "I know. Don't say it, Harry. There's no need. I think I understand. I want to understand." Again, tears ran down her face. Quickly, without noise, like beads of condensation on a window. She wondered if they were really for Marco or for her mother. Her mother would expect them. Mother wouldn't cry; no, she'd be drier than ever. But she would expect tears of others. What was death without tears?

"I have to go in," she said, kissing Harry's stubbly chin with dry lips. "Go home; get some sleep."

"When will I see you?" He felt foolish and very young.

"You'll see me," Sandra said. "As soon as you hear that Marco is dead, you'll come around to see us." She showed her teeth. "God, what a charade."

Harry watched the girl click out of the darkness into the antiseptic glare of the hospital lights and disappear through the front door under the blank gaze of the ambulance attendant. She didn't look back.

He continued to sit in the darkened car. Harry was tired, uncomfortable, wrinkled, slightly damp in spots, bruised and, above all, confused by the events of the week and especially that night. None of it fit. Time was necessary to sort it all out, but time was what he didn't seem to have.

Wearily, Harry slipped the car into gear and pulled away from the curb. He headed for home.

19

As his front door closed behind him, Harry remembered Hoerner. He was supposed to have gone back to the Lamplighter and waited there for a call from Hoerner. Harry looked at his watch. One o'clock. Just over six hours ago he'd talked to Hoerner. It seemed like six days. Harry dialed the number of the Lamplighter.

"Hank," he said, "Harry. Have there been any calls for me this evening?"

"Have there? Only about a dozen. Say, what happened to you? And what was with Marco? I thought you were coming back soon."

"It's a long story, Hank," Harry said. "I'll tell you all about it later. Right now I can't face it. Who were the calls from?"

"All the same guy, Harry. And he's here now waiting for you. He came in about an hour ago."

"Is he a tall, sort of mean-looking guy?"

"That's him. I wouldn't want him mad at me. Do you want me to call the cops or something?"

Harry laughed. "No, thanks all the same. But, Hank,

close up tonight at the usual time. Can you work tomorrow night?"

"Sure, but—"

"Okay," said Harry. "I'll ring you tomorrow. Now let me talk to my friend."

"Where the hell have you been?" Hoerner demanded. His voice was tight with tension.

"You wouldn't believe it," Harry said. "Look, Hoerner, I'm tired of talking on the telephone. Why don't you come over here to my house? You know the address."

"See you in ten minutes," said Hoerner. "I'll come in the back way." In just over that time there was a tap on the back door, and Harry admitted Hoerner to the dimly lit porch.

"Come in here," he said, leading Hoerner into the living room and switching on a floor lamp.

"Christ," said Hoerner, getting a look at Harry, "what happened to you? You look like you've been run over by a street sweeper—twice."

"Nothing serious," said Harry, dismissing the question. "Marco is dead."

Hoerner said nothing.

"He died maybe an hour ago at the hospital from the beating Rizzo's thugs gave him." After another silence, Harry said, "You don't seem to care very much."

"I don't," said Hoerner. "I never knew him."

"He was a good kid," Harry said, "but that's not the point. What I'm saying is that Marco is lying in the hospital stiff room with his head half-torn off. And all because I decided not to knuckle under to Rizzo. His mother and sister are wondering why he's dead. He was alive yesterday."

"They're not the only ones," Hoerner said. "There will

be some grieving going on at Rizzo's place tonight, too. After you called me this evening, I decided it was time to put a little heavy pressure on our friend Carlo. His little brother Steve had an accident tonight."

"Accident?" said Harry. "What do you mean?"

"If you have to know the details," Hoerner said, "a big, white Cadillac ran up over the curb on Sullivan Street tonight and knocked him over a stoop railing. Last time I saw him, he wasn't looking too healthy."

"Jesus!" said Harry.

"It had to be done, Harry," said Hoerner. "You saw yourself tonight that Rizzo means business. He apparently didn't learn anything from last night's experience, so he'll have to learn the hard way."

Harry looked at Hoerner with unbelieving eyes.

"You don't seem to understand, Harry," Hoerner said, "but we're fighting a war, you and I. In wars, people get hurt, people get killed. If we don't hit them, they'll hit us. It's as simple as that. They hit Marco Carradino, and he died. It's a damn shame. And so we had to hit back. Rizzo's pulled back into his shell; he's hard to get at. But his kid brother wasn't. So he was the target."

"Just like that," said Harry. "Like you'd swat a fly that buzzed around your head. What kind of person are you, Hoerner? I don't understand you at all."

"I guess you could say I'm sort of a soldier," Hoerner said mildly. "I'm hired to do a job, and I do it the best I can. It's not always pleasant, but then most of the jobs you get hired to do are the dirty jobs people don't want to do themselves. It was the same in Vietnam. I—" Hoerner abruptly changed the subject. "Look," he said, "there's no way of telling how Rizzo is going to react to what happened to his brother tonight. I'm moving up here until we see which way he's going to jump." He gave Harry a telephone number. "More likely, I'll be getting in touch with you."

"But what are you going to do next?"

"Right now," Hoerner said, checking his watch, "I'm going to get some sleep. I'll come by your place tomorrow morning just to see how things are going."

"But what about Rizzo? What if he gets back in touch with me?" asked Harry. "What the hell do I say to him? Apologize for having his brother run down? Blame him for killing Marco?"

"Do nothing like that," said Hoerner. "You don't know anything about that. Be reasonable but firm. Give him a chance to back down. You're going to have to play him, Harry, because you're his only point of contact. If he's willing to do the smart thing, you're going to have to help him save face. If you don't, this thing is liable to blow wide open. And even killing Rizzo might not stop it because he's not alone anymore."

"Not alone? What do you mean?"

"You may as well know, Harry. Gino Speranza, old man Speranza's youngest boy, has thrown in with Rizzo. Gino hasn't much of an organization, but he's a dangerous man all by himself."

"That's wonderful," said Harry.

"Yes, isn't it," Hoerner said. "But there's nothing to worry about yet, Harry. Rizzo is still under control. He's sore as hell about his kid brother, but he also knows that we're serious, that we'll do what we say. That's important. He's got to fear us a little."

"And he fears us a little, does he?" Harry asked wearily.

"Yes, I think he does. At least, he'd better. I'm going now. If you have to, you can reach me at that number." Harry followed Hoerner to the back door.

As Hoerner reached for the door, he turned back to Harry. "By the way, there's a couple of bozos in a black Chevy sitting across the street keeping an eye on this place. I passed them on the way in. One of them looks like he's sleeping, and the other one is listening to the radio. They look like a couple of kids. I could have zapped them both."

Harry blurted before he could stop himself: "But you didn't?"

"No," said Hoerner, "it's been a hard night. It's obvious that they're only keeping an eye on you or they'd have moved before this."

Hoerner opened the door, but Harry asked: "What are we going to do about them?"

"Let 'em sit," said Hoerner. "It will do them good. It's up to you, Harry. There are some things you're going to have to handle yourself. I'm tired." He slipped out of the half-opened door.

Left alone in the screen porch, Harry stood in the dark and thought for a moment. The idea of Rizzo's men keeping watch on the house all night gave him the creeps. He took Hoerner's revolver out of his pocket and looked down at it. Then he put it away again.

He walked into the front hallway and took up the Hudson County telephone book. Harry dialed a number and listened to the ringing of a telephone.

The voice that answered was bright and unnaturally cheerful. "Police. Sergeant Dennison speaking."

"Hello, police?" Harry said, not having to try to sound nervous. "There are some burglars outside my house. Come quick."

"What's your name, sir? And your address?

"Never mind that," said Harry. "There's a couple of very suspicious looking men sitting in a black Chevrolet in the middle of the 200 block of Elgin Street, and I think they may be armed. You'd better get over here quick."

Harry put down the telephone and turned to climb the stairs. In a few minutes, from the little window at the end of Lizzie's room, he watched a green-and-white prowl car come sliding around the corner and advance down Elgin Street swinging its spotlight from side to side. Then it stopped, and the car's white doors flew open like wings, releasing two patrolmen with drawn pistols.

He watched with satisfaction as one cop opened the driver's door and plucked Injun out like a winkle from its shell. Ruby came out more slowly, sleepily. At the sight of the cops, his big hands went up and up until he could have grabbed a handful of acacia leaves.

Ruby and Injun were ordered to lean with outstretched arms against their car while the smaller cop made sharp expeditions into their pockets and came out with interesting objects. One of these was Ruby's outsized pistol, which in the policeman's small hands looked like a cannon. Soon, still protesting, Ruby and Injun were prodded into the wire-caged back of the squad car. With a last twirl of the spotlight, the police car quickly covered the rest of the block and turned the corner.

Harry thought he'd never be able to sleep, but a minute after his ruined clothes hit the floor he was in a deep, dream-streaked sleep.

At one point, he was in bed with Sandra; her slim back was to him. Harry tried to turn her around, but the harder he pulled the more immovable she became and the higher his desire rose. With all his strength, Harry pulled at a shoulder like pliant marble, and slowly Sandra began to turn around. He pulled her close to his body and pushed his face to Sandra's.

But then the face was Marco's—bloody, battered, life-less. Henry closed his eyes in terror, but he couldn't stop seeing Marco's face, and he couldn't pull away. The body against his was hard and stiff. Paralyzed, unable to recoil, Harry desperately tried to look away, and finally Marco's face began to fade—to change—until he was Hildy. Smiling her hard, edgy, sardonic smile.

"Hello, Harry," Hildy said. "This is some movie, isn't it?"

Then, inches from his eyes, Hildy's face began to swim in meaningless shapes bearing all the faces he'd ever known. One face began to form from the confusion. Sandra's face. She was Sandra now— real, warm, alive. Timidly, Harry waited for further change, mistrusting his senses.

But it was Sandra, all right. Every inch of him could feel her body. She was as solid as she'd been a few hours before.

"You're real," Harry told her.

"Of course. I'm real," Sandra said, holding him in that strong-soft embrace he remembered. He felt every point of contact with vivid intensity, and he waited for the hunger to well up again within him.

But it didn't come. Nothing. It was as if he were the dead one, not Marco. It was more than impotence. Finally, Harry gave up and let his arms relax from around her.

"It's okay," she said.

But Harry didn't answer. He was looking at his own reflection in her eyes and watching heavy, glycerin tears pour down his expressionless face. Then they were both gone.

20

HOERNER WAS STANDING AT THE SPLIT AND PEELING door of a cottage near the Hudson River. It stood in a short row of similar buildings, more than shacks, not quite houses and all in an advanced stage of surrender to time and gravity.

Pounding on the weak door with a clenched hand, Hoerner shouted: "Come on, you scroungy bitch—open up!" When there was no immediate response, he added counter-rhythmic kicks to the bottom of the door. Under the double assault, the door buckled like the cheap plywood it was but didn't break.

Hoerner stopped banging, and he smiled when he heard the rusty heave of bedsprings inside and the shuffling pad of naked feet across linoleum. The door opened as far as a green-painted chain would allow, and the opening filled with dull blond hair, a pale, half-made-up face and sallow shoulders stuffed into a thin beach robe.

"Who is it?" asked the girl, looking up into Hoerner's face from a distance of two feet.

"Who is it?" Hoerner said. "Unlock that chain, Joy, or I'll rip off this door and throw it—and you—into the river."

"I can't, Alec," Joy said. "My husband is home."

"Your husband is the same place he was six months ago and the same place he'll be this time next year. Doing three to six on Riker's Island."

"He escaped."

"I'm going to escape in about a second, Joy, all over you and this shack, and there's not going to be much left of either of you."

"I really can't, Alec," she whined. "There's somebody here with me."

"Who?"

The girl looked up at his face, and her eyes were no longer soft and focusless. They were defiant and as hard as eyes like hers could manage. She jerked her sharp chin up. "My father," she said. Joy looked down at the burglar chain as if studying its mechanics.

"For Christ's sake," Hoerner said, not loudly but with so much force that the girl's hand grabbed for the chain and dropped it. She nearly fell as she stumbled back into the room at the same time.

Hoerner pushed the door, not worrying that he might hit her with it, and saw a dark-haired, under-chinned man sitting in T-shirt and trousers on the big, swaybacked bed, pulling on long, blue socks.

"It's all yours, kid," he said. "I got to get to work."

"O'Brien," Hoerner said, "when you go to work I'll start going to church. And when you stop humping your step-daughter, I'm going to run for pope. What do you think Mae is going to do when I tell her you're at it again?"

O'Brien looked up at Hoerner with black eyes with a hint of something half-wild and scared in them. He continued to tie the laces of shiny black, perforated-toe shoes that had cost Joy's mother forty-five dollars. His rounded, slightly twitchy face suggested a sophisticated rabbit. He was thirty-nine but looked a youthful forty-five.

"You know," he said, hastily jamming an arm into the wrong sleeve of a pin-striped shirt, "that Joy is like a daughter to me, Alec." He wrenched the arm out and tried to get it into the other sleeve.

"Yeah," said Hoerner, "you just fuck her to protect her reputation." He stepped back and opened the door which had bounced shut. "Finish dressing outside, shit-heel," he said, "or I really will tell Mae, and she'll cut your balls off. If you have any."

O'Brien gave up trying to button his shirt and dragged a suit jacket and tie from the bedside chair. "Sure," he said, "sure. I've got to be going." With his eyes fixed on Hoerner's face, he walked a long arc to the door and paused for a split-second. "See you, Joy," he said.

"Scram!" Hoerner yelled, slamming the door so fast it caught O'Brien on his right heel as he hopped clear of the doorway. Outside he knelt and tried to smooth the bruised leather with a spit-moistened forefinger.

Putting the chain back up, Hoerner turned back to Joy, who was leaning back against the grease-spattered stove watching him. Her limp robe had fallen open revealing a sagging, bruised breast with a tiny, pubescent nipple and below a scattered patch of sandy pubic hair.

"You staying long?" she asked.

"Long enough," said Hoerner. "If Jack O'Brien is waiting around for me to leave, he'll have a long wait." Joy shrugged. "The sheets," Hoerner said, gesturing to the bed. "Get them off."

"But, Alec, I just put them on yesterday morning."

"I don't care if you put them on tonight," Hoerner said. "I'm not sleeping on sheets used by that miserable little shit." He snatched the bedding to the floor. "And pillow cases, too."

With a shrug, Joy began rummaging in the bottom drawer of a warped bureau. As she sloppily remade the big bed, Hoerner watched her with weary eyes.

"Okay," he said, "that's good enough." Quickly stripping naked and hanging his clothes on a wooden hanger, Hoerner slipped into the far side of the bed facing the wall. The cheap sheets felt cool and clean.

Without turning around, he said, "Set your alarm clock for ten o'clock and don't mess up."

As he ordered his mind for sleep, Hoerner heard the girl winding the noisy clock and then felt her weight slip into bed behind him. The bedside lamp clicked the room into darkness. He felt her knee at the back of his thigh and a soft breast touching his back.

"Alec," she said, "is there anything you want?"

"Yes," he said, "some fucking sleep."

The girl moved back from Hoerner, not sharply or angrily, but as if she'd expected no better answer. She lay there watching him fall asleep.

21

IT WAS NEARLY NOON BEFORE GINO SPERANZA FOUND out what had happened to Ruby and Injun. He was just entering his apartment when the telephone rang.

"Yeah?"

"Gino?" a voice said.

"What's up, Vern?" he asked.

"It's Bonino and Carelli," the policeman said. "We've got them down here."

"What do you mean?" Gino asked, his voice rising.

"They were picked up, Gino," Vern said evenly, "over on Elgin Street early this morning. A citizen's complaint. Our men found them sitting in a car at close to two a.m with a loaded, unregistered pistol. They brought them in, and Dennison booked them."

"Booked?" Gino asked, genuinely surprised. "How booked, Vern?"

"You know, Gino, things are changing around here. New men. Dennison's even made sergeant, and he was on this morning. He booked 'em."

"Is the Chief there? Let me talk to him."

"He's here, Gino, but he says you better come on in and see him. He wants to talk to you."

"Talk to me? Vern—"

"Sorry, Gino," Hodges said. "I'm doing you a favor by calling."

"I'll be there," said Gino, dropping the telephone.

As he drove to the police station, Gino's mind was clashing, trying to sort out this thing that had happened. All he could figure out was that his men had been fingered by somebody, probably one of the guys who had taken Rizzo for a ride. Maybe the boss, the hard man Rizzo talked about. Gino's mind conjured up this man as a shadow, dark and commanding. The image brought to Gino memories of his father from the early days of his childhood.

When he appeared in the nursery, Baptiste Speranza had seemed like a superman to his youngest son. A dark, strong-smelling hero with powerful arms and a pocket full of silver coins. No matter how much the older kids clamored and hung on their father, Gino was never left out. Instead he was in the middle, caught up in the strong arms and pressed against a sandpaper cheek which left him with a glowing reminder of his father's presence long after he'd gone away.

That's how he remembered his father when Gino was sent, at the age of eleven, to that military academy in Ohio. Gino pretended not to remember the name of the academy. That was the same time his father had "gone away" for five years. Gino had known almost from the first that Speranza was in a federal prison. He'd been ashamed and proud at the same time, and had nobody in the world to talk about it with.

His father had been released just in time to see Gino—a short, rebellious, no-stripe cadet with too-long hair and nicotine-stained fingers—graduate with his class. There was a reunion with a gray old man in an expensive but ill-fitting suit who seemed only a weak shadow of his father.

Roy Beddell was sharpening a new pencil with a bone-handled jackknife, carefully dropping the shavings onto his spotless blotter, when Vern Hodges led Gino, looking very tight and controlled, into his office.

"Hello, Gino. Have a seat."

Gino sat down silently and watched the Chief bring the pencil to a needle point.

"Vern said you had a little problem," Beddell said, looking up at Gino.

"Vern said you wanted to see me." There was a silence.

"Yes, I did," the Chief admitted. "I understand we've got some friends of yours here. A couple of young fellows called"—he picked up a sheet of paper from his desk—"Bonino and Carelli. You know them, do you?"

"I know them," said Gino, not giving an inch.

"Okay, Gino," Beddell said, putting the paper into a manila file, "that's all I wanted to know. Was there anything else you wanted to talk about? If not..." Beddell left the rest of the sentence hanging.

"Chief," said Gino, bending, "what are you trying to do to me?"

"I'll tell you," Beddell said. "I'm trying to head you off from making some serious mistakes. I've a rough idea what you're up to, but there are some blank spots. Shall I tell you what I know so far?"

"Run it," said Gino, but he'd relaxed considerably.

"All right, I will. First, I know Charlie Rice is trying to move in on a fellow named Caster who owns a bar down on Parker Street. That was fairly obvious from the beginning. Charlie's not particularly subtle. But I gave him the benefit of the doubt. However, something happened last night that throws an entirely different light on his little operation. A young guy named Marco Carradino got himself badly beaten up—very badly beaten up."

"That's too bad," said Gino.

"So badly," the Chief went on, "that about midnight last night Carradino died at Parker Hospital." The policeman was watching Gino's face. He got no reaction, but he waited for Gino to say something.

"That's too bad, too.'

"It's more than too bad," Beddell said. "It's murder, or at the very least manslaughter. But the really interesting thing is that Marco Carradino was working in the same bar that Charlie Rice wants to take over. That's quite a coincidence."

"Seems to be," agreed Gino.

"And then, a couple of hours after the Carradino boy died, your friends are found sitting in a car across the street from Caster's house. At two o'clock in the morning. And Bonino is carrying a gun. They couldn't seem to come up with a convincing reason for being there, and Bonino was very embarrassed about the gun. I wasn't around, and neither was Vern, so Dennison did the only thing he could. He booked them."

"I know," said Gino. "Dennison is very keen."

"Yes, he is. But then he's new, you know."

"But you're not, Chief," Gino said, leaning forward in his chair. "You go back a long way in Parker's Landing. Back to days when you were a young cop struggling to raise a family on a hundred bucks a month, and we were the new wops in town."

"You don't have to remind me of the old days, Gino. I know them too well to forget. And I haven't forgotten what your father did for me. You should know that. And you should know, too, that my debt is to him, not to you. I don't owe you a damned thing, but we both owe the same man a hell of a lot. That's why I'm talking with you this morning. That's why I called your father this morning."

Gino tensed. "You called my old man? You lousy—"

"Cut it! You're not talking to one of your punks. Damned right I called your old man. Just as I did a few years ago when you put that 'borrowed' car through the front window of Egmont's Dairy. And kept you from going to reform school instead of that prep school upstate; have you forgotten that?"

Gino didn't answer, but Beddell could see that he remembered. "Gino," he continued, "you don't owe me a damned thing. But you're causing that old man a lot of worry, and it looks like you're set to cause him a lot more. If you've thrown in with Charlie Rice, you're buying yourself a lot of trouble. And your father will pick up the bill."

"What did he say—the old man?'"

"He wants to see you. He still thinks he can talk you into going back to college."

"That's funny," Gino said.

"No it's not, it's sad. And it's going to get sadder unless you use your head." His voice became harder, more official. "Now, get out of here, Gino, and keep clean. Don't think we won't be watching you. Obligation only stretches so far."

"What about my boys?"

Beddell sighed. "If I was a true friend to your father, I'd put you in with them and throw away the key. But I can't. Take them away; I don't want them stinking up my jail."

"Good," said Gino, standing up and turning toward the door.

"There's a price, Gino."

"Yeah?" Gino turned back.

"You're in luck there, too. Judge Ortiz wasn't hung over this morning so he allowed them bail. Five hundred for the gun-packing baby and two-fifty for the midget. He thought they were bargain prices; I think you're getting robbed."

Gino gave the Chief a bleak look and walked out of his office. He wondered whether to slam the door or leave it open. Instead, he shut it gently and went to retrieve Ruby and Injun.

22

ALEC HOERNER WOKE UP LATE. THE FIRST THING HE saw on opening his eyes was Joy's back. She was doing something at the sink, still wearing that sleazy robe.

"Coffee," said Hoerner, and he closed his eyes again. He remembered vaguely the tinny clanging of the alarm clock.

In a couple of minutes, Joy padded over to the bed and placed a cup of coffee on the paint-peeled bedside table. He could smell it. Then Joy perched herself on the very edge of the bed, ready to flee if necessary.

Alec pushed himself up against the pillows into a sitting position and took a sip of the hot, black coffee. Joy waited until he'd drunk nearly half of the cup.

"Alec," she said at last, "we go back a long time, me and you, don't we? I mean since I was just a kid on Forty-Seventh Street."

"Yeah," Alec said in a neutral tone, not angry or scoffing, "I guess we do."

Joy was encouraged. "Don't get mad or anything," she said cautiously, "but you've changed a lot. I mean from what you used to be before you went in the Army. I've noticed it a lot since you've been back. What is it—three years you've been home?"

"Closer to four," said Hoerner. "What do you mean I've changed?"

"Well—" Joy hesitated, and Hoerner smiled ruefully to himself. Having people scared of you was very convenient sometimes. It saved a lot of argument. But it could be overdone. Sometimes it was like living in a cage full of nervous hamsters.

"Go ahead, Joy baby," he said soothingly. "Say anything you want to. I won't bite your head off. I'm saving my strength for what could be a very wearing day."

"You sure?" she asked, looking up at him out of lowered eyes.

"I'm sure."

"Okay, then," Joy said, gathering resolution and sticking her weak chin out, "you have changed, Alec, you know you have. On the block, you know, you were always a tough guy. Hardly anybody was tougher, not between Forty-Fifth and Forty-Ninth Street, anyway. But..."

"You mean I'm not tough anymore, Joy," Hoerner said mockingly. "Is that it? You think I've gone soft. You think old Alec, the terror of the West Side, has turned pansy, is that it? I'm very hurt, Joy, I really am."

"No," she protested shrilly, "it's not that, Alec, and you know it." Joy was relieved to find Hoerner in such a good mood and was almost sorry she'd started questioning him. But she resolved to plow on. "What I mean, Alec, nobody's saying you're not still tough. If anything, you're tougher than ever. But that's not what I'm saying."

"So what do you mean?" Hoerner asked, finishing his coffee and setting the cup on the bedside table.

"I mean," Joy said, looking into his mocking eyes,

"inside you're different, Alec. You've gone all hard. It's as if —as if something in you that used to be sort of tough and springy is all gone hard and brittle. Like you were under some kind of terrific pressure inside." Joy stopped and looked away from Hoerner in embarrassment.

"Go on, Joy," Hoerner said, and she could tell from his voice that he meant it, that he wasn't angry with her. But she couldn't bring her eyes back to his, so she continued talking while looking away from Hoerner. Her hands picked at the frayed beading on her robe.

"Well, when you came home from Vietnam in uniform with all the medals and ribbons and all," she continued softly, "it seemed as if you hadn't changed much. But you had. You were all restless and moody, as if you were hunting for something, something that maybe didn't exist. Everybody noticed it, and they said so, too. Behind your back."

"What did they say, Joy?"

"They said something had happened to you in Vietnam," Joy said. "Something bad. And Johnny Fahey from over on Eighth Avenue said he'd heard things about you when he was in Vietnam."

"What sort of things?" asked Hoerner, lighting another cigarette.

"Johnny'd never really say. He just used to whistle, low like, and grin and say he was glad he wasn't no Vietnamese when you were around. Once, he said that the Army was happier to see you leave Vietnam than the Viet Cong were. I don't know what he meant by that."

"I can imagine," said Hoerner. "Go on, Joy. What else?"

"Well, then when you went for a copper. I couldn't believe it. Nobody could. There wasn't anybody in the neighborhood who could imagine the old Alec Hoerner in a cop's uniform. And me neither."

"But I did wear one, didn't I, Joy? For nearly two years," he said. "You saw me in it, didn't you?"

"Yeah, I saw you, Alec," Joy said, "but not much, because about that time Mom married Jack, and I came up here to live with them. But I heard a lot about how you weren't kidding, how you really were a cop, and how everybody around was nervous about you."

"Nervous about me?" asked Hoerner, genuinely a little surprised. "Just because I wore a cop's uniform? People scare a lot easier than they used to."

"No," said Joy, "not afraid of the uniform, Alec. Afraid of you. The uniform really had nothing to do with it. It was just you. What you'd become."

"What had I become?"

"That's what I don't know," Joy said. "That's what's got me puzzled. But you can tell me something—that is if you will."

"What's that?"

She looked down again; "What really happened with those two kids under the pier?"

Hoerner looked at the girl, his eyes blank. She was talking about the incident that had made the New York Police Department decide that Hoerner, despite his excellent record and prospects, was just a little too hot to handle. After Hoerner had won three citations in Harlem, they'd put him back on the West Side, and all had gone well. Crime had dropped considerably on his beat. But then at three one morning a cab driver reported a hot gun battle under Pier 86. When a squad car got there they found Hoerner on his feet but in a daze. Lying near a pier column were two local boys, members of a West Side gang, dying of bullet wounds.

One of the kids had a homemade pistol in his pocket,

but it had never been fired. Hoerner couldn't or wouldn't explain what had happened, so the department relieved him from duty and waited for the storm to hit. The shooting had come too late for the morning papers, and by that afternoon the evening papers were all tied up with an international plane hijacking. The Pier 86 story got lost among the underwear advertisements. A local youth worker and the mother of one of the boys tried to keep the matter alive, but nobody else was much interested. A couple of months later, Hoerner was quietly asked to resign, and it never made a ripple.

Hoerner relived it all in his head in a few seconds, and when he looked at Joy again it was with an expression so mild and unguarded that she hardly recognized him.

"You know," he said, "that's a question I've been asking myself ever since that night. The department didn't believe me, but I don't know what happened. You know who those kids were. They called themselves the Apaches. Well, a bit after two-thirty I busted four or five of them going in through the top of a Cadillac convertible on Forty-Sixth Street. They cut out for the piers, and the last I saw they ran into the darkness, and I went in after them. And then—I think—somebody started shooting at me. Several shots came out of the darkness under the piers. I remember pulling my gun and going in. And that's all."

"I never knew that," said Joy.

"I never told anybody," Hoerner said, "except the police department shrink, and I don't think he believed me."

"I believe you, Alec," Joy said so sincerely that Hoerner laughed.

"You would, Joy," he said. "You would." When Joy stiffened and started to turn away, Hoerner reached out and took her thin wrist. "Come on," he said. "I'm sorry."

Joy held back stiffly and looked Hoerner searchingly in the face. "Don't laugh at me, Alec," she said. "Please, don't." Her wrist between his fingers felt like a satin-smooth stick, and she still pulled away.

"I won't," said Hoerner, and he relaxed his grip on her arm. But instead of pulling out of his reach, Joy seemed to collapse on the bedcovers over his legs until she was lying nearly full-length with her cheek against Hoerner's abdomen. He felt her arms go around his waist and clutch tight. "I won't," he repeated, touching her badly-dyed hair.

23

HARRY CASTER WAS LYING IN BED STARING AT THE ceiling and trying to get up the energy and courage to rejoin the world when the doorbell rang. Harry lay very still. If he didn't move, perhaps they'd go away. No murder today, thank you. But the insistent ding-dong that Harry had hated since they'd moved into the house continued relentlessly. Even being shot was a little better than lying listening to that bell. Harry got up and crept to a small window over-looking the front porch.

Sandra Carradino was standing on the doorstep with her finger pressed firmly on the bell. Harry dropped the curtain, ran down the stairs, opened the door and jerked Sandra inside.

"Good morning to you, too," Sandra said, smoothing her clothes. "Do you always greet callers this way? I wouldn't want to be the Avon lady in this neighborhood."

"You're lucky I didn't shoot you," Harry said, leading her into the living room to the tattered leather sofa. "Some very strange things are happening on this street. There were two hoodlums sitting in a car across the street at two this morning keeping a watch on this house. One of them had a gun."

"How do you know that?"

"I saw the cops take a gun—a very big gun—off one of them. I called the police—anonymously—and told them there were burglars on the street."

"You're a very clever man," Sandra said. "But what's this business about my getting shot? Do you have a gun?"

"Yes," Harry admitted, and he told her how Hoerner had given it to him. "But I don't think I'd ever use it. There's something about shooting people that's so final."

"There is that," agreed Sandra.

"What I want to know," Harry said, "is what are you doing here? Aren't you supposed to be with your mother?"

"I was," said Sandra, "all night."

"Was it bad?"

"Yes, pretty bad," she said. "Have you ever been with someone who was terribly sick and wanted to vomit but just couldn't do it, just couldn't get anything up? That's my mother. Only with her it's tears that won't come. Thank God the clan has started arriving."

"The clan?"

"The clan Carradino," Sandra said, "every loving one in the tristate area. They don't just come and say vague things; they make a picnic of it with kids, dogs and vast amounts of food. My goofy cousin Leon even brought his football—he's thirty-seven, the fat slob—and right now he and his equally slobby kid are probably throwing it around in our garden."

"What does your mother think of all this?"

"She loves it. Now she's got somebody to organize, to boss. Besides, eventually my aunts, the dread Ferrara sisters, will make her cry. They'll work on her until she cracks, and I don't want to be there to see it."

"But won't they miss you?" Harry asked.

"Probably not until the funeral Sunday, and then only because it says in the book that the deceased's sister sits in such and such a place. But if they miss me, they miss me."

"And how are you?" Harry asked very seriously.

"I'm okay, Harry," she said. "I really don't believe it all yet, but I'm okay." She put a hand on his. "But right now, I'm very tired. Have you got a bed someplace in this palace where a person could lie down?"

"Sure," said Harry. "Alone?"

"Not necessarily," she said.

24

It was well after noon by the time Hoerner pulled up across the street from Harry Caster's house. He saw Caster's rented car in the driveway and knew he ought to go in and check with him, find out if anything new had happened. But instead he sat there in the car. Absentmindedly, he lit a cigarette and thought about that morning at the cottage by the river. You're getting soft, Hoerner, he told himself. All the same, it wasn't a bad feeling. Hoerner tipped his hat down over his eyes a little and slid back into reverie.

"Stupid," Gino Speranza was saying. "I never heard of anything so stupid in my fucking life." He'd just bailed out Injun and Ruby and was driving them back to Harry's street to their car.

"Somebody narked us," Ruby said from the seat next to him. He hadn't shaved, and blond stubble lay like golden powder on his cheeks. Injun sat in the back seat immobile and silent. His dark eyes burned into the seat back in front of him.

"Shut up," Gino snapped. "You're some operators, you are. I wouldn't send you out to heist a lollipop. Jesus, is Rizzo going to laugh when he hears about this. I provide him with a couple of men—good men, I tell him—and they can't even watch a house for one night without getting busted."

Ruby started to say something but closed his mouth and gritted his teeth. This was wise, because Gino was wound tight to the explosion point. The humiliation of his interview with Chief Beddell was eating away at his self-control like strong acid.

"Okay," Gino grated as the car turned onto Harry's block, "where is it?"

"Over there," said Ruby with a vague gesture of his hand.

"Over where, for Christ's sake?" Gino screamed, taking his eyes from the street to glare at Ruby. At that moment, the big Thunderbird swerved and hit the back of Hoerner's parked car with a crunch of collapsing metal. A hubcap popped off the Thunderbird and rolled erratically across the street.

Hoerner grunted with pain as he collided with the steering wheel of his car. The gun under his arm gouged into his armpit. "Shit!" he said, whirling out of the driver's seat onto the street to see who had hit him. Then he recognized Ruby's big blond head as it came back up over the dashboard. He didn't recognize the driver, but he knew the stabbing motion of his right hand toward the inside of his suit jacket.

Gino cleared his revolver first, but it struck the top of the half-open door he was leaning on and jarred out of his hand. Before the pistol could settle again into Gino's palm, Hoerner put two shots through the glass of the window into his pale mauve shirt front. Two red blotches appeared instantly, and Gino fell to a kneeling position in the street behind the door and stuck there, his hanging head leaning against the red-leather door panel. His gun clattered to the pavement and spun into the middle of the street.

Hoerner came swiftly around the door, saw that Gino would be no more trouble, and stuck his gun into the car, covering Ruby and Injun.

"Up!" he commanded. "Up. Grab a piece of the headliner."

Ruby and Injun silently did as they were told, keeping a wary eye on Hoerner's gun. The shots hadn't been loud, no more than two sharp cracks, but Hoerner knew he had to get moving before a crowd gathered. "Who's he?" He snapped his head toward Gino's body.

Neither spoke, so Hoerner arced his pistol across the back of the front seat to the point of Ruby's jaw. It connected with a sharp sound. Tears of pain appeared in Ruby's eyes, and he started to bring his hands down.

"Up," Hoerner ordered. He turned his eyes to Injun in the back seat.

"Gino Speranza," said Injun flatly, looking Hoerner in the eye.

On the street, a few faces had begun to appear at windows.

"Okay, crybaby," Hoerner said, turning to Ruby, "get over in the back with your buddy."

Ruby started to bring a hand down to open the door, but Hoerner stopped him.

"No," he said. "Over the top. You get in the far corner," he told Injun.

Hoerner watched as the big man struggled onto his knees on the front seat. Awkwardly, Ruby shifted his weight, threw a knee over the back of the seat and began to climb over.

At the same moment, Hoerner pushed the automatic gear lever of the still-running car down to reverse and jumped back. Slowly, the automobile lurched to a start and began moving backward. The open door pushed Gino's body to the street, and a front tire ran over his out-thrown hand. With the first motion of the car, Ruby lost his balance and fell heavily, trapping Injun with his broad shoulders.

Before Ruby stopped falling, Hoerner was halfway to his car. He jumped in and started the engine. At the same time, in the rearview mirror, he watched Gino's Thunderbird scrape along the side of a pick-up truck and keep going. As Hoerner wheeled around the corner, he heard the car hit a lamp standard with a crash and a shower of glass.

This new sound of impact brought Harry and Sandra to the window along with half of the housewives on the block. But few were looking at the automobile and the small, dark man struggling to get behind the steering wheel. Most eyes were on Gino's body where it lay face down a car and a half's width from the curb. They were momentarily distracted when Injun finally got into the front seat, shifted the Thunderbird into low and roared past Gino's body without a pause or a look.

"Who is that?" Sandra asked, looking at Gino's body. She stood unconcernedly naked at the window beside Harry. "Is he hurt?"

"I don't know," Harry said, struggling with the sleeve of his robe, "but I wish you'd put a little something on."

"I'll use some of yours," Sandra said, untangling the arm of the robe and slipping inside with Harry. Her naked hip, so warm in bed a few minutes before, was cool, and he felt her bare foot lightly on his.

"That's a little better," he said. "Now all I have to do is explain to the neighbors what I was doing sharing my bathrobe with a beautiful, naked young girl."

"It will do wonders for your reputation," she said. "Business at the Lamplighter will probably double."

"If there is a Lamplighter."

A black gardener from across the street walked out into the street and knelt beside Gino's body. Gingerly the gardener turned him over on his back. His whole chest was stained a bright red, but Gino's dark-jowled face was untouched. Even the tinted glasses were still in place.

Sandra clutched Harry's wrist. "I know him," she said, shrinking back from the window. "It's Gino Speranza. I met him at a dance last year. His father is supposed to be head of the Mafia around here."

"And I know where else I've heard that name," Harry said. "Hoerner said that Gino Speranza was working for Rizzo."

"Do you think so?"

"What else would he have been doing on this block with a gun? Not paying a social call. Anyway, I'm not going to stick around to find out. I'm getting out of here." Harry drew her away from the window.

"Where will you go?" Sandra asked.

Where will I go, Harry thought. Where do you run when you don't know what you're running from? "The city, I guess," he said. He thought of his brother Mickey.

"I'll go with you."

"No," Harry said. "I'll take you home. It could be dangerous with me. Besides, your mother may need you more than you think."

"I'll go with you," Sandra said.

Seven minutes later, the neighbors who crept out to the sidewalk to stare at Gino's corpse were surprised to see Harry Caster come out of his house with a young girl and drive away rapidly. This added considerable piquancy to the most exciting day Elgin Street had ever seen.

HOERNER DROVE AUTOMATICALLY, HIS ONLY GOAL TO put distance between himself and Elgin Street. He thought no more about Gino Speranza. Then he realized that he was retracing his path back to the river, going back to Joy's place. Hoerner shrugged. It was someplace to go.

He parked the car across the rutted tarmac road from the little house and strode to the front door. As he knocked, Hoerner smiled at the contrast between his arrival early that morning and this one. There was no answer. Hoerner knocked a bit louder. "Joy," he called. "Joy, it's me—Alec."

"You're wasting your time, son," said a voice not far from Hoerner's elbow. "Nobody's home."

Hoerner looked into the next yard and saw no one.

"Down here," said the voice, and he saw that it belonged to an old woman, not much higher than the leaning green fence. Gray puffs of hair stood out from her head like explosions of rusty steel wool. She wore an ancient gingham dress tied around with a patch-pocket apron into which her hands were jammed.

"Where is she?" Hoerner asked.

"Couldn't say," the old woman said, squinting up at him. "She left about twenty minutes ago with that rabbity, dark-haired fella who's always hanging around. She was carrying an old suitcase, and it looked heavy."

"You don't miss much, do you, Granny?" Hoerner asked.

"Nope," she said. "There's not much else to do on this block but spy on the neighbors. Not that they're that interesting. Best show we've had in months was when you got here last night."

"Glad you were amused," Hoerner said. "I'd have thought you'd be mad because I woke you up."

"I can sleep any time," said the neighbor. "Is he really her father?"

"Stepfather."

She looked a little disappointed. "If you want to get in," the old woman said, "my key fits. They're all just skeleton keys."

"I don't want to get in," Hoerner said as he turned and kicked his way through the hanging gate and onto the ruined sidewalk.

"Son—" Hoerner turned and looked back. The little woman was on her porch now, a twin to Joy's. "Take an old woman's advice, boy," she said. "Don't—"

"Stuff your advice, Grandma," said Hoerner, and he walked back to his car. The old woman was smiling as she turned to go back into her house.

Once in his car, Hoerner didn't know where to go next. With Gino Speranza cold and dead in front of Caster's house, everything had changed. No longer was it a case of preventing a war. Now the important thing was to win.

The thought of cutting and running, of leaving Harry Caster to sort out his nasty little problems himself, crossed Hoerner's mind. But he couldn't do that. He needed the rest of the money Mickey Caster had promised, and he knew Caster wouldn't pay for a half- finished job. No, the last thing Rizzo would expect would be another attack so soon, but that was what he was going to get. Only this time Hoerner was going to hit him so hard that Rizzo would be glad to call it off. How he was going to do this, Hoerner had no idea. But he knew where he had to be: at Rizzo's. And as soon as it grew dark, that was where he was going to be.

Then he felt hungry, and Hoerner knew he had some time to kill before this evening. He turned the car around, decimating a row of bedraggled lilies, and headed away from the river.

25

CARLO RIZZO WAS SITTING ALONE IN HIS LIVING ROOM angrily reliving the night before with his family. His brother would pull through, the doctor said, but Rizzo's family had been on him fiercely, blaming him for Steve's injury. His sisters had been worst of all, the worthless bitches. And their two-bit husbands hadn't been much better. They hadn't been too proud to take the crumbs he'd thrown them when things were going better. Finally, he had stomped out at three in the morning after telling them all to go to hell. He could still see his mother's face—cried out, stark, pleading.

Now Rizzo heard loud voices out on the front lawn, and he carefully peeked out of the side window and saw Pete standing off Injun and Ruby, who were trying to explain something. Then Rizzo heard the words, "They shot him," and he hurried to the front door.

As soon as they were in the house, Rizzo turned on them. "Who's been shot? What the hell is going on?"

Ruby and Injun exchanged glances, and Ruby said: "It's Gino. Somebody burned him on Caster's street. Just a few minutes ago. We came right over." Ruby quickly told Rizzo all that had happened.

"Who was this guy?" Rizzo asked. "Did you recognize him?"

"No," Ruby said, "but he was a pro, that's for sure. Gino only bumped his car a little, and he came out shooting. He must have been guarding Caster's house."

"Yeah," said Rizzo, "I'll bet he was." He turned to Injun. "Where's Caster now?"

"When we got out of there, he was home," Injun said. "At least I think he was. But I doubt if he stuck around for long."

"You're really clever," Rizzo said, "to figure that out all by yourself." He thought hard for a moment while the two youths eyed him uneasily.

"You're working for me now," Rizzo told them.

Ruby and Injun looked at each other again and then both nodded okay. There didn't seem to be anything else to do.

"I've got a job for you," Rizzo said. "First we've got to get rid of Gino's car. Pete will give you his car, Injun, and I want you and Ruby to take the Thunderbird and lose it somewhere. Then you both come back here, and I'll have work for you. Don't be too long getting back."

Pete reluctantly handed over his car keys to Injun. With Ruby following in the Thunderbird, the driver's window rolled down so that the bullet holes didn't show, they rolled off toward the river to find a place where the big car wouldn't be found for a while.

All went well until they got to Guilford Avenue. Injun squeezed through on a red-orange signal, but Ruby, under the eye of a traffic cop, chickened out and stopped. He tried to look innocent and hoped that a report wasn't out yet on

Gino's car. Injun drove on slowly, expecting Ruby to catch up with him in a couple of blocks.

But while he was sitting nervously at the signal trying to keep an eye on Pete's car through the traffic-filled crossing, Ruby saw Harry and Sandra drive across the intersecting street heading south out of Parker's Landing. For once in his life, Ruby reacted without hesitation. To the annoyance of a woman driving a Volkswagen bus, he edged into the curbside lane as the light was changing green and turned right to follow Harry's car.

CHIEF BEDDELL ARRIVED ON ELGIN STREET WHERE Gino's body still lay in the street. He looked down at the form beneath the olive-drab tarpaulin with no other feeling than weariness. He hadn't meant to be so right in his prediction of Gino's fate. After a word with his sergeant confirming that Harry Caster was not in his house, Beddell got back into his unmarked car and drove away.

The old man was having his afternoon nap when Beddell arrived at the Speranza house. He said he'd wait, and Carmen, the daughter, still attractive at thirty-five but going middle-aged around the eyes and mouth, led him into the living room and got him a cup of coffee.

Beddell sat back on the leather sofa and looked around at the expensive furnishings, the big color television set, the well-framed oil paintings on the walls. I should have taken that job he offered years ago, he thought. Maybe I did, he added ruefully to himself, or I wouldn't be sitting here now.

Carmen sat down on the other end of the sofa and looked at him.

"You've never been here before," she said.

"No," said Beddell. "This is the first time." There'd been plenty of invitations at first, but after he'd refused them all without making excuses, the invitations had stopped coming.

"What do you want here?" she asked directly.

"I think I'd better wait for your father."

"Yes, I suppose so," Carmen said. She started to say something else when Baptiste Speranza appeared in the doorway wearing the clouded face of the newly awakened. His gardening clothes had been replaced by a pair of baggy, soft-gray trousers and a checked woolen shirt.

Beddell stood up automatically as the old man entered the room, and Speranza came toward him with his hand extended. His mouth was smiling, but Beddell knew from his eyes that Speranza sensed that this was no social call.

"Roy," he said, "it's good to see you again."

Beddell took the old hand and shook it. "Hello, Baptiste," he said. The grip was gentle, but beneath the soft padding Beddell could feel a ghostly reminder of the vise that hand had once been.

"Sit down, sit down," Speranza urged, still gripping Beddell's hand. "Carmen," he said in the same soft voice, but it was definitely a command.

"But, Papa—"

"Carmen," Speranza repeated, no louder than before. Carmen sighed, and with a glance at Beddell she left the room.

"Carmen's the only one I can push around these days," Speranza said after the door closed. He didn't smile. "Even the little one tells me what to do, and I do it." Then he smiled. "But, Roy," the old man said, "I'm glad to see you after all this time. A telephone call this morning and now a visit. "Is it"— Speranza's face darkened—"still that business about the boy?"

"It's about Gino, Baptiste," Beddell started, and he tried to summon up one of those useful phrases employed to avoid handling the naked blade of truth. But he couldn't this time. "Gino's dead, Baptiste," he said. "Somebody shot him to death a little while ago over in Parkland."

Speranza took the news, absorbed it as rich earth absorbs rain. His eyes lost their contented dullness, becoming not sharp but keen. His face seemed to shed the flaccidness that had crept into it in recent years. Speranza looked slightly ludicrous in the clothes of an old man, like an actor backstage.

"What happened?" he asked quietly.

"We don't know yet," Beddell replied. Now he was all policeman. "Gino came in this morning after I talked to you and bailed his two punks out."

"You let him have them?"

"I didn't have any choice. Ortiz set bail, and Gino had the money. So he took them with him. A little while later we got a call that there'd been a shooting on Elgin Street where that Caster fellow lives. It was Gino. He didn't suffer, Baptiste; there was no pain." Speranza did not rise to this easy bait. Beddell went on. "We don't know exactly what he went there for. But there was some sort of collision. Gino went for his gun—he died with it in his hand—but the other fellow got his shots in first."

"This Caster you were telling me about—the bar owner," Speranza said. "Did he shoot Gino?"

"No," Beddell said. "Witnesses say definitely not."

"You've talked to him?"

"Not yet. The shooting scared him off, and we haven't been able to locate him yet. But we will."

"He hired a gun?"

"I don't know," Beddell said. "He's a pretty frightened man."

"And Rizzo," Speranza said, "he knows that Gino is dead?"

"He probably does by now." The situation had changed. Beddell had turned from bearer of bad news to an informant. "The two men with Gino beat it right after the shooting in Gino's T-bird. Probably it was Bonino and Carelli heading straight for Rizzo's."

"Have you seen Rizzo?"

"I came right here."

"I am grateful, Roy," the old man said. He laid a heavy hand on Beddell's arm. "I know you won't let me do anything for you, but—"

"There's something you can do for me, Don Baptiste," Beddell said. He hadn't often used the tide of respect, and Speranza's face registered suspicion. "You can do me a big favor by staying out of this. Please, you can't do anybody any good by getting involved. Leave it to me. It's my job."

Speranza smiled gently. "So you're telling me what to do, too, Roy. You and the little one," he added without meaning to insult. Speranza stood and offered his hand. Beddell stood, too, and he knew he'd been wasting his time. "You've been a good friend, Roy," Speranza said, taking his hand, "a good friend. And I'm very grateful."

"I'd have been a better cop if I'd been less of a friend," Beddell said, and he knew he was speaking the truth. "And probably a better friend, too."

Speranza wasn't listening. His ears were tuned to inner thoughts in which Roy Beddell didn't figure at all. "Thank you, Roy, thank you very much," he said, drawing Beddell toward the door.

"Baptiste!" the police chief said sharply as they got to the thick door. Speranza raised his eyes to his face, but Beddell saw no recognition there. In vain, he continued: "I have to warn you. Keep out of this. I enforce the law in Parker's Landing—you don't. I'll take care of Caster and Rizzo and the guy who killed Gino. I guarantee you that. If you or any of your people take a hand, I'll stop you."

"Goodbye, Roy," Speranza said, opening the door.

"Goodbye, Baptiste," Beddell said with resignation, walking down the path toward his car.

Speranza turned back to the large hallway and found Carmen waiting for him at the entrance to the living room. Her face was a worried void.

"We have bad news. Carmen," Speranza said gently. "Gino is dead. He was shot to death a short while ago. You had better inform the family." Almost before she could react, he added, "I'll tell you all about it later. Now, I must lie down for a while. If I fall asleep, wake me when the girl comes home from school." He walked past his youngest daughter into the back of the house.

26

"I TELL YOU, I DON'T HAVE ANY IDEA WHERE HE WENT," Injun said to Rizzo's unbelieving face. "We were driving out Adelaide to dump the Thunderbird near the river when Ruby got hung up at a red light at Guilford."

"You told me that," said Rizzo.

"Yeah, well, I was going slow, but he never caught up with me. So I turned back, but I couldn't find him."

"He's a stupid bastard," Rizzo said, "and so are you."

Carelli flushed and started to say something, but then the bell chimed.

"Christ!" said Rizzo. "What now?" Easing over to the side window, he lifted the edge of a thick drape and saw Pete shrugging at him in consternation and Roy Beddell standing at his doorstep.

"It's Beddell, the Chief of Police," Rizzo said. "If he followed you here—"

"Nobody followed me back here," Injun told him sullenly.

"I guess I'll find out about that in a minute," Rizzo said

as the doorbell sounded again. "You fade out into the kitchen while I see what's on Beddell's mind." When Rizzo opened the door, Beddell was just pushing the button again. "Hello, Chief," Rizzo said.

"Hello," said Beddell under careful control. "May I come in?"

"Sure," Rizzo said, opening the door wide.

Beddell followed Rizzo into the anonymous living room. "Can I get you a drink?" Rizzo asked.

"No," Beddell said. "This is not a social call."

"No?" Rizzo said coolly. "Well, sit down anyway." Rizzo seated himself in a chair and gestured Beddell to the green-tufted sofa. "Now, what can I do for you today, Chief?"

"You can lay off Harry Caster," Beddell said, "and you can do it starting right now."

"Chief—" Rizzo began, but Beddell rode over his words.

"Let's not kid each other, Rizzo," he said. "It's no secret that you're trying to cut in on Caster's bar. I'm surprised that it's not in the goddamned newspapers."

Rizzo said nothing. He sat looking at Beddell with polite interest, but Beddell knew there was something working behind those flat eyes.

"It's not going to work," Beddell said. "There's a lot more involved now than a simple muscle job. You ought to have realized that after what happened to Gino this morning."

"Gino?"

"Don't bullshit me, Rizzo," Beddell said wearily. "Just don't bother. I've just told Baptiste Speranza that his boy was cut down and I don't need any more hassle." Beddell looked Rizzo hard in the eye. "And neither do you. You think you've got problems with the muscle Caster has hired.

Wait'll you see what you've got when Speranza finds out that you put Gino in a position to get snuffed. He's sure to blame you."

"Speranza's a joke," Rizzo said. All pretense had gone out of his voice. "And you're wasting my time."

"I'm not going to waste much more of it, Rizzo, or my own. Gino Speranza was with a couple of punks named Bonino and Carelli when he was killed. Have you seen either of them today?"

"I never heard of them."

"I'll bet," Beddell said. "Do you mind if I look around the house?" Out in the hallway, her ear pressed to the living room door, Angie Rizzo started nervously, but she forced herself to stay at the door, listening. She had never eavesdropped on Carlo before. But then, the Chief of Police had never come to the house before, and Angie felt she had to put some order to the whirl of fears and suspicions in her mind—even if it had to be this way. Now she knew at least part of the situation, and she felt better.

"Not at all, Chief," Rizzo said. Angie's hands automatically pushed her away from the door, but she relaxed when her husband's voice continued, "If you've got a search warrant in your pocket."

"I can get one," Beddell said, getting up. Out in the hall the telephone began to ring. Then it stopped, and a few moments later, the door to the hallway cracked slightly and Angie Rizzo put her head into the room.

"Carlo," she said shyly, not looking at Beddell, "it's for you."

"Thank you, Angie," Rizzo said. His wife started to close the door, but Rizzo stopped her. "No, darling, don't go. I want you to meet someone." He held out his hand, and

Angie obediently came forward to meet it. Rizzo wheeled, holding her hand.

"Chief," he said as coolly as if they were at a party, "you haven't met my wife, Angela, have you? Angie, this is Roy Beddell, the Chief of Police."

"Hello," said Angie timidly.

"Angie," Rizzo said, "you keep our guest company while I answer the telephone. I'll be right back." He walked through the hall door and closed it behind him. Once he was in the hallway, the polite look left Rizzo's face. He picked up the telephone. "Hello," he said impatiently, "this is Charlie Rice."

"Mr. Rice," said an excited voice, "it's me. Ruby."

"Where the hell are you?"

"In Manhattan. Listen, Mr. Rice—"

"No, you listen, Bonino," Rizzo said. "You're crazy. I sent you out to dump a car, and you—"

"But wait," Ruby started again, "I've found Caster. I saw him in a car in Parker's Landing and followed him. I didn't have time to tell anybody, and this is the first chance I've had to telephone. I didn't want to lose him, so I—"

"Okay, shut up," Rizzo snapped. "Where are you right now?"

"On the East Side, Lexington and Sixty-sixth. Caster put his car in a garage, and they're in a restaurant eating. I can see the door from this phone booth."

"They?" Rizzo asked.

"Caster and some girl. Long black hair. She was with him at the hospital last night. I think she might be related to that Carradino character."

"How long have they been in the restaurant?"

"Maybe five minutes. I saw they were going in to eat

and jumped over here to call you. What do you want me to do?"

Rizzo lowered the receiver to his side and thought for a moment.

"Mr. Rice," he heard Ruby's voice thin and metallic.

"I'm here. You stay with Caster wherever he goes and call me whenever he stops for even five minutes."

"Can I get some lunch? I haven't had any yet."

"Sure," said Rizzo, "if you can keep an eye on Caster at the same time. If you lose him, Bonino, you'll be sorry."

"I won't lose him."

"Don't." Rizzo put the telephone down.

When Rizzo returned to the living room, Beddell noticed that his confidence seemed deeper and less assumed. Something in that telephone call cheered him up, Beddell thought.

"Thank you, dear," Rizzo said, dismissing his wife.

Obediently, Angie got up and said goodbye to Beddell. "Goodbye, Mrs. Rice," Beddell said. "I hope Bobby is feeling better soon."

"Thank you," said Angie and left the room. Beddell noticed Rizzo's puzzled expression.

"Your son Bobby," Beddell said. "Your wife tells me he's not feeling well enough to play in the football game tonight."

"Oh, yeah," Rizzo said. "It's nothing serious. You know how teenagers are."

Beddell nodded.

"Now, what were we talking about?" Rizzo asked briskly. "Oh, yes, Gino Speranza. It's a shame about him. Gino was a nice boy. Not very bright, but always polite to me. I certainly hope you catch the guy that killed him, and I won't keep you if you want to get back on the job."

Beddell didn't respond. There was no point in arresting Rizzo yet. His lawyer would have him out in an hour.

"I will, Rizzo," Beddell said finally. "I'll get whoever shot Gino. But I'll tell you something. You're riding for a heavy fall. And when it comes, I'm just going to mark another cheap punk off my list." Rizzo stiffened, then relaxed and smiled.

"Thanks for dropping by, Chief," he said. "Any time you're in the neighborhood."

By this time Beddell was nearly in the hallway. Rizzo followed the policeman and watched the front door close behind him. Through the little window, he watched Beddell get in his car and drive away.

Rizzo found Injun sitting in the back kitchen eating a big dish of lasagna. "I've got a job for you," he told him.

"I'm eating," Carelli protested.

"Hurry it up," Rizzo said. "As soon as Ruby calls again, I want you to go someplace."

"Ruby called?" Injun asked through a mouthful. "Where is that jerk?"

"Manhattan. That jerk has picked up Harry Caster, and when Caster comes to a stop, I've got work for you to do."

IT WAS A LONG EVENING OF WAITING FOR RIZZO AND Injun. Ruby was just finishing a sandwich he'd bought at a delicatessen on Lexington Avenue when Harry and Sandra came out of the restaurant.

"Where are we going now?" Sandra asked.

"Do you want to meet my big shot brother with the razor-cut hair and the sexy secretary?"

"No."

"Then that's where we'll go," Harry said, taking her hand. "You'll love him."

"I'll hate him," Sandra said, squeezing Harry's stubby fingers.

At the discreet building, Harry led Sandra through the massive doors and confronted the gray-haired receptionist for the second time that week. She showed no sign that she recognized him. To her polite query, Harry said: "Harry Caster to see Mr. Caster." He felt a bit foolish still holding Sandra's hand.

"I'm afraid no one is in at the moment, sir," the receptionist said. "But we're expecting Mr. Caster this evening. May he telephone you some place?"

"No," said Harry, "I don't know where I'll be. Just tell him I was here and that I'll call him later."

Ruby was in a booth on the far side of Madison and Sixty-Sixth, banging on the telephone to get a dial tone, when he saw Harry and Sandra emerge from the building. To his dismay, they turned and started walking directly toward him. They were coming to the telephone booth. As quickly as he could, without actually running, Ruby got out of the booth and started walking west on Sixty-Sixth. He fought the urge to look over his shoulder.

Harry dialed the last number Hoerner had given him, but there was no answer. He listened to the ringing for a long time and then hung up.

"No luck," he told Sandra. "Nobody's home today."

"I don't care," she said. "What do we do now?"

"I don't know. Central Park is only a couple of blocks away. Do you like the park?"

"I heard it was full of muggers."

"Come on, then," Harry said, grabbing her hand. "I'll introduce you to some very nice muggers I know."

At Fifth Avenue, Ruby turned away from a magazine rack and began to follow Harry and Sandra toward the park.

"Did you have a nice read?" the newsdealer asked him, but Ruby didn't hear.

27

BAPTISTE SPERANZA OPENED HIS EYES AND KNEW THAT Carmen had disobeyed him. It was nearly dark outside, and faintly he heard the new electric carillon of St. Peter in Chains. In vain he listened for the tiny pauses Fred Mapes, the old carillon player, used to make between phrases. Some said the pauses had been due to alcoholic uncertainty, but Speranza didn't care. They were human; the new machine ground out the sacred music like so much sausage meat.

It was a tiny room Speranza slept in, and sometimes at night he felt like a monk looking at the bare, brown walls. A low, rough-cut Spanish chest in the corner helped to further the illusion. Speranza had lived in this room for over three years now, since shortly after his wife, Rosa, died. In another time and another world, it had been a maid's room. Gradually, unconsciously, Speranza had made it his, first by napping there. Then he'd stopped climbing the stairs to the room that had been his and his wife's.

Most of his belongings were still in the big bedroom. The inhabited chests and closets like costumes for a play that would never reopen. Speranza had often urged

Carmen to take the room, but it remained empty, dusted daily, cleaned once a week like the rest of the house.

Gino is dead.

The thought came back into his head, and Speranza moved his lips with the words as children do when they read. Dead like Rosa and most of the people he had known. Speranza had been thinking about death a lot lately, but for himself, not for Gino. For Gino, death had been as unthinkable as for the little one. But there it was: Gino was dead. Like so many things in his life these days, that was final, unchangeable. But the fact lay on his chest like a stone; he hadn't yet learned to wear it.

Speranza knew they'd be waiting for him in the living room, as many of the family as could be hastily gathered. He tried to rouse himself to face them. The sooner he did, the sooner they'd leave him alone. But the stone was heavy, and his bones were heavy, and the flesh on them seemed to weigh him down more than ever. Finally, he pushed his legs over the side of the hard, narrow bed and felt them strike the floor like two heavy sticks.

The noise in the big living room was an emotional buzzing of bees when Speranza opened the door, and for a time none of them noticed him. He'd always known that Rosalie, the oldest, would run to fat, and she had. Ridges of flesh writhed beneath an exclusive tweed suit as she told her little sister Doris for the tenth time: "I just can't believe it, Dor; I just can't believe it."

Doris dutifully patted the great white hand that had been forced upon her and wondered how much the new emerald ring had cost. "We're all mortal," she said. "We're only mortal, Rose. But he was so young, so young."

In the corner near the big window looking out on Speranza's garden, the sons-in-law were talking in low, fervent tones about the left knee of the New York Jets' quarterback.

"It's like a matchstick," Lou Altomare, Doris's penny-pinching husband, was saying. "It'll snap like this." He twisted an extended forefinger until it popped loudly.

"Yeah, but," Bruno Fisher, once Frischetti, said, "don't forget that it's the arm that counts." He grabbed his biceps and gave it a shake. "He don't throw with his knee."

On a window seat at the far end of the room, a slim blonde woman not quite thirty years old sat close to Carmen Speranza, talking intently in a voice that couldn't be heard three feet away. Her clean features claimed a perfection for which a professor of plastic surgery at Stanford University felt a warm glow of accomplishment. In the field, it was quietly gaining a reputation as "Ledbetter's Nose," but it was Dominic Speranza's checkbook that had made it possible.

"I'm sorry Dom isn't here," Delia Speranza was telling Carmen. "I called the Dorado Beach Hotel and left the number here for him to call when he gets back to the hotel."

Sitting on the thick carpet in a corner, two grandsons of prep-school age discussed the curious demise of Uncle Gino in cool accents they hadn't learned at home. From the garden came the voices of Kathy and the younger grand-children.

Someone saw Speranza standing in the doorway and sounded the alarm. The family surged toward him, a wall of humanity mouthing various degrees of sympathy. All except Delia. She remained poised in front of the window seat. But her calm, gray, plain-girl's eyes read Speranza's face with accuracy and compassion.

The family clung to Speranza, pulling him into the room, but Carmen soon dropped back. She saw in his face a tinge of annoyance at the tumult and probably at being allowed to sleep so long. But all else was concealed behind a mask which frightened her more than anger or grief would have. Then Carmen slipped away to the kitchen. The eating would begin soon. Whether gathering in sorrow or joy, the Speranza family would have to eat.

In the midst of the confusion, the doorbell rang. With carefully learned grace, Delia walked to the front hallway to answer it. She knew who it would be.

"Hello, Abe," she said as she opened the door.

Abe Montara deserved the nickname—the snake— which wasn't as unknown to him as many thought. There was something reptilian in his small, bright eyes, in his slim, spring-like body, in his smooth cap of dead-black hair which never seemed to need cutting.

He inspired fear.

Of all the non-family minions, only Abe would come today. The telegrams from friends and foes had already begun to pour in, but this was a family-only gathering. Abe was as close as he could be without being a Speranza, closer than the in-laws. His hooded eyes showed no grief at the death of Gino Speranza.

"Mrs. Speranza," he said as he stepped into the front hall.

Delia and Montara knew where they stood with each other. He knew that at a word she would leave Dom Speranza and come to him. She knew the word would never be spoken. They both saw the acid humor in the situation.

"How is he?" Montara asked.

"Tight, very tight," she said. "He's not showing it, but he's very hard hit. It's going to be bad."

"Can you blame him?"

"Gino was Gino," she said. "He didn't learn. If it hadn't been today, it would have been tomorrow."

"You're a hard one, Mrs. Speranza," he said with the sharp smile which seldom indicated humor and which could disappear like a water snake sliding into a shadow. "I hope you won't feel that way when it's my turn."

"It won't happen to you, Abe," she said with certainty.

He dipped his eyes in recognition of the compliment. "I'd better get in there."

The family was still crowded around old Speranza when Montara stepped down into the room. But when they saw his presence reflected in the old man's face, the family fell back willingly and then turned to the long table in the dining area which Carmen had just finished stocking.

"Abe," Speranza said, holding out his hand.

"Don Baptiste." Montara moved quickly across the room and took the hand. Their eyes met, and there was no need for words of sympathy.

"We must talk," Speranza said, retaining Montara's wiry hand in his own. "Come, we'll go to my room." The two men left without a word to the others, who had begun to settle into the dining table. Delia and Carmen watched them go. Each wore a different kind of concern on her face.

"Sit," said Speranza. He indicated the narrow bed still rumpled from his nap.

Montara sat down, marveling at the hardness of the bed and the austerity of this little room where Speranza had chosen to spend the last years of his life. Abe's own house had the sleek, cold comfort of a new car. No one would call it ascetic.

Speranza sat himself down near the head of the bed and placed his big hands on top of his thighs. Montara had never seen the old man look so bleak.

Speranza broke the silence. "Well, Abe, what are we going to do?"

"I heard just a few minutes ago when I got back from the city," Montara said. "You'd better fill me in."

This wasn't an answer the old man liked. But he restrained his impatience for a time. "I'll tell you what I know," he said. Speaking slowly, but with some of the command he'd once had, Speranza told of the visit from Rizzo that Wednesday morning, how he had refused Rizzo's plea for help, and that apparently this was when Gino got connected with Rizzo. "I never saw Gino again," he said, "or heard anything until Beddell called this morning."

"What did you tell Rizzo when you turned him down?"

Speranza raised his eyes to Montara's. "I told him that you were the only one who could take him off the hook." The statement was an admission of weakness and a challenge at the same time.

Montara acknowledged this with a shrug and asked, "What about this Caster? Where's he?"

"I don't know. Gino was murdered in front of his house. I sent Renzetti over to find out for me. He—" Speranza saw a blank wall rise up in Montara's face and stopped short.

"You shouldn't have done that."

"Why not?" the old man demanded stubbornly.

"You know why not. That block is not only crawling with local cops, but by now the feds have heard that your boy got himself killed. They're just waiting for you to react. We've got enough problems without that."

"Problems," the old man said scornfully.

"Yes, problems," Montara repeated. "Unless you want to go back inside and take a lot of people with you, you've got to stay clean. The investigators are going to come to a decision about prosecuting very soon, and it's not all going to depend on what the accountants say."

The old man said something obscene in Italian about investigators and accountants.

"I agree," Montara said, laughing involuntarily. "But there are too many of them. They—"

"This is no laughing matter, Abe," the old man said gravely. Montara knew he'd gone far wrong. "My son is lying dead, and you're joking. I want revenge. I want somebody to pay for this. Are you going to help me?"

"Don Baptiste—"

"No, Abe, don't. Don't call me 'Don Baptiste.' You say it to humor me, to push me back to my garden and leave everything in your hands. Leave it to Abe...Abe knows how. Well, maybe I've left everything to Abe too long. If I can't avenge the death of a son, I'm nobody's Don. But I will see his death avenged. This is still the Speranza family, Abe, and I'm still the Speranza."

He looked Montara in the face with eyes which seemed as hard as they'd ever been.

Montara didn't flinch or look away. Since Speranza had interrupted him, he'd sat quietly listening and watching the old man's face. In the real sense, Montara was more of a son to Speranza than either Dom or Gino. Although he'd been young at the time, it had largely been Montara who had held the family together during Speranza's years in prison. At first, he'd relayed orders to the other lieutenants. But when he recognized that Speranza was growing more and more distant and losing contact with the outside, Montara had begun to initiate policy that he pretended was Speranza's. Finally, the trips to the prison became an empty ritual. And they both knew it.

"Don Baptiste"—there was no cajolery in his voice—"I

owe you the respect due a father, but I also owe you the truth." He saw the old man's face harden in rejection of the words to come, and Montara purposely put more edge to his voice as if to grind them into that granite exterior. "You've been away from the business a long time..."

"I am no businessman," Speranza burst out angrily.

"...and things have changed. You are the head of the family, and I honor you. We all honor you. But these are difficult times. The feds —the Treasury Department, Customs, even the FBI—have never been tougher. They mean business."

"Business," Speranza said, pretending to misunderstand, "always it's business."

"That's why"—Montara tried to soften the words yet give them special emphasis—"I cannot allow you to start an action now. It's the worst possible time. It's—"

"You cannot allow." Speranza said the words totally without inflection, as if by deadening them he could remove the sting. "You cannot allow."

"I'm sorry," Montara said. "I didn't want it to come to this. We can't risk trouble at this time. Later, in three months maybe, we can move. We can punish those who killed Gino. It will give me great pleasure. But now—"

"You cannot allow me?" Now it was a question, and Montara thought for a long moment before he answered. He knew no other answer.

"No." He said it with finality. "Don Baptiste..."

"I have nothing more to say to you," Speranza said, and he swiveled his heavy head to look away from Montara into the corner of the bare room at the shadow of a wardrobe which had been removed years ago.

Montara sat looking at the back of Speranza's thick neck

where the gray hair sloped unevenly over the collar of his shirt. Then he got up silently and left the room.

In the dining room, the family was still eating. The uproar grew as the strong red wine took effect. At a separate table in the corner, the children, with the two prep-school boys as their captive tyrants, drank their watered wine and giggled into their plates.

Abe ignored the tumult at the table except for a glance exchanged with Delia who had been silently watching the door. Rosalie looked up and saw him going away. "Abe," she cried through a mouth half full of salad, "come have a bite." But Montara didn't pause. The door closed quietly behind him.

Carmen, sitting opposite Speranza's empty chair, started to get up, but Delia put a restraining hand on her arm. "Let me go— please." Delia slipped away from the table without causing a ripple in the flow of talk and food. Carmen watched her go, with hatred tempered by the knowledge that Delia was right. Papa would never listen to her, but he would listen to Delia, the charmed outsider.

Delia touched the door with her slim knuckles and said, "Papa?" Without waiting for an answer, she turned the knob and entered the dark room. Speranza was sitting as Montara had left him, but the firm old chin seemed to have slipped like an undermined cliff. She sat down beside the old man, her sleek thigh not quite touching his leg. She put a hand on top of his where they lay useless in his lap.

28

AFTER HE REJOINED THE FAMILY, SPERANZA SEEMED much the same as before: kindly, distracted, saddened, slightly aloof. More family arrived, and Speranza greeted them gently, accepting their sympathy.

But all this time, Speranza was deep within his head trying to come to terms with the shattering insight he'd gained from the talk with Montara. When it came to important things, Speranza had imagined that he withheld some final authority that would be respected. Now he found that he hadn't, and the knowledge stuck in his throat like a flat, sharp bone.

Speranza worked himself deeper and deeper into a feeling of helplessness and depression until he was responding with only a vacant stare and a mumbled word or two. Thinking that it was grief that preoccupied the old man, Rosalie and Doris stopped by from time to time to pat his brown-spotted hand or touch his lined cheek. The sons-in-law argued their own diagnoses of the old man's state under their breath near the bar.

"I tell you," Lou said, "he's not drunk. He's old, and he's had a hell of a blow. What do you expect?"

"You're crazy," Bruno said. "If he's senile, I'm senile. I wish I was as sharp as that old bastard. Go up and get a whiff of his breath, why don't you! I bet it'll knock you over."

"Five bucks?" Lou asked.

"Make it ten."

Lou won the bet, but they were both astonished a few minutes later when Speranza came to life and took complete charge of the family gathering. It was as if twenty years had fallen from him. He was everywhere in the room: consoling, joking, teasing the children, drawing forth recollections of events and people that everyone else had forgotten.

"Hey," Speranza cried, "why is it so quiet? What is this —a wake?" He gave the old booming laugh they knew so well. "Let's have some music, Rosalie! You and I used to be a great dancing team." He held out a hand. "Come! Dance a tarantella with me like you used to."

"Oh no, Papa," Rosalie laughed, flashing her big black eyes. "I couldn't."

But the old man caught her hand and pulled her to a space in the middle of the room made clear by scurrying relations. An old record was started on the hi-fi, and Speranza whirled his heavy daughter around until he made her laugh and throw her head back shamelessly revealing her aging neck.

"What did I tell you," Bruno whispered. "The old man will put us all in the grave." He wondered how he could get his ten dollars back.

"Especially Rosa," Lou said. "She can't take too much of that."

From that point, the gathering became a party, the first real party the house had seen in several years. Only Carmen and Delia exchanged worried looks as they moved about serving food and drinks. Both thought the old man was putting on an act. What would happen when the party was over?

But it wasn't an act. Speranza had simply made up his mind what he would do. And the relief had made him light-hearted. Besides, he loved his family. They would cry at the funeral, but he wanted them to laugh tonight.

The party went on until late, and the last relations had to be practically ejected. But when the time came when he thought they must go, the old man was just as vigorous in getting rid of the family as he had been in making them lively.

"Good, good!" he cried as, unbelievably, Lou Altomare danced Rosa down the front walk toward their big Chrysler trailed by their sleepy and embarrassed children.

Delia was the last guest to leave the quiet house. Kathy had been driven tearfully up the stairs to her room by whis-pered threats, and Carmen was in the living room begin-ning to repair the damage from the party. When Delia, her near-black sable coat thrown over her shoulders, came to the door, Speranza took her hands in his. He looked into her eyes silently.

"Papa," she said softly, "may I stay tonight?"

"No, my darling." Speranza continued to hold her hands in one of his and touched a lock of her ashen hair with the other. "You must go. But thank you for coming. You are kind to an old man."

"Papa—"

"Yes?"

"Nothing," Delia said, standing on tiptoe to kiss his

cheek. "Good night. Papa." She gathered the collar of her coat around her throat and hurried down the front walk, her thin heels tapping like a telegrapher's key.

Speranza closed the door behind her and switched out the hall light. He walked back into the living room where Carmen was working.

"Carmen. It's late. Leave all this. Go to bed. Let Ella help you with it in the morning."

"There's not much to do, Papa," Carmen said, emptying another ashtray into a plastic bucket.

"Leave it, I say," Speranza commanded. "It's time you were in bed. It's time everybody was in bed."

"All right, Papa." Carmen put down the bucket. "Good night, Papa." She threw her apron on the back of a chair and walked toward the stairs.

"Carmen," said Speranza, stopping her.

"Yes, Papa?" Carmen turned and looked at him with anxious eyes.

Speranza walked over to his youngest daughter and put a hand on her arm. "You're a good girl, Carmen," he said. "You've always been a good girl. Give your papa a good-night kiss."

Carmen put her dry lips to his chin. "Good night, Papa. I love you."

"Bless you, Carmen," Speranza said, and he let her go. He stood watching as she disappeared up the stairs. Then, flicking off the last lamp, Speranza sat down in his big leather chair and listened to the sounds of the house. Finally, he heard Carmen's footsteps going down to Kathy's room. Then, a door closed, a few more footsteps, and a final door closed. He sensed that the last light in the house had gone dark.

Speranza walked noiselessly up the stairs to the big

room that had been his and his wife's. He walked to the big desk near the window and snapped on a small, downward-thrust desk lamp. Sitting down, he unlocked the wide central drawer and withdrew several big manila folders and stacked them at the side of the desk. Taking one from the stack, he began to pore over the papers it held. Occasionally, he wrote something with the thick black fountain pen he'd owned for so many years.

Before long, Speranza had been through all of the folders. Shoving them to one side, he drew out a clean sheet of paper and filled the fountain pen. In a large script, he wrote the date at the top of the sheet of paper and then paused to think. Nothing came. He wanted to say something, but nothing came. Crumpling the paper, he threw it into the wastebasket and capped the old pen. Then he squared the folders in the middle of the desktop and placed a rectangular slab of magnifying glass across them diagonally as a paperweight.

He reached down and opened another drawer. From it, Speranza lifted a chamois bag which clanked softly. From the bag he drew a large revolver and a handful of loose bullets. Speranza spun the cylinder and smiled with satisfaction at the smooth action. Then he broke the gun and began to fill the round chambers with fat cartridges. Fixing the safety, he snapped the revolver shut with a gratifying snap and put it into his large trouser pocket. Speranza then relocked the middle drawer, threw the key ring on top of the file folders and killed the light. He sat waiting a moment for his eyes to readjust to the dark and then walked out into the hallway.

Speranza moved down to the room at the end of the hall and opened the door slowly and quietly. At first, the small bed seemed to be unmade but empty. But then Kathy's slight form became apparent, curved into a U halfway down the thin bed. By morning, she would be down to the footboard.

Speranza stood watching the covered hump that was his favorite grandchild. He mouthed something toward her and then stepped back out of the doorway. Walking swiftly, a man going somewhere, Speranza passed Carmen's room and moved on down the stairway to the main floor. In the front hallway, he took a jacket at random and transferred the revolver to the jacket pocket. Outside, he silently lifted the garage door and rolled the small sedan, usually Carmen's automobile, down the driveway to the street and then down the sloping street. He started the engine in second gear, flicked on the headlights, and drove toward a house not many blocks away.

Upstairs in Speranza's house, Carmen dropped the window curtain and turned back to her bed. She slipped between the still-warm sheets and lay there open-eyed and thinking.

29

Bobby Rice was red-eyed from crying and red-faced with shame. He hadn't cried in years. He was a big boy for sixteen, heavy in the shoulders and arms but nearly as slight as a child below the waist.

Now Bobby sat on his bed and looked at himself with pity and disgust in the dresser mirror. Beside him was a small bag packed with the necessaries for the night's football game: a fresh jockstrap, clean woolen socks, his own cleat tightener and four extra cleats, lampblack to cut the glare from the stadium lamps, and a small white hand towel. It was packed as carefully as a doctor's bag.

At the dinner table a few minutes before, Bobby had refused to eat and had come to the table only after his mother had begged him with tears in her eyes. He didn't mind not eating. He felt so devoid of hunger that it seemed impossible that he would ever eat again. Bobby stolidly watched his family eat the cheese-and-tomato laden pieces of veal as if they were machines chewing up cardboard. Finally, his father left the table without a glance at him, and Bobby climbed back up the stairs to his room.

He had known for years that there was something funny about his father's business. Rizzo had tried to keep his affairs secret, but Bobby was a clever boy who had fitted together all the pieces and decided that his father was some kind of crook. At first, when he was nine or ten years old, Bobby was thrilled by this discovery. But as he grew older, he became ashamed of Rizzo's shady dealings and tried to block out all knowledge of them. If anybody asked, he said his father was a businessman and let it go at that. He often secretly wished that his father would die in an accident. Father Cony urged him to fight these fantasies and to try to understand.

The older he became, the more Bobby cherished the name Rice. When Donald Mofilitt, in the ninth grade, learned his real name and started calling him Rizzo, Bobby caught him behind the boathouse and beat him relentlessly. He was never called anything but Rice after that.

Bobby looked at his watch: seven o'clock. The team would be arriving at the gymnasium, laughing and going to Doc Blundell for their freshly laundered uniforms. Bobby could see his own uniform—tight-fitting golden pants and white jersey with the big, blue "14" on the front and back—laid out like a bullfighter's suit of lights on the scarred wooden bench.

He could even smell the wonderful odor of the gym, a mixture of ancient sweat, strong liniment from Doc's blue bottles, a whiff of after-shave lotion and the fresh-bread aroma of the newly laundered jerseys.

Bobby knew that his knees would have been shaking as he stood with the starting team facing Coach Blundell. The coach had a habit of talking directly to the starters and letting the rest of the team eavesdrop. He could hear himself being asked: "Rice, on the R-34 draw, what do you look for if Hokanson doesn't move his fat ass quick enough to get you some running space?"

"Elliot Carlson on the left flank, Coach," Bobby answered aloud, "and—" But he couldn't go on. His throat wouldn't produce the words his mind was feeding it. He sat there feeling choked and hopeless. He looked at his watch again and knew that the coach would be worried and wondering where he was. Starting players were never late.

Unable to stand the tension, Bobby jumped up and slammed the punching bag hanging in the corner with his right hand. He instinctively spared his passing arm. He felt the punch tingle all the way back to his shoulder. The slight pain felt good. And with that punch, Bobby made up his mind. He would play in the game tonight. To hell with his father. He could still make it if he hurried. And the team would win. He'd worry about facing his father tomorrow. Nothing he could do to him would matter after tonight.

Bobby leaped over to the bed, zipped open his bag and checked the contents. Then he slipped into his leather jacket and opened the window. He felt the sharp needles of the cool evening sting his face. It was a beautiful night for football.

It was a dozen feet from Bobby's window to the ground, but the drainpipe was strong. Bobby knew that Pete and another of his father's men were patrolling the house. He had to evade them.

He tied his old Boy Scout rope to the handle of his bag with a slip knot and carefully lowered the bag to the ground just past the dark window of the downstairs spare room. When the bag touched, Bobby flicked the rope and felt it fly free. He drew it up swiftly. Looking around the room for something sturdy, Bobby tied the rope to the leg of his bed and pulled the bed up against the wall under the window.

Getting back up the drainpipe would be tough without the rope.

Bobby threw a leg over the windowsill, tested the pipe with half of his weight and found it did not give at all. He began to lower himself, hand over hand, sneaker-shod feet clamped to the pipe, down the side of the house, keeping as flat to the stuccoed wall as he could. The shadow of the house next door made the wall under his window a fathomless black.

Slowly, with an athlete's control, the boy edged down the pipe and then jumped to the ground into a silent crouch. He tied the rope taut to a strut at the bottom of the drainpipe. He retrieved his bag from the flower bed.

Still crouching, Bobby tried to determine the safest way past his father's sentries. He started to move toward the fence of the yard next door with his bag in hand when he saw a shadow pass the corner of the front of the house and heard a voice call: "Did you say something, Pete?"

"Naw," said Pete, "I think it was somebody in the house."

As the shadow withdrew, Bobby uncurled and stretched for the fence again. He switched his bag to his right hand. Then, with a measured step, Bobby gracefully vaulted over the fence, broke his fall with his right foot and crouched noiselessly to the ground, bag in hand.

Bobby was exposed for only a moment in the bright light of a near-full moon at the top of the fence before slithering back into the darkness. But it was long enough for Alec Hoerner, hidden in the recesses of a screenless porch across the street, to spot him.

Stiff, bored, cold and getting increasingly pissed off, Hoerner had turned his mind inward to other endless nights in Vietnam and on the West Side of Manhattan. Sometimes it seemed as though he had spent half his life in the dark waiting for something violent to happen. Keying himself up to the point where if nothing happened you made something happen. Anything. So long as it resolved the hard, aching knot of tension. Hoerner saw something move swiftly on the right periphery of his vision. Bobby Rice. Suddenly he wasn't cold or bored. He was a highly trained hunting animal acting on his own. He was alive to the possibilities of the chase.

Alec sat still for a moment and waited for Bobby to appear again. When he didn't see the boy, Hoerner knew that he'd come out on the side street and that it was time to move fast. This was his chance to strike. Across the street in the bright moonlight, he could see one of the thugs patrolling the front of the house. He knew there was at least one other.

Stepping from the side of the porch into a bed of lovingly planted dahlia bulbs, Hoerner fell flat on his stomach onto the rough concrete driveway and wriggled quickly into the safety of more shadow. Putting a thick tree between himself and Rizzo's house, he set out in pursuit of Bobby Rice.

30

INJUN WAS CRUISING SLOWLY DOWN CENTRAL AVENUE drumming a rhythm on the steering wheel and humming the fill-in melody. On the seat beside him was a bag full of leak-proof containers of Chinese food—dinner for Pete, Ernie and himself. Bored and restless, Injun had volunteered to get the food. Rizzo said all right, but don't screw around.

He wasn't exactly screwing around, but Injun was driving very slowly in the curb-side lane watching the flow of kids heading for the football game at the municipal stadium. He'd been too small to play football himself, and he couldn't see much in the game. Injun was giving special attention to three short-dressed pompon girls practicing a routine and singing as they jogged along in the early dark when he saw Bobby Rice. Bobby was on the other side of the street, moving at a half-trot toward the stadium, and a group of boys were running to keep up with him.

"Bobby," one of them panted, "are you going to score some touchdowns tonight?"

"I hope so," said Bobby, looking over his shoulder in

hopes of spotting someone in a car who could drive him the rest of the way. He could feel his shirt clinging to his sweaty back under the leather jacket.

"You're late," another kid said, spurting ahead and turning around to run backward ahead of Bobby. "It's only twenty min—" The boy caught his heel and fell, and Bobby had to shift to avoid stepping on him.

"I know," said Bobby, not tired but worried. "I know."

Nearly a block behind Bobby, Hoerner was having difficulty keeping up without attracting attention to himself. Hoerner knew he had to grab the kid before Bobby got to the stadium ahead or he might never get another chance at him. He figured that once he had Bobby, and Rizzo knew it, the pressure would come off Harry Caster in a hurry.

"Young bastard!" an old man with a heavily-laden string bag shouted at him after being jostled.

"Get laid," Hoerner muttered, sidestepping to get around a clot of giggling young girls.

"What's your hurry?" the boldest of them called to him.

Hoerner had just broken through a string of sidewalk-hogging boys too timid to do anything but mumble soft protests, when Injun braked the car sharply to halt across the street from Bobby Rice.

"Hey, Bobby," he called out.

For a moment, Bobby thought it was a friend from school, and with a grateful grin he cut through a covey of admirers and ran toward the black car. Halfway across the street, he recognized the driver, saw that Injun was opening the door to get out, and Bobby's smile turned into a grimace.

"No!" Bobby cried and swiveled to get away from the car and Injun. But then Injun was out of the car and had hold of Bobby with his short but powerful arms. "Let go!"

the boy shouted, trying to stiff-arm his way out of Injun's grasp, but Injun held on and dragged him toward the car.

Still nearly half a block back, Hoerner saw Bobby run into the road toward the waiting car. "Damn!" he said, startling a chemistry teacher and his wife walking in front of him. Alec thought, I'll lose him sure as hell if he gets into that car. He cut from the sidewalk into the street and began running.

Then he saw the little man from the car grab Bobby and instantly recognized him as one of the punks with Gino Speranza. Hoerner automatically drew his pistol and held it flat against his right thigh.

At nearly the same moment, while grappling with Bobby, Injun saw Hoerner over the boy's shoulder, saw the flash of the gun as it slid back into darkness. He forgot Bobby, shoving him away with such force that the boy fell sprawling on the cobbled street and lay stunned for a moment. But then Bobby realized he was free, jumped to his feet and sprinted at full tilt toward the lights of the stadium. Injun scrambled back into his car.

Splitting his vision, Hoerner saw the punk go back into the car, but most of his attention was on the shifting back of Bobby Rice as he raced toward the sanctuary ahead. Catching him was out of the question, Hoerner knew, especially after he had been spotted by Rizzo's man. He knew that within seconds he would have to deal with that danger. But right now he could concentrate only on the fact that he had either to let Bobby go or bring him down. Hoerner made a blind, instinctive decision.

Hoerner dropped to his left knee and brought his gun-carrying arm in front of his body like a short lance. Grasping his right wrist, he aligned the sight of the pistol with Bobby's shifting back and squeezed the trigger at half-second intervals.

The first bullet hit Bobby on stride and seemed to speed him up rather than slow him. But a split second later his regular gait turned wobbly like that of an exhausted runner. The second bullet increased the staggering and started his fall to the rough-cobbled pavement. The third shot caught Bobby high on the shoulder as he went down, accelerating his plunge and sending him scudding across the cobble-stones on his smooth cheek until he shuddered to a stop with his eyes wide open, not in pain but in disappointment.

Still able to move, Bobby threw his right hand out toward the stadium. "Coach!" he cried through a froth of blood. Then Bobby Rice died with the tall arc lights of the stadium reflected in his wide-staring eyes.

When he heard the first shot, Injun was already back in the car about to wheel it around and go after Bobby. But at the sight of Hoerner's crouching figure, the boy was forgot-ten. Jabbing the starter button, Injun pushed the gear shift into low and floored the accelerator. As the car peeled out, he flicked the car lights out.

Hoerner noted with clinical satisfaction that he had been right to drop the third shot a shade. He frowned as he saw the fourth shot miss the boy and spark as it shattered against a cobblestone. He didn't notice a girl farther down the street crumple as a fragment severed her spinal cord.

He thought no more of the boy as he began to recover from his shooting position. Hoerner's senses were raw to the danger of his exposed situation in the middle of a well-lighted street. He kept his pistol leveled, but so far all atten-tion was on Bobby's body. Someone urged someone else to call an ambulance, and several boys ran out into the street to kneel over the boy.

"It's Bobby Rice," a stunted freshman said in wonder. "He's been hurt."

Hoerner was nearly erect and turning to deal with the menace of Injun, but he wasn't quick enough. A speeding black object became a car, abruptly veering toward him, and Alec raised his pistol to aim.

The hammer was not quite all the way back when the left fender hit Hoerner full on and drove him backward off his feet. The gun flew from his out-flung arm, spun brightly in the air and skidded to a stop next to the curb.

With a grunt of pain, Hoerner felt his pelvis crack and tried to cling to the front of the car as his feet were swept from under him. But as the pelvis bones grated under the assault of the car, a thin, sharp knife shot through his body. With a shrill moan, Hoerner tried to push off the smooth black fender like a gored matador high on the horn of a bull.

He needn't have bothered. For as Injun fought to get the car back on the other side of the street, Hoerner, still conscious, was hurled backward under the front of an oncoming bus. The crunch as a big wheel passed over his chest brought welcome blackness from the searing pain that rode him to the ground. The back wheel, unchecked by the frightened bus driver, also passed over his body, but the jolt bothered the passengers more than it did Alec Hoerner.

Cutting off a terrified boy in an MG, Injun regained the right side of the street and floored the accelerator again. Switching the lights back on, he jumped a red light and at the next corner braked into a controlled slide which shot the car into a narrow side street.

Rizzo was sitting in the living room trying to figure out his next move when he heard the banging on the door.

"I'll get it," he told Angie who was sitting under the lamp knitting a sweater. As Rizzo opened the door, Injun nearly hit him as he lowered his fist. "What do you want?" Rizzo demanded.

"It's your boy," Injun gasped. "He's been shot. Down near the stadium."

"You're crazy," Rizzo said. "Bobby's in his room." But he knew Injun was telling the truth. Rizzo turned his head and saw his wife standing in the doorway to the living room. "Angie," he said, pushing his arm toward the stairs leading to their son's room, "Bobby..."

"You'd better go, Carlo," Angie said. Her white face was prepared for the worst.

"I'll be right back," Rizzo told her. Pushing Injun out of the door ahead of him, he strode toward his car at the curb. "You guys stay with this house," he told Pete and Ernie without pausing. "If anything goes wrong, I'll have your balls." He said to Injun: "You come with me," and ran to the car.

Angie Rizzo listened as the car roared down the street. Then she turned and walked up the stairs to the hall in front of Bobby's room. Biting her lip, she first tried the door and found it locked. Then she knocked feebly and called: "Bobby? Bobby? Are you there, Bobby?" There was no answer, and she'd expected none. She lowered her arm and stood looking at the door.

Just then the telephone rang. Absentmindedly, Angie lifted the upstairs extension from its cradle on the hall table.

"Hello?" she said automatically.

"It's me—Ruby, Mrs. Rice. I'm down in Greenwich Village. Caster and the girl are still wandering around. I wanted to ask Mr. Rice what I should do next."

Angie responded without a pause. "Kill them, Ruby. Kill them both."

"Mrs. Rice?" Ruby said in confusion. "Did you—"

"I said kill them both. Ruby," Angie said with force. "Hit them. Burn them." She used the slang awkwardly. "I want them dead." She put down the telephone.

"Okay, Mrs. Rice," Ruby said into the dead telephone. He looked across the square to the brightly lit sidewalk cafe where Harry and Sandra were sitting.

31

Hours of wandering and telephoning had passed, and Harry and Sandra sat wearily at a small round plastic table surrounded by tourists.

"Just to cheer us up," Sandra said, stirring her cooling coffee for the fifth time, "why don't you try to call your brother again?"

"Again?"

"Yes, and if he's not there this time, we'll commit suicide by jumping off a high curb."

Harry fished a dime from his pocket and dialed Mickey's number again on a telephone hanging next to the scarred restroom door. He didn't hope for anything better than the same old recorded message, but to Harry's surprise he heard the rasping tones of a busy signal. "Hey," he called to Sandra, "you're not going to believe this, but somebody seems to be at Mickey's place. The line is busy."

"Hurrah," said Sandra flatly.

Across the square in the shadow of two power poles, Ruby looked anxiously at the couple in the glassed-in enclosure of the restaurant and gripped the carved handle of a

.32 automatic in his coat pocket. The safety lock of the pistol was firmly on and had been checked and rechecked a dozen times in the last half hour. The square was busy with casual strollers, and Ruby dared not chance shooting. So he watched and worried.

Harry dialed again. This time the monotonous ring sounded and then was broken and a voice answered.

"Hello?" said a woman warily, and Harry recognized the voice.

"Alison?" he said. "It's Harry—Harry Caster. Is my brother there?"

"Hello, Harry," she said. "No, he's not here right now. I'm expecting him any second, but—"

"I've got to see him," Harry said. "Everything has gone wrong."

"Things are falling apart here a bit, too," the secretary said, "but okay, come over and take your chances. But I'm not guaranteeing anything. I've got to go now, g'bye." She hung up the telephone.

"What did he say?" Sandra asked when Harry came back to the table.

"He's not there," Harry said, "but his secretary said to come and Mickey will probably be there soon."

"Let's go, then," Sandra said. Harry paid the bill, and they walked out onto the cold sidewalk.

A yellow cab appeared like a shark in clear water, and Harry jammed two fingers into his mouth and let blast a piercing whistle. The taxi swerved to a stop, and they climbed in.

"Sixty-Sixth and Park," Harry told the driver, a middle-aged black wearing a faded Dodgers cap with the bill turned to the back, and the cab plunged up Sixth Avenue.

This move caught Ruby unaware, and he gaped at the

disappearing red tail light of the cab. Recovering, he leapt out into the rough-paved square and looked wildly about for a taxi. It was five minutes before one crept slowly into the square from West Eighth Street, and by that time Ruby was almost frantic. As the cab rolled to a stop, he nearly ripped the door off and threw himself into the back seat.

"Take it easy, fella," said the driver, half-turning around. "Where to?"

Ruby sat stunned by the question. His soft mouth dropped open.

"Well," said the driver sharply, "don't you know where you want to go? You were in a big hurry a minute ago." He was a little guy with a sharp, drooping nose and hairy ears.

Ruby's mouth snapped closed. "You shut up and just sit there," he told the driver savagely. "I'll tell you where to go when I want to. You open your face again and I'll put my foot in it."

"Okay, okay," said the driver, turning back and snapping the meter onto waiting time.

Caster and that broad could be going any place. Ruby thought in anguish. If he didn't find them, Rizzo would have his head. Then he knew where they must be heading. They had to be.

"Okay," he said to the back of the driver's head, "take me to Sixty-Sixth and Madison, and make it fast. And keep your mouth shut."

32

WHEN RIZZO AND INJUN GOT TO CENTRAL AVENUE, the street was cleared of traffic. Police cars were parked at odd angles in the middle of the street, and officers were directing drivers into side streets.

"What'll I do?" Injun asked as a tall cop tried to flag them to a stop.

"Keep going," ordered Rizzo, and the cop had to jump out of the way. He followed Rizzo's car with angry eyes as it drove into the center of the square created by the police.

Lying at an angle on the white center line was a long object covered by a shiny tarpaulin. A swiftly circling red and blue light on top of a nearby squad car flickered across the cracked reflective surface of the tarp. Ignoring Chief Beddell, who stood to one side talking with a subordinate and a slight but athletic man in gym shoes, sweat suit and bulky blue jacket, Rizzo walked toward the covered body on the cobbled street. Injun stayed behind the wheel of the car.

Stopping, Rizzo picked up one corner of the tarp and revealed a foot wearing a dirty-white tennis shoe with diagonal blue and yellow stripes. He knew it was Bobby without looking further, but Rizzo knelt and folded the cover about a third of the way back.

The first adult to reach Bobby, a local veterinarian, had turned him over to feel for a heartbeat. When he found none, he closed the boy's wide-staring eyes with his thumbs. Now, as Rizzo knelt and looked into his son's face, he tried to imagine that Bobby was only sleeping. But it was death, not sleep, that Rizzo saw in the young face with its bloody cheek and soft, half-formed mouth hanging open in eternal surprise. Rizzo was dimly aware of the sounds of the football crowd coming from the stadium.

"Hey," said a sergeant, grabbing Rizzo's shoulder from behind. "What do you think you're doing?"

Rizzo shrugged off the policeman's hand and bent from the waist to kiss his son on the mouth. It was still warm. Then he straightened up, replaced the tarpaulin neatly over Bobby's face and got to his feet. Ignoring the sergeant, Rizzo walked over to where Beddell and the others were standing.

Beddell was talking with Coach Blundell when Vern Hodges nudged him. He looked up and saw Rizzo coming toward him from his son's body. Blundell instinctively moved back a step when he saw Rizzo's face, but Beddell stood his ground.

"Where is he?" Rizzo demanded.

Beddell jerked his chin in the direction of the near curb where a crowd of high-school students stood their ground against a cop not much older than they were. Another tarp, half on the curb and half on the street, covered a sprawled heap in the gutter behind the policeman. Oblivious of the crowd and the policeman, Rizzo put a toe under the edge of the tarp and kicked it half off of Hoerner's crushed body.

As hard as he tried, Rizzo couldn't hate this still body which looked as if life had escaped through its face. It was nothing but a piece of meat. Half-heartedly, he drew back his foot as if to kick Hoerner.

"Look! Look!" kids on the curb were yelling, pointing at Rizzo. Others turned away as they caught sight of Hoerner's uncovered body. For a moment, the cop refused to pay attention, but then he glanced back and caught sight of Rizzo.

"Hey, mister," he said, half-turning, "you can't—" The crowd surged forward behind him to fill the gap. Rizzo turned and walked away, and the cop started to follow until Beddell called him off with a gesture. The young policeman wheeled and chased the gawking crowd back to the sidewalk with his truncheon raised.

As Rizzo approached again, Blundell said huskily, "I'm very sorry, Mr. Rice." But Rizzo spoke to the Chief of Police.

"Who was he?"

"His name was Hoerner," Beddell replied. "Alec Hoerner. That's about all we know so far."

Rizzo's eyes showed no interest. "I'll make the arrangements for my boy," he said. He walked back to the car where Injun waited hunched low behind the steering wheel.

33

The same gray-haired woman greeted Harry and Sandra at the building on East 66th Street. Harry thought she must be like some enchanted gatekeeper maintained in a state of suspended animation until needed.

"Mr. Caster," she said routinely as they stepped into the foyer. "Your brother is expecting you." The receptionist motioned them both to the small elevator.

The door leading to Mickey's office was half-open, and Harry led Sandra through it. The large room had lost its look of executive serenity. Every surface was covered with business papers. The door to Alison's apartment was open, and they could hear voices inside.

Harry and Sandra stood quietly in the middle of the office unaware that they were holding hands.

Then Mickey Caster walked through the doorway to the apartment, talking over his shoulder: "Whatever you say, sweet. Just pack them, and I'll wear them." He saw Harry and Sandra.

"Hello, kid," he said. "Sorry everything is such a mess, but we're in a bit of a hurry. Fix yourself a drink." He gestured toward the low glass table. "No, don't. The whiskey is under all that crap. I'm afraid, and if you disturb it we'll never get out of here." He put some papers on the edge of a chair and walked over to Sandra who had self-consciously dropped Harry's hand. Harry introduced them.

"Miss Carradino," Mickey said, taking her hand, "I'm happy to meet you, but I wish it could have been under better circumstances."

Sandra nodded. She was conscious of the hard muscularity of Mickey's small hand. He was less than impeccably groomed at the moment. His expensive jacket was on the bed in the other room, and his fitted shirt was riding up between thin braces. Mickey's razor-cut hair looked as if it had been buffeted by a costly breeze.

"What the hell is going on?" Harry asked.

"A little trip, Harry," Mickey said, riffling through a pile of papers. "Going on a little trip in about—" He looked at his thin watch. "Christ, Alison," he called loudly, "do you know that we've got only an hour and forty-five minutes to catch that damned plane?"

"Don't worry, darling," Alison said as she walked into the office. "We'll be out of here in another twenty minutes. You just find those bonds. Hello, Harry," she said. "I warned you that this wasn't the best time to call, but it's good to see you again. Did you get that little matter straightened out?" She looked at Sandra in a cool but not unfriendly way.

"Not exactly," Harry said. He turned to his brother again. "That's what I'm here to see you about. Can we talk for just a minute?"

"Got the little bastards," Mickey exclaimed, putting some papers into a slim attaché case. "Hell, Harry," he said, looking at his watch again.

"Baby," he said to Alison, "why don't you ask Miss Carradino to give you a hand with the final packing while Harry and I have a little chat? But when we're done, I want you out here with the cases ready to go, right?"

"Right," answered Alison. She turned to Sandra. "You really can help me," she said. "I can buy clothes, but I can't decide which ones to leave behind. You help me be brutal about it." Sandra followed her into the apartment.

"There's got to be something to drink around here," Mickey said, pulling open cupboards with both hands. "Aha." He pulled out two bell-shaped glasses and a decanter half full of dark liquid. "This ought to be either brandy or furniture polish." He poured two drinks, downed one and refilled it before giving the other to Harry. "We're in luck," he said. "It's furniture polish and a very good year, too." Failing to find a place to sit, Mickey leaned against the front of his crowded desk and raised his glass to Harry, who stood awkwardly in the middle of the room. "Here's to us, Harry," he said. "Screw the rest of them." He took another sip and asked: "What's on your mind, kid?"

Harry held the glass but didn't drink. The light from surrounding buildings made him feel as though he were in a well-illuminated fishbowl. He didn't know where to start.

"Mickey." He hesitated. "Mickey, everything is going wrong. I thought that guy you got for me was only going to scare Rizzo off. He's going crazy." He quickly told his brother about Steve Rizzo and the gunning down of Gino that day. "I don't know what Hoerner or Rizzo is going to do next, but I'm afraid to go home."

Mickey swished a little brandy around in his mouth and swallowed. "Yeah," he said, "it's been that kind of week. I think Hoerner has been trying a little too hard. But look, you've still got the bar, you're still alive and so are Hildy and the girls. That's not so bad. Look at me."

"Yes, you," said Harry. "What are you doing? What do you mean you're going on a trip? A trip where?"

"Harry," his brother said wearily, "that's something nobody knows but me and Alison, and it's better that way. If you don't know, they can't make you tell in court."

"In court? What court?"

"Kid," Mickey said, "I told you it's been a rough week for me, too. Only for me it's been a rough year. And if we don't get out of here very quickly, the next year—or maybe five—is going to be even rougher. In blunt terms, Harry, Alison and I are doing a midnight flit. In less than an hour and a half, we're going to disappear."

"But what about your businesses? And Esther and the kids?"

"My business interests," Mickey said, "are over there in that fat little satchel on the chair. Take a look."

Harry twisted the copper hasps, and the leather bag jumped crisply open. It was full of tight bundles of bills, high-denomination bills. The bundle on top looked to be all hundred-dollar bills. "It's money," he said stupidly.

"That's right, Harry boy, you'll be a success yet. Anybody who can recognize money is well on his way. If you need some, help yourself. But don't be greedy. It may be some time before I have a regular source of income."

"I don't need any," Harry said, closing the bag and snapping shut the twin locks.

"I didn't think you would. Harry, you're a refreshing experience. Better than two weeks at the seashore. And as for Esther, her interests are as well looked after as ever. What is Esther's has always been Esther's, and let no one doubt that. She won't miss me for long, kid, maybe a hot minute."

Harry didn't say anything, but he turned his eyes in the direction of the apartment.

"Alison?" Mickey said. "Sure, I'm no fool, Harry. Don't go all moral on me at this late hour. You're not exactly alone, yourself. Harry, give me a break. I've got enough problems. I know you're thinking: What about the kids? So am I. And I tell myself that they don't need me anymore, that they'll be okay. I've got to believe that, so don't you start confusing the issue."

Mickey jumped up from the edge of the desk with a fresh burst of energy. "And now, Harry, I'm sorry but I've really got to hit it if we're going to make that plane. Stick around and see us off, but excuse me if I go on with my packing."

"But, Mickey," Harry said, "just a second. What am I going to do about Rizzo? Christ, how can I go home?"

"You'll be okay, kid," Mickey said. "Hoerner is a tough cookie. He'll see you through. And I'll give you your money back."

"I don't want my money back. I want the whole thing stopped. Rizzo can have the goddamned bar."

"Too late for that, Harry. It's an old story, and sad, but if you buy a ticket you've got to ride it to the end."

"Like you are?" Harry asked sharply.

Harry expected anger, but Mickey looked at him soberly, even fondly. "If you but knew it, kid," he said, "this is all part of the ride." He started snatching up papers. "Alison," he shouted, "where the hell are you and those suitcases?"

Harry stood and watched.

34

ACROSS THE STREET IN THE DARK SHADOW OF A HALF-basement door, Ruby Bonino crouched and watched the lights go out in Mickey Caster's office. It was getting colder. For the tenth time. Ruby took the black automatic out of his pocket and checked the cartridge clip and safety. He'd used a gun before, but never alone.

While Ruby's head was down, the big front door across the street opened, and Harry and Mickey came out, each carrying two large suitcases. Alison and Sandra followed with smaller cases. Alison had the money satchel firmly in hand. Down the street, a darkened limousine turned on its parking lights and began moving silently and smoothly toward the small group on the sidewalk. Ruby lowered his pistol and waited.

"We'll take you to the airport," Harry said.

"It's okay," said Mickey, "here's our car and driver."

The limousine pulled up, and the driver got out and said: "Mr. Kastransky?"

"That's right," said Mickey. "Open your trunk for our bags." The big, hollow-looking driver quickly stowed the bags away, except for the satchel with the money, and got back in the driver's seat. Alison quickly said goodbye and slid into the limousine. Mickey stood with his hand on the open door.

"Well, kid," he said, "there's a lot we could say, but there's no time to say it. Take care of yourself."

"You, too, Mickey," Harry said. "You, too." He held out his hand.

Mickey put his manicured hand in Harry's and gave it a strong, expressive squeeze. He winked at Sandra and then ducked swiftly into the big car.

"Go," he told the driver.

As the elongated Cadillac pulled away from the curb, Ruby once more laid the barrel of his pistol on the cold, wet iron railing. He squeezed the trigger.

Harry felt a quick burning sensation at the side of his neck and then heard two loud cracks which echoed in the nearly empty street. Two small, many-pointed stars appeared in the curtained window behind them. Harry put his hand to his neck. It came away dark with blood which reflected a street light. A third shot cracked, and Harry reacted at last, pulling Sandra down into the doorway out of Ruby's line of fire.

Several yards down the street, the black limousine rocked to a sharp stop, and the right-hand rear door opened. It remained open for a few seconds, then slammed again, and the big car sprinted to the corner and disappeared.

"You're bleeding," Sandra said.

"I know," said Harry. "Stay down. Where the hell is that doorbell?"

Disgusted at having missed with three shots. Ruby saw lights going on across the street and a terrace door open. He knew that if he was going to finish the job, it would have to be now. He didn't want to. But then behind him in the half-basement kitchen a light went on, startling Ruby and pushing him up the wrought-iron stairs with the gun in his hand.

"He's coming," Sandra cried, trying to burrow under Harry's arm as she saw Ruby's big figure appear on the sidewalk.

Where the hell are they, Ruby thought nervously, peering into the darkness inside the doorway of the building opposite. The street wasn't lit brightly, but he felt as if there were searchlights trained on him. Advancing slowly at an angle, he saw Harry and Sandra crouched in the corner of the entranceway.

"Your gun, Harry, your gun," Sandra cried. "Do something."

Ruby brought his gun up. He wasn't going to miss again.

Harry's hand gripped the revolver and brought it out with surprising ease. Almost blindly, Harry extended his arm and jerked the trigger as fast as he could.

The deafening noise and echo of the five shots died down, and the stink of gunpowder drove Harry and Sandra out of the doorway. The first thing they saw was the big form of Ruby Bonino lying face down in the middle of the street. His gun lay in the gutter a few paces from his head.

"Harry," Sandra said, clutching him, "you hit him."

"Yeah," said Harry softly, still not believing it.

"Do you think he's dead?"

"I'm afraid to look."

Ruby groaned loudly and rolled cumbersomely over onto his side. "Help me," he said weakly. "My leg." He was curled over, reaching toward but not touching his blood-soaked leg. "I'm bleeding to death. Call a doctor."

Looking up at Harry, Ruby started to plead once more

and then saw the gun in Harry's hand. "You shot me," he said.

"I'm sorry," said Harry lamely.

"You bastard," Ruby said. "Call a doctor."

Harry became aware that up and down the street people, most of them in nightclothes, were standing looking silently at them. Unable to look at them, Harry kept his eyes on the man he'd shot. Then he heard his name called softly.

"Mr. Caster." It was the receptionist of Mickey's building. She came out onto the sidewalk. "I think you'd better go. Walk east to the corner and circle around to the garage. You'll be less conspicuous that way."

"But—" Harry began.

"You'd better," she insisted, still calmly. "The police are bound to have been called, and I shall call them myself in a moment."

Like obedient children, Harry and Sandra turned their backs on Ruby and moved to the sidewalk.

"Mr. Caster," the receptionist said again, and Harry looked at her quizzically. She glanced down at his hand, and Harry realized that he was still holding the pistol. Hurriedly, he jammed it back into his pocket.

It was less than fifty yards to the corner, but to Harry and Sandra it seemed like a mile walked on a high wire. At any second they expected to be hailed from behind or headed off by the police. But neither happened, and once around on Sixty-Seventh Street, they stopped near a huge trash receptacle, and Sandra bound his neck with a handkerchief and arranged his coat and shirt so that a minimum of blood showed. His neck had stopped bleeding, but it felt raw and stung like a bad burn.

"Do I look respectable?" Harry asked.

"Don't ask for the impossible."

At the parking garage an incurious attendant brought the rented car sliding down the curving ramp to the exit. "Oh, no," he said when Harry tried to pay him. "Mr. Caster will take care of it. Mr. Caster always pays for his guests."

That's what you think, buddy, Harry said to himself as he started the car.

"Where are we going?" Sandra asked.

"Where do you go when the party is over?" Harry asked. "Home."

35

Rizzo was silent on the short ride home, and Injun didn't dare to speak. When they got to the house, Rizzo jumped out of the car and strode inside, leaving Injun to tell the others what had happened.

"Angie," Rizzo called softly. When he got to the top of the stairs, he knew he had to look no further. The lock on Bobby's door was smashed, and the open door was splintered in several places.

Rizzo stood in the doorway and felt for the light switch. "Please don't turn on the light, Carlo," Angie said. Rizzo edged into the room. He could see her dark silhouette against the side window. As his eyes became accustomed to the dark, Rizzo saw that his wife was sitting on Bobby's bed with something in her hands. It was Bobby's hand-muscle builder which he had spent hours squeezing. She was holding it by one red handle, aimlessly twisting and turning it.

"I broke the door open, Carlo," she said. "With the hatchet. I'm afraid I made an awful mess of it."

"Angie," Rizzo said, sitting on the bed beside her, "Bobby—"

"Please don't say anything, Carlo," she murmured. "I know. I know. But don't say it. We'll talk about it later."

They sat in dark silence for a while, and then Rizzo spoke again. "I'm sorry, Angie. I can't tell you how sorry. I never thought..."

"I know. Carlo," she said, putting her hand on his in the dark. "It's not your fault."

They both knew she lied, but the words helped. Rizzo put his arm around his wife's defeated shoulders.

"I've got to go out again, baby," he said, "for just a little while. I won't be long."

"No," said Angie firmly, "you don't have to go. It's okay."

"What do you mean?"

"After you left. Ruby called from Manhattan. I told him to kill Caster, kill both of them. You don't have to go, Carlo. It's all over. Stay with me, please."

Rizzo was silent. Ruby kill Caster? He wanted to believe it, but he couldn't. At the same time, he hoped Ruby hadn't succeeded. He wanted to kill Caster himself. Rizzo got up and put his hand on Angie's shoulder.

"It's not that, Angie," he lied. "It's something else. I have to go."

"All right, Carlo," she said. "Don't be long; I need you."

"I won't, Angie," he said. Rizzo left her sitting in the darkness behind him. He didn't hear her start to cry again.

Downstairs, in front of the house, Rizzo spoke briefly with Pete, and a small wooden carton was taken from the garage and placed in the back of his car. After strong words to his men, Rizzo got back into his car and peeled away from the curb.

Several minutes later, Rizzo pulled up at the curb in front of Harry Caster's house. The house was dark, and he sat in the car staring at it and trying to summon up the intensity of hate he felt for its absent owner. A house was a poor substitute for a man.

Rizzo got out of the car, opened the back door and took two gasoline-filled soda bottles with cotton wicks from the wooden carton on the floor of the car. He carried them carefully to a spot in the middle of Harry's badly-kept front lawn some fifteen feet in front of the big picture window.

Setting the bottles firmly on either side of his wide-spread legs, Rizzo stood looking into the bottomless depths of the big black window. In one corner, he could see himself and the street lamp behind him reflected as if they were the only things left in the world.

Deliberately, Rizzo reached into a coat pocket and pulled out a pistol, a big .38 with a snub barrel. He half-extended his arm, but at that moment the telephone inside the house began to ring. He let the trigger slack off and stood listening intently, counting thirteen rings before it cut off in mid-ring. When the sound was gone, Rizzo methodically emptied all six chambers into the plate-glass window until all that remained were the corners and a long, cutlass-like shard of glass defying gravity from the upper left corner.

By the third sharp report, lights were going on all over the block, but Rizzo ignored them as he pocketed his hot pistol and knelt to the bottles. With a cigarette lighter, he ignited both wicks and stood again with a bottle in each hand. Rizzo sent the first bottle in a flickering arc toward the gaping window, but the throw was short. The bottle rebounded from the sill to the wet bushes where it guttered ingloriously. Shifting the other bottle to his right hand, Rizzo hurled it.

This one was true to the target. It vanished through the window, struck the far wall with a hollow crack and spread a blanket of flame over the wall and the piano below it.

At the first sign of flames, Rizzo turned without another look and walked back to his car. By that time, several of Harry's neighbors stood on their porches or front lawns staring at the Caster house and Rizzo. Ignoring them, Rizzo slipped back behind the wheel and started the car.

"Stop him, John," said Mrs. Barnett from the safety of her porch across the street. But John Barnett, golf club in hand, remained where he was and watched Rizzo's car speed down Elgin Street and around the corner.

When a car pulled up in front of Rizzo's house, Pete and Injun were ready. But as an old man wearing a heavy lumber jacket got out of the car, they relaxed. Pete walked to the sidewalk to confront him.

"Evenin', pop," he said. "You looking for something?"

"Carlo Rizzo," he said, not speaking to Pete but through him. "This is where he lives?"

"Maybe," Pete admitted, "but he's not home right now. Why don't you come back some other time?"

"Mrs. Rizzo is here? I have to talk with her."

Pete took an exaggerated look at his watch. "It's late, pop," he said. "Mrs. Rizzo has had a very bad day, so why don't you..."

The old man said deliberately, "I want to see Mrs. Rizzo, and I want to see her right now."

Pete wasn't impressed. "I'll bet you do," he said, "but—"

Angela Rizzo's voice cut in from the front porch. "Let him pass, Pete. I want to talk to him."

"But Mr. Rice said—"

"I say let Mr. Speranza come in," she said firmly.

Speranza began to move his bulky body forward, but Pete was still in his way. "I'll have to frisk you," Pete told him, looking the old man stubbornly in the eye.

"I am armed," Speranza told him, returning the look but speaking very softly, "but you won't search me. If you don't get out of my way right now, boy, I will kill you."

Speranza began moving again, and Pete melted out of the way like a phantom. As the old man passed him on the way to the porch, Pete turned back to Injun. He looked closely for signs of derision on Injun's dark face.

Angie met Speranza on the steps.

"Don Baptiste," she said, "it was good of you to come." She reached out for his hands and walked with Speranza into the hallway. "Come, sit down," she said, leading him toward the dimly lit front room. "Would you like coffee?"

"Angie," he said, studying her face in the muted yellow light, "something's happened. You've been crying. It's not about Gino."

Angela looked puzzled. "No, Papa," she said. "But then you don't know. Our Bobby was shot and killed this evening on his way to the football stadium."

"Your Bobby?" Speranza asked. "But who? Why?"

"I don't know," Angie replied. "He shot Bobby down like an animal." Tears began to streak down her face again.

"My dear," Speranza said, taking Angie in his big arms and pulling her to him.

"I'm sorry about Gino, Papa," she said in a muffled voice. "So sorry. I talked with Carmen earlier this evening."

"I know," Speranza said. He patted her shoulder lightly.

When Angela had stopped crying, she sat back on the couch and dabbed at her eyes with a small handkerchief. She asked: "Do you know this man Harry Caster, Papa?"

"No," said Speranza, "but I'm looking for him. That's why I came here tonight. Where is Carlo?"

"I don't know, but I think he's looking for Caster, too. He left quite a while ago, and I haven't heard anything." She paused. "Have you, Papa?" she asked anxiously.

"No, Angela," Speranza said gently, "nothing."

The telephone in the hallway rang loudly, and Angela jumped back. Her eyes went to Speranza's face in alarm.

"I'll answer it if you like," Speranza offered, and she nodded. "Hello," she heard Speranza say, and Angela held her breath as she waited. "No," he said, "Mr. Rice isn't here. Can I help you?" Angela stopped consciously listening; she was too busy with thoughts of her own.

Then she heard the name Bonino and started listening again. But Speranza was speaking very softly. Angela started to get up, but she heard Speranza say goodbye and put down the telephone.

"What is it?" she asked as Speranza returned to the living room. "Ruby Bonino, one of Gino's friends, was shot tonight in Manhattan. They found Carlo's business card in his pocket."

"My God," Angela said, putting her hand to her mouth.

"What's the matter?"

"Ruby was following Caster tonight for Carlo," she explained. "He called tonight right after we heard—heard about Bobby—and I told him to kill Caster."

Speranza shook his head. "I must go," he said, taking Angie's hand once more. She held on tightly.

"Don't, Papa," she said.

"I'm an old man, Angie," Speranza said, putting his other hand on top of hers. "That boy out front probably thought I'd been dead for years. In a way, I suppose I have been. But I'm not dead tonight. Gino is dead, but I am alive and I must do something. It's been a long time, but I haven't forgotten. I am still a man."

Angie released her grip on his hand. "All right. Papa," she said meekly, "if you must go."

"Yes," Speranza said, stooping to kiss her forehead gently. "If I see Carlo, I will send him home."

"Carlo's a man, too," she said, and she lowered her eyes from his face.

Out front, Pete and Injun were standing in the shadow talking quietly when Speranza came out of the house and got into his car.

"I wonder what that old fart is up to," Pete said as Speranza drove away.

36

NEITHER HARRY NOR SANDRA SAID MUCH ON THE RIDE home to Parker's Landing. The streets of Manhattan were crowded as Harry fought to get to the West Side, but once they got on the Expressway they were virtually alone.

Harry couldn't help glancing again and again in the rear-view mirror in search of a persistent set of headlights which would mean that the big youth whom he'd shot on Sixty-Sixth Street hadn't been alone. But every time he spotted a likely shadow, the lights either turned off at an exit or swept by on the left and disappeared in the dimness ahead. On the other side of the Hudson River, the New Jersey palisades were thinly studded with points of light.

"How does your neck feel?" Sandra asked, breaking a long chain of silence.

"It still stings," Harry said, "but it's stopped bleeding. I think I'm going to have a very stiff neck in the morning. But I guess I should be grateful that he wasn't a better shot."

"You'd better be sure to see a doctor when we get to Parker's Landing," Sandra said. "You could get lockjaw or whatever it is people get from gunshot wounds."

"Gunshot wounds," Harry said. "What a glamorous expression. I've had every other ailment you can think of, but I never thought I'd have a gunshot wound. Even in the Army the worst I got was a sprained ankle."

Parker's Landing lay in pre-midnight darkness when Harry slipped off the parkway and into its quiet streets. He quickly threaded his way until they were approaching Sandra's house. It was the only house on the block still illuminated. Passing the big mansion, Harry pulled around a slight curve in the winding street and stopped the car. He cut the engine and doused the headlights.

Neither of them spoke for a long time, and then Sandra asked: "What are you going to do?"

"Go home, I guess," Harry said, "and change into something a little less gory."

"Do you think it's all over?"

"I don't know. I suppose that depends on Rizzo. I have no idea where he is or what he's doing. For all I know, he's watching us right now." Harry looked nervously behind the car. "I don't even know where Hoerner is."

"But can't you try going back to Chief Beddell? After the shooting this morning and tonight, he's got to believe you."

"He believed me before," Harry said. "I'm pretty sure of that."

"Now he'll have to do something, won't he?"

"That I don't know," Harry said. "I just don't know. I may try him again. What about you? What are you going to do?"

Sandra smiled wryly. "Go back in there and be the grieving sister. I've got a lot of catching up to do."

"Will they ask a lot of questions about where you've been today?"

"No," Sandra said. "They'll think a lot of questions, but they won't ask them. In my family, grief is an excuse for any amount of eccentricity. When Great-Aunt Rosaria died, my cousin Ethel, the spinster, jumped on her racing bicycle and rode around the block for nearly six hours. Finally, she got a flat tire, wheeled the bicycle home and came into the house as if she'd been out for a walk."

"I guess you're safe then," Harry said. He looked at the luminous dial of his watch without meaning to.

"Harry," Sandra said, "I don't want to go in."

"Where else would you go?"

"With you."

Harry laughed. "Where's that? I don't even know where I'm going, not really. Somewhere out there Rizzo and Hoerner are probably shooting it out, and I feel like I'm about to move into the middle of it. The only reason I came back here was because I didn't know where else to go. If I was twenty years younger or like Mickey, I'd never have come back at all. You and I would be on a plane to some- where—anywhere."

"Let's do that," Sandra said quietly and seriously. She was staring straight ahead.

"Sandra," he said, "I can't—you know—"

"I know, Harry," she said. "You don't have to explain. Even if there weren't Rizzo and Hoerner, there's Hildy, the girls, et cetera and et cetera. I always knew the reasons why not. But I wanted to ask just in case. Just for the record, as they say."

"Sandra," Harry said, wanting to touch her, "aside from all that, you wouldn't want to be with me. Not for long. I'm only what you saw when you walked into that waiting room: a middle-aged nobody who's spent most of his life selling people something they'd be better off without. If

Rizzo lets me, I'll probably spend the rest of my life doing the same thing. You know you want more than that."

"What I want," Sandra said, "is not really the question here. What I can *get* is. I'm not complaining, Harry, I'm just sorry. And now I'd better go. But first I'm going to tell you something." Sandra faced Harry in the near dark. Her face was shapes and shades of gray. "You're not the funny little man you think you are, Harry. You're much more, and you've proved it in a crazy way by standing up to Rizzo. You never should have done it, but in a queer way I'm glad you did. You're a man, Harry, and that's a lot."

Sandra cracked the door open on her side. "You know where I live. I'll be there for some time, not exactly waiting for you, but all the same I'll be there." She leaned over and lightly kissed Harry's mouth. "Try to stay out of the way of bullets, hey?"

"Yeah," said Harry softly. He watched her until she disappeared around the curve of the street.

WHEN HARRY DROVE ONTO HIS BLOCK HE KNEW something was wrong. The acrid smell of fire defeated by water invaded the car. And he knew instinctively whose house had burned. Harry pulled up and parked in front of his house. He saw that it hadn't literally burned down. The house still stood, but the front of it gaped at him like an empty eye socket. Harry got out of the car and leaned against it, surveying the havoc.

The front yard looked as if the burning house had vomited the contents of the living room out toward the sidewalk. He recognized the charred remnants of the hi-fi, the sodden hulk of the sofa, still smoldering slightly, and the piano listing among the rose beds like a sinking aircraft carrier.

Before Harry could go on with the inventory of the remains, a figure detached itself from the darkness of the side porch and walked toward him. It was a fireman, complete with long-billed helmet, rubber coat and fire ax. Like the house, the fireman seemed to smolder still, and as he crossed the lawn his high rubber boots squeaked. "You Mr. Caster?" the fireman asked.

"That's right."

"My name's Coogan, Parker's Landing Fire Department. Had a pretty nasty conflagration for a while here tonight."

"So I see," Harry said. "What's the damage?"

"Living room gutted, smoke and water damage on the rest of the ground floor, suspected deterioration of first-floor beams and chance of collapse."

Almost idly, Harry asked: "Okay if I go in and take a look?"

"Sorry," Coogan said, "no one is allowed on the damaged premises until arson investigators complete their work in the morning."

"Arson," Harry said.

"Suspected arson," the fireman corrected. "There is a strong suspicion that the fire may have been initiated by a type of fire bomb—what is popularly known as a Molotov cocktail."

"Oh."

"With this sort of suspicion, we can't allow anyone in your home—not even you—until investigations are completed. That's why I'm here, as well as to deal with any fires which may rekindle."

"All right," Harry said. "Thanks very much."

"Any time," said the fireman.

As Harry turned to go back to his car, the fireman spoke again: "You been away from Parker's Landing this evening, Mr. Caster?"

"Yes, I've been in the city. Why?"

"It's been one hell of a night. A local boy got shot and killed this evening on Central Avenue. On his way to play in the football game. Bobby Rice, the quarterback, it was. Some fella shot him three times in the back and then got run down and crushed by a bus. You never saw such a mess in all your life."

Harry couldn't react with surprise, so he just said: "It sounds like it."

"Sure was," said the fireman. "And the boy's father was really broken up, so I heard. A terrible thing. He was dead before anybody got to him."

"The guy who shot him," Harry asked, "who was he?"

"A stranger," Coogan said. "Nobody I ever saw before. I didn't catch the name exactly, but it was Harney or something like that. I don't know what he'd want to shoot a boy like Bobby Rice for. It doesn't make sense."

"No, it doesn't," Harry agreed. "No sense at all. But then a lot of things don't make sense."

"You're right there," said Coogan. "Good night now."

"So long," said Harry.

Harry got back into his car wearily like a gypsy being pushed on yet another time. The dried blood on his shirt and undershirt was scratchy, and the slight wound on his neck still bothered him. He sat for a moment wondering why one of the peaceful, darkened houses wasn't his. Then he turned the key to start the engine.

Baptiste Speranza wheeled the car stiffly around the corner. It had been years since he'd driven. He was so intent on what he was doing that for some time he didn't notice the red-and-blue light flashing behind the car. It took a long blast of the horn to get his attention and make him pull over to the side of the road.

What a nuisance, Speranza told himself as he shut off the engine. He slipped the big gun from his pocket to the seat beside his thick thigh and began to fumble in his wallet for a long-invalid driving license. Rolling down the window, Speranza looked up at the policeman who'd parked behind him and walked up.

"Officer," he started to say, and then he recognized Beddell. "So, it's you, Roy."

"Yes, Baptiste," Beddell said, looking down at the old man. "What do you want?"

"You know," Beddell said.

"Carmen called you," Speranza said almost petulantly. "I should have known."

"No, she didn't," Beddell said. "Nobody called me. I wasn't looking for you—didn't even know you were out. I'm looking for Carlo Rizzo. He burned out Caster's house a little while ago."

"Caster killed Rizzo's boy," Speranza said. "And my Gino."

"That's not the point," Beddell said. "What I'm saying is that it all has to stop right now. Where's Rizzo?"

"Have you tried his house?" Speranza asked. "He might be there."

"I was just there, but Rizzo wasn't. He had three punks staked out at the house, but now they're on the way to the lockup."

"You left Angela without protection?" Speranza asked anxiously. "Roy—"

"My men are there," Beddell said. "She's protected.

There will be no more killings—on either side—in Parker's Landing."

"My Gino is dead," Speranza said.

"I don't care. Gino was asking to be killed. If you want to blame someone for his death, blame me. I should never have let him have those two hoods this morning. Or blame yourself, Baptiste, if you want to."

"Me?"

"Yes," Beddell said. "You bought me a long time ago. I had a debt to you that I could pay only by staying bought. That's why I didn't take the situation in hand on Tuesday as I should have. Then there would have been no killings at all."

The old man said nothing.

Beddell continued: "I was wrong to think I could sell only a little bit of my soul. I'm taking it back right now."

Speranza looked up into the policeman's face. "Roy," he said softly but forcefully, "maybe you're right. But if you want to buy your soul back, get in that car of yours and leave me alone tonight. I'll never ask anything more of you."

"I'm sorry, Baptiste," Beddell said. "I can't pay the debt, so I'm canceling it. You'll have to accept that fact. Now, I want you to give me your gun and go home, or, so help me, I'll take you into the station."

"Arrest me? What for?"

"It doesn't matter. You know I'll find a charge and make it stick."

"You'll be ruined if you do."

"I'm ruined already," Beddell said undramatically. "I'm just trying to stop the rot from spreading. Baptiste, give me that gun." He gave his revolver a little hitch in its holster. "I don't want to have to take it from you."

"You'll have to, Roy," Speranza said calmly, and he leaned forward to start the car.

Beddell cleared his gun from its holster and leveled it at Speranza. The old man leaned back from the steering wheel and laid his hand lightly at the side of his thigh. He looked up again at Beddell.

"You'd shoot me, Roy?" he asked. His eyes lowered to the gun in the policeman's hand.

"I'll shoot you if I have to, Baptiste," Beddell said evenly. "Give me that gun." He held out his left hand.

Only then did Speranza understand that Beddell really meant what he said. Without further thought or hesitation, he swept his gun up from the car seat and brought it across his chest. He pulled the trigger and then pulled it again.

Beddell saw the stiff motion in plenty of time. Almost in slow motion, he saw the gun in Speranza's hand travel up from his thigh and turn until he could see the darkness of its large barrel.

It was then that Beddell should have pulled the trigger. It was the last thing his brain told him. Even he couldn't have said why he didn't.

Beddell rocked back at the first shot, but he felt no pain, only a numbing sickness. He stared at Speranza and then down at the gun in his own hand. He didn't hear the second shot.

Speranza watched his old friend fighting the rising flame. He knew the feeling and he knew it wouldn't last. He watched Beddell rock back and come forward with a creeping red stain spreading across the taut front of his gabardine shirt.

"Baptiste," Beddell said, leaning stiff-kneed against the car door.

"I'm sorry, Roy," Speranza said. "I didn't want to."

"Baptiste," Beddell repeated. Then he slumped forward, momentarily filling the window with his bloody torso. Then he rolled off to the right, grabbing the rear door handle of the car. His body twisted and he fell face up alongside the car with an arm propped up toward Speranza. His face was as blank as a burned-out light bulb.

Speranza looked down at the dead policeman and then at the bloody smear at the bottom of the window. His face showed no expression except fatigue. Dropping the gun on the seat beside him, Speranza leaned forward and started the car's engine. He raised his eyes to the street ahead and started to press down on the accelerator. But something stopped him. He switched off the engine and doused the car lights. It was dim in the little pocket holding the two cars. Speranza let both hands drop from the wheel into his lap.

A sleepy milkman found the two men exactly like that two hours later and called the police.

37

Harry let himself into the darkened Lamplighter by the front door and slipped behind the bar without bothering to turn on the lights. The only illumination was from a blue-lit globe advertising a mixer. Reaching blindly for the whiskeys, he grasped the neck of a bottle and poured two inches into a highball glass. He raised the glass to his lips.

"Enjoy your drink, Caster," said a voice from the darkness. "It's the last one you'll have." Carlo Rizzo came out of a booth with a pistol pointed over the bar at the middle of Harry's body.

"Hello, Rizzo," Harry heard himself say. He was surprised at the calmness of his voice. "I thought I'd be seeing you someplace." He took a drink from the glass.

At the first taste, Harry shuddered convulsively and had to fight the urge to gag. He spat the rich, fruity liquor into the stainless steel sink and poured the rest of the drink after it.

"What's the matter?" Rizzo asked sarcastically.

"I got the wrong bottle," Harry said. "It was a peach liqueur. Do you mind if I find some Scotch?"

"Go ahead," said Rizzo. The easy voice didn't go at all with the gun he was holding. Harry shook his head to try to bring back reality. It didn't help. Switching on a small lamp, he located a bottle of expensive Scotch and reached out for it.

"Only the bottle," cautioned Rizzo. "Don't try anything."

"Only the bottle, Rizzo," Harry said, showing him the richly crested label. "Do you want a drink? It's on the house," he added with heavy irony.

"Pour it out."

Harry poured two heavy drinks and carefully set the bottle down. Then he looked up at Rizzo and really saw him for the first time since he'd spoken.

Rizzo was as sharply dressed as ever. But there was something markedly different about him. Before, Rizzo had been confident that he could ward off disaster. Now that confidence had been worn through like a cheap veneer. But with Rizzo, the veneer had been ripped rather than worn, and something naked and ugly showed through.

They drank. Rizzo drank carefully, keeping his pistol aimed at the middle of Harry's body. "You're going to die, Caster," he said.

Harry didn't answer. He thought of the revolver in his coat pocket with one shell left in the cylinder.

"You don't seem to care very much," Rizzo said. "Or are you just playing it cool? It won't do you any good."

"I'm not playing it cool, Rizzo. I'm scared of dying. But so much has happened that I haven't any emotions left. If you're going to kill me, kill me. I won't put on a show for you."

Rizzo thought this over, but he wasn't ready yet to kill Harry Caster.

"You know what that goon of yours did to my boy tonight?" he asked. "Did you tell him to do that? Did you?"

"I know," said Harry, "but I didn't tell Hoerner to kill your son, Rizzo. I didn't even know where he was tonight. Hoerner must have gone crazy."

"Hoerner," Rizzo said. "Yes, that's the name—Hoerner. Where did you get ahold of such a guy, Caster? To shoot a boy like that?"

"Where did you get the men who beat Marco Carradino to death?" Harry asked boldly, not caring about Rizzo's reaction. "I'm sorry your boy was killed, Rizzo, but I don't see a lot of difference."

"You don't," said Rizzo.

"No."

Rizzo thought this over for a few moments. "You'd feel different if it was your son. You don't have a son, do you, Caster?"

"I did once," Harry said, "a long time ago. He died when he was fourteen months old."

Again Rizzo was silent. "You can tell me something else," he said. "How did you come to hire a gunsel like this Hoerner? I mean, what made you decide to fight me?"

"You didn't think I would?"

"No," said Rizzo. "I didn't think you had it in you."

"Do you mind if I pour us another drink?" Harry asked. "I could use one."

"Go ahead," Rizzo said. He still pointed the gun at Harry, but the hand holding it rested on the bar in front of him.

Harry poured two more stiff drinks and then returned the bottle to the service counter below the bar. He picked up his glass with his left hand. As he drank and Rizzo drank, Harry stealthily took the revolver out of his pocket, the move hidden from Rizzo by the high bar. As he put his glass down on the bar with a clink, Harry laid the revolver softly on a towel in the shadow of the bar.

"No," Rizzo said, "I really didn't think you had it in you. Who would have thought a two-bit guy like you would fight it out just to keep a crummy joint like this?"

"It's all I've got, Rizzo," Harry said. "What would you have done in my place?"

"You really want to know?"

"Yes."

"I would have fought, too. I'd have blown your head off if you'd tried to muscle in on my rackets." Rizzo laughed bitterly. "You want to know something really funny, Caster?"

"What's that?"

"I don't even need your lousy joint now. I don't need it. Do you know who Abe Montara is?"

"I've heard of him."

"Well," Rizzo said, "Abe's the guy who squeezed me so hard that I came on to you. He was very mad at me for a couple of small reasons. But when he hears what happened tonight— that Bobby was killed—he's not going to be mad at me anymore. He's going to give me my piece of the action back, Caster. And maybe a bit more. What do you think of that?"

"It's crazy," Harry said.

"Yeah, it's crazy. But Abe Montara's got a heart—he's a snake with a heart—and he's going to forgive Carlo Rizzo. And Carlo Rizzo is going to be a good boy from now on." His laugh could have etched glass. "A very good boy. Pour us another drink, Caster." Harry did, and when he put the bottle back down below the bar, he let his hand fall on the butt of the revolver.

"Drink," ordered Rizzo. "Drink to my good luck. I'm a very lucky guy."

Harry drank silently. His other hand remained on the pistol grip. Rizzo let his gun hand relax, and the pistol lay canted on the bar. "You know something else, Caster?" he said.

"No."

"I'm not going to kill you." Rizzo looked at his pistol and then returned it to the holster between his arm and his chest. "Not tonight. I'm going to give you your life, Caster. Do you know why?"

Harry shook his head. He didn't trust his voice.

"Because it's not enough," Rizzo said. "I kill you, and you're gone. I can't reach you anymore. No, Harry, I want you alive. I want you to think about how you got my boy killed tonight. Think about it good. And think about me, Harry, still around. And this." He gave the gun in its holster a thump with his knuckles. "Imagine me behind you with a gun wherever you go. Because I might be."

Rizzo pivoted a little unsteadily and started walking along the bar toward the front door of the Lamplighter.

"Rizzo!"

Rizzo turned with a sour smile on his face and found Harry Caster pointing a revolver at him from behind the bar. Harry held the gun well out from his body at shoulder height as if he were taking target practice.

Rizzo's hand jerked, and his fingers splayed in anticipation of a gun butt.

"Don't," warned Harry deliberately, "or I'll kill you."

"I believe you," said Rizzo. He let his hand drop to his

side. From where Harry stood, Rizzo was perfectly framed in the Lamplighter's glass door.

"So?" said Rizzo.

"I listened to you, Rizzo," Harry said. "Now, you listen to me. I didn't start all this; you did. I fought you, and now I'm sorry that I did. Nobody won a damned thing. But I want you to know that I'll do it again if you don't leave me and mine alone. You're not the only one who can use a gun. You'd better think about that. Now get out of here, Rizzo. Go home to your wife."

Rizzo said nothing, only raised his eyebrows and walked out of the bar onto the sidewalk.

Harry waited until the sound of Rizzo's car died out in the street. Then he put his pistol back on the service counter. Ducking under the bar, he followed Rizzo's path out of the door, locked it behind him and got into the rented car. Starting the car, Harry made a wide U-turn on Parker Street and headed north to the Expressway and Hildy.

THE END

BECAUSE REVIEWS ARE CRITICAL IN SPREADING THE word about books, please leave a brief review on Amazon if you enjoyed *Fighting Back*. Thanks.

SIGN-UP FOR THE FREE NEWSLETTER (NO SPAM, NO BS) to receive news and exclusive discounts on the latest Charles Alverson books: watchfirepress.com/alverson

. . .

THE WORD: WHEN LIFETIME CRIMINAL JOE DIXON is released from Folsom Prison, he vows never to return - but with no skills and no prospects, Joe turns to the best grift of all: the word of God.

Buy *The Word* on Amazon at watchfirepress.com/theword

ABOUT THE AUTHOR

Charles Alverson's writing career has spanned over five decades, during which he has written for publications such as *The Wall Street Journal*, *Rolling Stone*, and *HELP! Magazine*. Alverson has written ten novels, two children's books, and helped co-write the screenplays for Terry Gilliam's cult films *Jabberwocky* and *Brazil*.

Alverson currently lives in Serbia, where he has resided with his wife since 1994.

Download Alverson's anthology of short fiction *Ryan's Way & Other Short Stories* when you sign up for his free author newsletter at watchfirepress.com/alverson.

www.ingramcontent.com/pod-product-compliance
Lightning Source LLC
Chambersburg PA
CBHW031708170626
46808CB00005B/1655

* 9 7 8 1 9 4 0 7 0 8 2 9 4 *